# JUSTICE FOR LIZZIE

KARI H. SAYERS

JUSTICE FOR LIZZIE
Copyright © 2022 by Kari H. Sayers

ISBN: 978-1-955784-88-7

Published by Satin Romance
An Imprint of Melange Books, LLC
White Bear Lake, MN 55110
www.satinromance.com

Published in the United States of America.

Cover Design by Caroline Andrus

# 1

RECONNECTING WITH AN OLD FRIEND

The russet glow of dawn crept over the eastern ridge when I came out on the deck with my laptop and a steaming cup of coffee one morning. Fluffy clouds hung over the lake like balls of cotton wool; the air was cool and crisp. It is my favorite time to write. I put my cup on a small table and sat down on a deck chair to plot out my new mystery novel:

*A young black lawyer, Nabila Brown, was found dead in a pool of blood, stabbed to death, in her upscale condo on the Esplanade in Redondo Beach. A neighbor had heard Nabila's phone ring all afternoon and when she went out to run some errands, she was surprised to see that the lawyer's car was in the garage. When the neighbor returned and saw that Nabila's car had not been moved, she knocked on Nabila's door and called her name. No one answered, so she decided to call the police.*

*My sleuth Jule McCormick, a petite ex-nun turned psychology professor, stopped by Nabila's place that same afternoon to discuss a contract dispute with the young lawyer. She found the building surrounded by police and the entrance blocked by yellow crime tape. She recognized the officer in charge, Detective Wilkinson, a big burly man with thinning gray hair and a beginning paunch. He knew who the professor was and told her what had happened. As was her custom, McCormick offered her assistance. She had often helped the LAPD with their investigations, and Officer Wilkinson, who now worked for the Redondo Beach Police Force, allowed her to enter the lawyer's well-appointed condo. Several emergency personnel were standing around the bed where the body still lay half-dressed in a heap of bloody sheets.*

———

As the sun rose, the low clouds slowly dissipated. The daffodils and tulips that were in bloom everywhere came into view. It was springtime in our mountain resort, deep in the San Bernardino Mountains.

I put down my laptop and checked my phone. There was a text from Susie, my old friend from graduate school at UCLA:

*Just learned that Elizabeth Wurtz now lives in your little mountain resort. Remember her? We used to call her Lizzie. She failed the comps the first time even though she had passed the very difficult Foreign Service Exam earlier and had worked overseas somewhere. When she returned, she studied for her master's with us and worked part-time in a doctor's office where she met her husband, one of the doctors there. He was very handsome. I think his name was Ray Khazin from somewhere in the Middle East. I just learned that he has taken a job at the hospital up where you live, and I thought y'all should get together. I don't have her number, but they'll have it at the hospital.*

I remembered Lizzie well. After we graduated, we taught together for a while too, and we were all good friends. Lizzie was a little older and had served in consulates in France and Lebanon. She was more worldly than the rest of us, and she and I talked often before my first husband Robert and I moved to Africa. I remember meeting Lizzie's husband, but also remembered I didn't particularly like him. He appeared to be such a gentleman on the surface, but he was overly flirty and too slick for my taste. Even so, I immediately decided to look him up on the hospital website. And there he was: Dr. Raymond Khazin. I would call him later.

By now, I had lost my inspiration to write. I closed my laptop and went back inside, checking on my little son John Patrick, or JP for short, who was still sound asleep in his new big-boy bed in the corner of my bedroom. He had just turned three and was looking more and more like his father Chris, a contractor I had met up here after Robert died in a plane crash. Sadly, Chris was crippled after a burning beam fell on him during a fire in this very house. About a year ago, he succumbed to an infection.

I let JP sleep and walked into the kitchen. As soon as I started rattling around trying to fix myself a piece of toast, our dog Duchess whimpered softly. I went to her pen beside the house and let her out for a short early-morning run. She was quick, for she knew it was soon feeding time. When I came back inside again, I heard a key turn in the front door.

*"Hola, Miss Megan,"* a cheerful voice called from the living room. It was Maria, my Mexican housekeeper and nanny, who had worked for Chris's family since Chris and his brother Ed were in elementary school. She went straight to the bedroom and got JP up. The three of us had toast and juice before Maria helped JP dress. Then the two of them waved goodbye and were off to nursery school.

It was after nine o'clock before I called the hospital to ask for Dr. Khazin. He was preparing for his first surgery, I was told, but the receptionist took my number and said he would call back after an hour or so.

I walked over to my piano, actually my mother-in-law's grand piano that I inherited. I wiped the keys with a tissue, then I sat down to play through my usual warm-up exercises before I launched into a couple of Beethoven's etudes.

I had gone out on the deck again when the phone rang. I saw the hospital number on the screen. "Hello, Dr. Khazin," I said as I picked up the phone.

"Yes. Hello," he said with some hesitation in his voice.

"It's Megan Viets. Remember me? I'm an old friend of Elizabeth's from UCLA. I just heard you'd moved up to our resort where I've lived for over three years now."

"Oh, yes. Of course, I remember you, Megan."

I recognized his polished voice and his slight accent right away.

"I just heard from our friend Susie that you and Elizabeth had moved up here."

"Oh, yes. I didn't know that you lived around here."

"A lot has happened since I saw you two last, but I know you're busy, so I'll come straight to the point."

"Oh, but I always have time for pretty women, Megan," he said with an affected and oily intonation. "It's been a while."

"Yes, true." I paused for a second. "Can you give Elizabeth my phone number? I'd like to get in touch with her."

"Of course, but why don't I give you her number so you can call her?"

I agreed, and he gave me her number. I thanked him and said goodbye. However, I decided to wait until the evening to call to give Ray time to tell her first.

Even though Lizzie probably didn't recognize my number, she picked up right away. She was surprised to hear from me.

"Didn't Ray tell you I'd call? I talked to him at the hospital this morning, and he gave me your number."

"No, he didn't tell me. Are you ill?"

"Oh, no. Susie—you remember Susie the redhead at UCLA, don't you?"

"Oh, yes, of course, I remember her."

"She told me that you had moved up here. I waited until evening to call. I thought Ray would be home and would have told you."

"No, he's not home. He's hardly ever home." She sounded wistful. "He's probably down in San Bernardino at the restaurant he bought some time ago. He's really busy these days. He meets with a group of Lebanese expatriates to discuss politics in the Middle East. I hardly ever see him."

"Oh, I'm so sorry. And, yes, I've read the news and know it's terrible over there now. I lived in Beirut for a while too, remember."

"Yes, I remember."

"Well, with your experience, you ought to be their advisor."

"Oh, no, it's fine. I'm used to spending my evenings alone. Ray and I aren't on great terms these days. But what about you? What are you doing up here?"

"I live here, too. I've lived here for over three years now, but it's a long story. Why don't we get together for lunch or something?"

"That would be nice." Her tone of voice was flat. I had expected her to be more enthusiastic.

"Lizzie, are you alright?"

"Oh, it's nothing. I'm good. When do you want to get together?"

"Are you free tomorrow?"

"Yes. What time?"

"Why don't you come over here for lunch about noon?"

"Okay. What should I bring?"

"Nothing. I have a wonderful housekeeper and nanny who will help me prepare something good. It will be better than the cafeteria food at UCLA."

We both chuckled.

"Did I hear you say something about a nanny?"

"Yes, I have a small son now. He just turned three a couple of months ago."

"How nice! I didn't know. Ray and I weren't able to have any children. Ray may have been disappointed. You know how Arabs love children. But it's okay with me. I'm no mother hen."

"Right. Not everyone needs to have children in this over-populated world, and I have only the one, and there will be no more. But let's talk tomorrow."

She told me where she lived, but I wasn't sure where her street was, so I explained how to find my house from the hospital. The GPS doesn't always work well up here.

———

I was in the kitchen with Maria, preparing Chinese chicken salad and setting the table for lunch, when I heard a car door slam. I went outside to meet my old friend and was immediately struck by how much weight she had gained. Her face appeared puffy, and her skin pasty and pale. Her hair was a little darker but still thick and wavy, and she had the same crooked smile that added to her charm. She wore a loose multi-colored top over blue pants and blue slip-on shoes. We embraced, and I led the way inside.

"Wow!" she exclaimed. "What a nice house you have! You have come a long way since our college days."

"Thanks. My father-in-law built it himself. He has a contracting business up here."

"Really?" She glanced over at the piano and added, "That looks like a much grander piano than your old upright."

I laughed. "Yes, remember that old honky-tonk?"

"Sure do. We all used to play on it."

"Well, this one is a Steinway Grand. It belonged to my mother-in-law who I never met. It's great. Try it."

She shook her head. "No, not now. Maybe later. I guess you still play then?"

"Yes, now and then—as time permits."

"Yes, I know you're busy. Written several books, I heard."

I smiled. "Yes, that's right. Have you read any of them?"

"Not yet, but I will now." She took a couple of steps into the cavernous room. "And that's a serious fireplace, isn't it? It practically fills up the entire wall. So mountainy too, just like the furniture." She walked closer and touched the stones as if she wanted to see if they were real.

"Well, we're in the mountains, aren't we?" I said. "And that fireplace keeps the room really warm in winter. We were lucky it survived a big fire we had a little over three years ago now."

"Fire?" Her eyebrows rose.

I pointed to the black spots that still marred some of the rocks and the side of the mahogany grand piano. "See those black spots? They're soot marks that we haven't been able to remove yet." I brushed a soot mark on the mantel piece.

"What happened?"

"My husband's first wife was crazy. She was actually in an asylum down in San Bernardino but escaped and came here to set fire to the place. When Chris came home and saw the flames billowing out from the upstairs windows, he ran inside just when a burning beam fell. He was trapped under it and injured his spine. He was in a wheelchair until he died about a year ago."

"I'm so sorry, Megan. That must have been a difficult time for you."

"That's true," I said with a deep sigh. "It took me a while to get over it. But I'm okay now. Life goes on, and time heals every wound, as they say." I paused. I didn't want to dwell on tragedy and sadness now. "But let's go into the kitchen, and you can meet Maria."

The kitchen smelled like freshly baked bread and fried chicken that Maria had cut up for our salad. The table was set. In the middle sat a basket of homemade rolls and a pitcher of cranberry juice. Maria had a big, cheery smile for Lizzie as they exchanged greetings.

"I hope you don't mind eating in the kitchen, Lizzie. It's really more comfortable," I said apologetically.

"Not at all. And what a great kitchen you have too with all the latest stainless-steel appliances." She suddenly leaned over as if she had lost her balance and had to steady herself on the back of a chair before she sat down. Because she appeared to be all right, I didn't think anything of it. Maria excused herself. "I run some errands, and I pick up JP later," she said and left. I filled our glasses with juice, and we helped ourselves to the chicken salad and rolls.

Lizzie took a bite of the roll. "Yummy. It's delicious."

"Yes, Maria is a gem. She's very close to the family." I paused and took a bite of salad. It was good too. "So," I continued, "the last time we were together, I was with Robert as we were going back and forth to Africa. You gave us some good advice, remember? 'Don't drink the water.' 'Wash everything you eat!'" I wagged my forefinger and chuckled. Lizzie smiled faintly. "You heard that Robert was killed when he crashed his plane in a sandstorm in North Africa, right?"

"Yes, I heard. You've had your share of tragedies, Megan. I remember your stories about how he flew into the African bush. I don't recall who told me the news that he had been killed. It must have been Susie."

"Yes, Susie keeps us informed." I took a bite of my roll before I continued. "Of course, Robert's death was a shock. Fortunately, we didn't have any children, and somehow I got him home and his ashes scattered over the Pacific Ocean where he so often had practiced flying."

"You always were such a practical and resourceful woman, Megan."

We ate in silence for a few moments.

"So, how did you end up here?"

"Well, before Robert died, we bought a cabin up here. When the situation became more dangerous in Africa, I came back to LA and started teaching again. After Robert was killed, I sometimes came up to this little resort by myself and met Chris, the father of my little boy." I finished my salad and took another roll. I offered Lizzie another one too, but she declined.

"It's all very delicious," she admitted. "But I'm on a strict diet. Ray doesn't like that I have gained so much weight." Her tone was melancholy. I filled her glass with more cranberry juice.

"So, what's going on with you and Ray?" I asked as I bit into my roll.

"Well, you know that I didn't want to go back into the Foreign Service, so I continued teaching after you left. Ray worked in different hospitals, and we moved around quite a bit. I decided to quit working to try to get pregnant. Ray prescribed fertility pills and gave me steroid shots. That's one reason why I think I gained so much weight. Ray doesn't like it. He hardly ever comes near me, even when he's home." She paused to take a few sips of juice before she went on. "Without Ray's knowledge, I went to see a gynecologist who told me I was as fertile as they come, but when I told Ray afterwards, he became furious for some reason. Maybe he thought I avoided getting pregnant on purpose."

"Really? That's too bad," I said and added cautiously, "I remember he was—and I assume he still is—a very handsome man."

She nodded. "Yes, I always thought so. My whole family fell in love with him. He was so considerate, brought my mother flowers and showered her with compliments and gifts. He has a brother who lives in Rancho Cucamonga, but the rest of his family lives in the Middle East. That's why I think he kind of adopted my family."

"He is Christian and not Muslim, right? I remember he stressed that."

"Yes, it is important to him. His whole family is Catholic, and that was important to my family too." She put her napkin on the table and pushed her chair back a little. She seemed to have some trouble getting up.

"You seem a little pale, Lizzie." I looked at her more carefully. "Are you alright?"

"I'm okay. But I do need to lose fifty pounds."

"Well, maybe not fifty, but a few perhaps," I said and tried to avoid her gaze.

"Ray is giving me some diet pills, but they give me a headache and make me feel dizzy."

I didn't say anything but decided to change the subject. "Let's have some coffee and take it out on the deck."

"That would be lovely."

"Cream and sugar?"

"No, thank you, just black." She steadied herself on the back of the chair once more. "Sometimes I don't take the pills Ray gives me. I pretend to take them but put them in my pocket instead. I'll be okay in a minute."

"Quick tour?" I gestured toward the other section of the house, wondering if she could make a tour without falling over.

At her nod and quick smile, I showed her the bathroom. She peered into the master bedroom with JP's new big-boy bed in the corner half hidden by a screen. Then we looked into the large dining room.

"You could probably seat twelve people around that big dining table," she commented. "What's upstairs? Bedrooms?"

"Yes, and a media room with a big-screen television."

We moved out onto the deck, and I got Lizzie situated in a comfortable chair before I went back for the coffee.

"What a view you have, Megan," Lizzie said as I returned. She was standing by the rail, looking out on the lake. I set one cup on a small table next to her chair. "You can almost see our house from here." She pointed to the north side of the lake.

"And if you had a kayak, you could paddle right across to the commercial center on the south side to do your shopping instead of going all the way around the lake," I said, and we both laughed. "You know, I'm really into hiking around here," I continued. "Want to come along sometime?"

"But I'll slow you down." She returned to her chair and sat down awkwardly

"Nonsense," I assured her and sat down opposite her. "Forget pills, Lizzie. I believe in the common sense diet: eat less, work out more."

"Yes, but it's easier said than done." She took a sip of her coffee. "Good coffee," she commented.

We talked some more about school, our old teachers and friends, until we heard the chirp of a siren from the driveway.

"What's that?" Lizzie looked at me with a bewildered expression.

"Oh, that's Ed."

"Who's Ed?"

"Ed is my brother-in-law, Chris's brother. He's the town sheriff."

Lizzie looked flushed. "What's he doing here?"

"Well, Ed and I have sort of a relationship."

Lizzie's eyebrows rose even higher, and her cheeks reddened when Ed came out on the deck. In full uniform, he cut an imposing figure. I rose to greet him.

"So this is where you're hiding," he said jovially as he came over and put his arm around my shoulder.

"Hi, Ed. Meet my friend Elizabeth Khazin. She's an old study buddy from UCLA. Her husband is the new surgeon at the hospital."

Ed moved over to her, and they shook hands. "How do you do," he said simply.

Lizzie's cheeks reddened a little more, and she looked uncomfortable although she soon regained her composure.

"Do you want a cup of coffee, Ed?" I offered.

"Sure, but I'll fix one myself." He turned to Lizzie and continued, "Can I make you another cup too?"

"Thank you, but I'm good. I should be getting on my way."

"No," I protested as I sat down again. "You have to stay and meet JP."

She smiled and turned to Ed. "Okay, I'll take another cup then. Just black, please."

"No problem. What about you, Megan?"

"Okay, a small cup for me too, please."

"Coming right up," he said as he walked inside.

"He's certainly good-looking, Megan," Lizzie commented when Ed was out of earshot.

"Not as handsome as his brother," I said playfully. "But steadier and a few years older than me."

"Over forty?"

"Yes, a little, but as you can see, he's in good shape."

"Be careful with handsome men. They often get too full of themselves," she mused philosophically.

She looked at me seriously, but before she could comment further, JP came running out on the deck. I could hear Ed talking with Maria in Spanish before he came out, balancing our coffee cups. We all played with JP for a while. Lizzie soon finished her coffee and rose, ready to leave.

"Walk tomorrow, Lizzie?"

"Okay. Where shall we meet?"

"I'll pick you up. Just explain to me how to find your house. As I'm sure you have discovered, GPS doesn't work so well up here in the mountains." We agreed to meet at eleven o'clock.

Little did I know Lizzie's life was more a bed of weeds rather than roses, even with a handsome, successful husband.

2

# HIKING THE TRAIL WITH LIZZIE

L izzie and Ray's two-story house sat on a big lot only a stone's throw from the water. It looked new, and it was painted light beige with dark blue shutters. Like most houses in our resort, it had an expansive terrace that overlooked the lake.

It was a warm day, and Lizzie was well dressed for the occasion in a coral-colored top over loose beige pants with black sneakers and a black cap. I had brought Duchess with me and barely managed to put her leash on and introduce her to Lizzie before she jumped out of the car. She whimpered impatiently, and I let her loose to chase gophers and squirrels. I too wore beige pants, an old T-shirt with our village's logo and, of course, my hiking boots. We were both slathered in sunscreen and had plenty of water with us.

"So what did Ray think about our hiking trip today?" I asked casually.

"Oh, I don't know. I didn't see him this morning."

"Really?"

"I didn't see him last night either. As I told you, he's hardly ever home any more. He usually goes down the hill to his restaurant that I told you about after his last appointment at the hospital."

"What kind of restaurant?" We were walking slowly down toward the path that snaked around the lake. "Is it Middle Eastern?"

"I don't know, Megan. I've never seen it."

"Why not?"

"I don't think Ray particularly wants me to."

"Maybe we should both go down together one day."

"Oh, I don't know if he would appreciate it. I think he views it as his private sanctuary. He's there almost every day."

"Driving up and down the highway in the afternoon rush hour?"

"Well, I guess there's no other way to get down there, is there?"

"I guess that's true," I said thoughtfully.

"As you may know, Megan, a lot is going on in Lebanon right now. I think…I think Ray is involved with a group of people that are up to no good."

I made no further comments as we trudged on, taking deep breaths, but I wondered what Ray could be involved in. What was he doing with a restaurant? Why was he there all the time? A restaurant? He was a doctor.

Duchess ran ahead of us, sniffing, wagging her tail, and chasing everything that moved, including dry leaves that fluttered around whenever there was a gust of wind. Soon we sat down on a fallen tree trunk for a water break.

The fresh air had done Lizzie good. Her face had more color, and she seemed more energetic.

"I need to find a job or something to do here, Megan. I can't just sit around. That's another reason why I've gained weight. Do you know of anyone looking for someone to help them out in an office or something?"

"Sure. Give me some time to think about it. What do you have in mind? I think they're looking for substitute teachers at the schools around here."

"Anything really. Anything to get me out of the house."

We rose, but without anything to lean on, Lizzie fell. I helped her up on the tree trunk again, and she brushed the leaves and twigs from her pants.

"Lizzie. I should have Ray's cell phone number just in case."

"All right, but I'm fine now." She gave me the number, and I entered it into my phone.

"Okay, let's start on our way back."

The outdoors always gave me a boost of energy too, but after a while, I could see that Lizzie was tired. Beads of perspiration had formed on her forehead, and her breathing was heavy. We were more than a mile above sea level, although Lizzie ought to be used to the altitude by now.

When we got to Lizzie's house, I put Duchess back in the car. We agreed to hike the next day too at the same time, but I suggested we take turns and meet at my house tomorrow.

When Duchess and I returned home, I filled her water dish and poured a big glass of water for myself. The rest of the afternoon, I worked on my mystery novel.

*My sleuth Jule McCormick was assisting the Redondo Beach police, going door to door, asking neighbors if they had seen or heard anything. Except for the neighbor who had heard the phone ring and had called 9-1-1, no one had seen or heard anything out of the ordinary. One neighbor who also lived alone did seem a little odd and said he could sometimes see the beautiful black woman from his own condo. McCormick asked him if he sometimes spied on her and watched her go to bed, but he just gave her a lurid smile.*

———

The next day, I waited for Lizzie outside my house as we had agreed, Duchess impatiently tugging on her leash. It was past eleven o'clock, but Lizzie had not shown up, nor had she called to say she was late. At quarter after eleven, I called her but got no answer. I took Duchess for a short walk, constantly checking my phone for messages. There were none. At twelve-thirty, I put Duchess back in her pen and drove over to Lizzie's place. I had a feeling that something bad had happened. Something was obviously wrong, or she would have called.

As soon as I had passed the last bend in the road, I saw two police cars and a fire truck parked in front of the main entrance. Deputies were busy putting yellow tape around the house. Ed was standing over on the side, and I went over to him. He turned, apparently surprised to see me.

"What's happened?" I asked, fearing the worst.

"There's been an accident," he said somberly and put his arm around me. "It's your friend."

"Is she badly hurt?"

"It's worse than that, Megan."

"What do you mean *worse*?"

He didn't say anything but looked at me seriously, shaking his head.

I covered my face with my hands. "Oh, my God." I just stood there, not knowing what to say or do. Blood rose to my face, and I felt sick to my stomach. I was afraid I was going to vomit. "What happened?" I said finally. "Can I see her?"

"Not yet. Her husband just returned from the hospital and found her on the bathroom floor all covered in blood. She had evidently slipped and fallen, hitting her head on the ledge of the shower stall. He called 9-1-1." Ed took my arm as if to steady me. "I'm sorry, Megan."

"We were supposed to go hiking again today, but she didn't show up. I tried to call and text, but she didn't answer so I decided to come over." I pulled a Kleenex from my pocket and wiped my eyes and nose.

"Yes, I overheard her give you directions to her house when I was over the other day," he said and looked over at the house. "That's how I realized it had to be your friend."

I saw the ambulance and firetruck leaving. "Did they take her with them?"

"No, the doctor pronounced her dead, and now the coroner's car will pick her up and bring her body to the morgue."

Oh God. The *body*. The *morgue*. He said it so casually. Lizzie was dead. What on earth had happened?

"Can I go in and see her now before they take her away?"

"Okay, I'll go with you. Be careful not to touch anything."

The house was not yet fully furnished. We passed the master bedroom. I was desperately trying to wrap my mind around what could have happened before we entered the bathroom. A bloody scene met us, and I had to stop and take a deep breath to keep my composure.

"Dr. Khazin covered her up after he examined her," one of the paramedics explained. "He was here when we arrived and was pretty shaken." The medic lifted the sheet just so I could see Lizzie's bloody face before he continued. "She was only partly dressed, probably getting ready to take a shower or something."

"Oh, Lizzie. I'm so sorry," I exclaimed. I felt faint as I knelt down beside her. I detected a faint smell and saw that her face was already blue, as if she had been dead for a while. I wanted to lift the sheet a little more, but Ed held me back and helped me stand up.

As the medics took Lizzie out, I briefly noticed that Ray was following them. Two deputies were dusting for fingerprints. A towel bar lay on the floor. It had apparently been ripped off the drywall as there was a big gash where it probably had been. I also noticed fleetingly that there were blood stains on the wall that someone had tried to wipe off, but whoever it was hadn't done a good job of it. There were marks of a bloody handprint too, and other marks, straight lines going this way and that. It looked as if someone had tried to write something with a lipstick or most probably blood.

"You'd better get out and get some fresh air," Ed said and pulled me away. "How well did you know these people?"

"Him not very well. I knew Lizzie very well. Dr. Khazin and Lizzie were married when we were in grad school. She used to work for him. That's how they met. I don't know what drew them to our little hospital up here." We continued down the driveway, ducking under the yellow tape and walking over to my car. "Do you think he had something to do with it? I saw the deputies dusting for fingerprints."

"We have to look at all possibilities. You're a mystery crime writer. You know the drill. We'll have to question him."

I unlocked my car remotely, and Ed opened the door. "I'll stay and talk to the deputies before they leave and find out what they saw. I'll come by later and let you know what they say." He leaned down and kissed my forehead.

I looked at him and managed a faint smile. "Dinner?" It was Friday and our date night.

"Okay."

I got in the car and left. I remembered Lizzie's demeanor and tone of voice when she talked about Ray. According to her, they didn't have a good relationship.

I had planned to tell Lizzie about Ed and me on our walk today. How we'd taken a trip to Paris to meet James, his son, who had just finished a summer course in Norway. How we had taken James to London for a semester abroad, a semester that turned into a year. How Ed had asked me to marry him, but we hadn't made our engagement public yet. Now I would never have a chance to tell her anything. Life is so full of unexpected changes

I had certainly seen my share of death. I accepted Robert's remains after he crashed his plane in that terrible Saharan sandstorm and brought what was left of him back to the States. It was all just a blur in my memory now. Chris had died in my arms at the hospital. Even so, one is never really prepared for death, least of all the death of a long-time and relatively young friend.

The van was in the driveway as I drove up to the house. JP came running up to me as I entered the front door. I picked him up and hugged him before he squirmed down. "How was school, JP?"

"Good." Then he ran out to the deck to play with his toys.

"Ed will be over for dinner, Maria," I said as I walked into the kitchen. "Can you stay?"

"No, I better go home. I know he come, and I make Chicken Alfredo for you guys. It's one of Ed's favorites."

"Thank you, Maria." I paused. "Remember my friend Lizzie who came to lunch the other day?"

"Yeah, we make fried chicken salad."

"Yes, and it was very good too." I went over to the stove and inspected the casserole. "My friend had an accident today. She slipped on the bathroom floor and hit her head." I took a deep breath. "She died."

Maria looked at me with her big brown eyes. "*O dios mio.* That's terrible. I'm so sorry, Miss Megan."

"We went to school together many years ago."

"Yes, you tell me."

Maria spoke fluent English and had a large vocabulary, but for some reason, she had no use for the past tense. She had been like a mother to Ed and Chris after their own mother died of breast cancer when they were little. Maria had taught them Spanish, and both Chris and Ed spoke the language fluently. Now JP also spoke both English and Spanish too, while I was still learning Spanish.

After Maria left, while waiting for Ed, I texted Susie with the news, and she called right back. She was speechless and seemed just as numb as I was. "Ed is coming over for dinner," I said finally. "Let's talk more tomorrow. I'll keep you updated on any funeral arrangements. She had family. Do you remember where?"

"No, I can't remember, but I'll try to find out and let you know."

"Thank you. I'll try too. And I'll follow up with Ed. One of the deputies has talked to Ray. He was evidently close to her family. I'll follow up with Lizzie's family as well."

———

Ed finally showed up after six. As always, he announced his arrival with a short chirp of his siren. I was in the kitchen but went into the living room, as JP came running in from outside to meet his uncle at the front door. Ed lifted him up high and spun him around until he squealed.

"What are you up to, Big Man?" Ed inquired as he set my little boy down and turned toward me with a smile, but JP took his uncle's hand and pulled him outside. With no time to talk to Ed, I returned to the kitchen to set the table.

When Ed came back, he had unbuttoned his uniform jacket. "Something smells good," he said as he gave me a hug and a kiss. "Is Maria still here?" he asked as he headed for the fridge to grab a beer.

"No, she left a little while ago."

He set the beer on the table and looked at me for a moment before he put his arms around me and pulled me close. "How are you holding up, Megan? It's been a rough day, hasn't it? You may still be in a state of shock."

"Yes, maybe. I feel numb in a way, but JP keeps me grounded. I still can't believe that Lizzie is dead. I was stunned when I saw her in all that blood, but I'm slowly processing it. Now I'm wondering what really happened this morning."

Ed let me go and leaned against the counter. As if on auto-pilot, I put the Chicken Alfredo casserole that Maria made in the microwave on reheat.

"Yes, it was an unpleasant sight," he said. "I worried it might be too much for you." He hadn't shaved since this morning, and his five-o'clock shadow made him look scruffier than usual. "I'll stay with you tonight. I don't want you to be alone." He reached for the beer and drank it slowly before he headed for the bedroom. He always kept civilian clothes in Chris's old closet because he often spent the night. This was, after all, the home where he grew up. He reappeared in his jeans and a white T-shirt and came over to the table. I was holding our plates but set them down to give him a warm kiss.

"I'm so sorry about your friend." He slipped his arms around me and gave me a gentle hug.

"Thank you."

"How long had you known Mrs. Khazin?" Ed asked.

"We studied linguistics together at UCLA with Susie and some other friends. Lizzie was a little older and had already lived abroad. She had worked in a couple of consulates in Strasbourg and Beirut. We talked a lot before Robert and I headed for Africa. She worked in a doctor's office where she met Dr. Khazin. As you know, he's the new surgeon at our hospital."

"Actually, I didn't know that until you told me."

JP came in, and Ed lifted him up in his booster chair while I put the casserole on the table and poured milk into his plastic cup that he grabbed out of my hand. Then I filled two glasses of ice water for Ed and me. I helped JP get started before we served ourselves Chicken Alfredo and a simple salad.

"I'm surprised that the hospital keeps a full-time surgeon up here," I said between bites.

"They have a private practice associated with the hospital, I think, and do minor surgeries only. People go to Colton for bigger things."

I had no comment to add as we both laughed at JP who was trying to balance his food on a fork. He had no trouble eating with a spoon but insisted on using a fork.

"You know that your friend had an accident not long ago, right?" Ed asked casually and shot me a quick glance. "One of the deputies reminded me this afternoon. I remembered it because her name was Elizabeth."

Elizabeth was the name of Ed's deceased wife, the mother of his son. She passed away a little over two years ago. That's how Ed and I were thrown together, so to speak: two single parents with a son each; as well as being brother- and sister-in-law.

"No, I didn't know. What kind of accident?"

"A car accident. She drove a fairly new Lexus—the report verified it as her car—into a tree on Cedar Point Road on the North Shore in broad daylight. No other car was involved. The road is pretty straight where she crashed." He looked at me with raised eyebrows. "She didn't tell you?"

"No, she didn't tell me anything about that. When was it?"

"Oh, I don't remember exactly, a couple of weeks maybe. The highway patrol officer thought she was drunk, but he didn't smell any alcohol. Do you know if she took pills?"

"She was overweight and was trying to lose weight. She told me that her husband had prescribed some diet pills for her. She may also have felt faint from not eating. Was she hurt?" I realized that it couldn't have been serious since she hadn't mentioned it and seemed fine when she came over for lunch, but I did remember her bewildered expression and restlessness when Ed showed up in his uniform.

JP started to scoot down from his chair, wanting to return to his toys. He was pretty independent.

"You go and play, big man," Ed said. "I'll join you later."

"I don't think Lizzie and Ray had a particularly loving marriage." I hesitated to add that, but Lizzie mentioned it so that relationship—or lack of one—could mean something to the police.

"Really?" Ed said thoughtfully. "See." He looked at me mischievously. "The minute people marry, the romance is all gone."

"So, that's what happened to you and Elizabeth?"

"Well…" He looked down and sighed.

"Right. And it didn't happen to me and Chris either."

"Women were all over Chris."

"Hm. They seem to be all over you now too. And as long as you're not married, you are fair game," I said teasingly. "I guess you want to have your cake and eat it too."

"You're being unfair, and you know it." He tried to look crestfallen but didn't succeed.

"So, what happened after I left this afternoon?" I asked in an effort to change the subject.

"The doctor and the medics deemed it an accidental death. Not that I think that the medics looked at her that carefully. The husband—the doctor—got there first."

"I guess that's understandable," I said. "They saw the doctor examine her and deferred to him. That's what they're supposed to do, isn't it?"

"The husband usually wouldn't be able to examine her even if he is a doctor."

"Maybe the medics felt a bit awkward about it."

"Maybe. They said they had checked her thoroughly before I got there and confirmed that she was dead, but I don't know how good a job they did. They should not have let a possible suspect do any checking at all. They said the doctor ordered them to take the body down the hill to the morgue. The coroner will give a final report."

"Do you think there could be foul play here?"

"So far, no, but I am concerned about the sloppy procedure. The deputies dusted for fingerprints, of course, a common procedure, but I'd be surprised if we found any others besides the husband's and Lizzie's. Maybe a housekeeper if they had one. Any others would be suspicious."

"Well, actually, I mentioned Lizzie and Ray's poor relationship to you because it could be used in a further investigation."

We rose, and Ed looked at me, shaking his head.

"Were you close enough to her face to notice a strange smell?"

"I did notice a smell, but if there's anything out of the ordinary, the medical examiner will note it in his report."

While Ed cleared the dishes and cleaned up the kitchen, I gave JP his bath and got him ready for our bedtime routine. For his story time, JP wanted to hear about The Three Bears. Ed joined us for a while, but soon he proclaimed in no uncertain terms, "And now, it's time to go to sleep, big man. Tomorrow, we'll go out in the cop car and get coffee and doughnuts for Mommy."

I smiled as we tucked in the little boy and kissed him good night. JP was wonderful at any time, but in times of sadness, he cheered me up even more. I kept thinking about Lizzie and her life cut short. I remembered the day Chris died too. Ed was with me then as well.

I joined Ed in the living room.

"Let's have a glass of wine," he suggested. He brought a Cabernet from Chris's wine cabinet, and we sat down on the big couch in front of the fireplace.

"So, what did you observe at the scene this afternoon, Megan? You're probably plotting out a whole scenario for your next book." He spoke sarcastically as he twirled his wine glass.

"Ed, my friend died today," I said reproachfully. "I want to find out exactly what happened. For one thing, it looked like somebody had torn the towel bar off the wall."

"Yes, she grabbed it to try to prevent herself from falling." Ed took a sip of wine.

"Maybe. And what was that strange red smear on the wall? It looked like blood or lipstick or something. There might be DNA there."

"Yes, it was blood that had splattered on the wall from her head wounds. Tests will find that the blood is your friend's."

"Yes, but it also looked like someone had tried to rub it off. There was a mark of a hand and some funny lines."

"Yes, good, you are very observant, Megan."

"Well, to me, it stuck out, even if it was over on the side." I bit my lip and just sat there for a few moments. Ed was toying with me, and blood rose to my face. "And what about footprints? Other than from the medics." I tried my best to stay calm.

"Well, there was also the husband's. He was the one who found her. The medics and the doctor estimated the time of death to be somewhere between 9 and 9:30 am, no later than 9:45."

"Interesting," I said,

"It will all be in the report, Megan."

I looked into my wine glass and swirled it around as if I thought the answer would be in the Cabernet. Why was I beginning to feel that something was not right? *Stop it, Megan. This is not one of your books.*

Ed woke me up from my daydreaming. "Why don't you play something on the piano?" He leaned back. "That will take your mind off of this terrible day."

I went over to the piano and sat down on the piano bench. The only piece that came to mind was "Largo" by Handel.

"That's a sad song," Ed complained. "Play something livelier."

For some reason, "Amazing Grace" in the key of G came to mind, and I played it several times over with different accompaniment.

"That's beautiful," Ed said. "I know it well. My mother used to play it too, but I don't remember the words."

I sang the first verse and stopped. "Sorry, Ed. I can't think of anything else." I went over to the couch and sat down next to him again. We drank a toast to Lizzie and one for Chris. Then we toasted his wife Elizabeth and my first husband Robert, as well as a toast for Ed's mother.

"I guess you have seen your share of death too, huh." I said. "I suppose you go out on the highway every time there is a fatal accident."

"Not so much anymore, but I used to. The worst is when young people are involved." We set our empty glasses down on the table. With a meaningful glance at the hallway, he ended our night. "But enough doom and gloom," he said, and pulled me up. Hand-in-hand, we walked together into the bedroom.

## 3

# THE MIDDLE EASTERN NIGHTCLUB

As he promised, Ed took JP out in his car to buy coffee and doughnuts to bring back to the house for breakfast. Ed had the day off, and we all, including Duchess, went for a long hike along the lake trail. Later, while JP and Ed lay down for a nap, I called Ray at the number Lizzie had given me. It rang for a while before I realized that this was perhaps Lizzie's number, but he finally answered. I offered my condolences. He accepted them politely and formally.

"You have contacted Elizabeth's family, I presume," I said

"Yes, of course. We are very close."

"Actually, I'd like to call them too, if you think I should."

"Yes, by all means." His tone was flat, and he sounded tired.

"You know, Elizabeth—we used to call her Lizzie—and I go way back to graduate school at UCLA." I paused, but he did not respond. Of course, he already knew that. "Do you have her parents' phone number handy, by any chance?"

"Certainly." He gave me the number.

"Thank you, Ray. Are you staying at the house, or is the yellow police tape still up?"

"I'm not staying there. I'm staying with my brother in Rancho Cucamonga."

"Of course, I can understand that." I cleared my throat. "I imagine you still have to look after your restaurant." I knew I was being pushy, but I was on a mission. I wanted to find out exactly what had happened to my friend and make sure her death really was an accident and nothing else. "Elizabeth promised to take me down to see it one day and surprise you. Now I have to go there by myself. Where is it exactly?"

"Oh, it's not really a place for women. It's a bar and club. A place for men."

"For men only? What do you mean?"

"It's a Middle Eastern bar, a place where you can go and smoke a pipe. You've lived over in that part of the world and know what they're like."

"Now you really have me intrigued. Do you serve food? I love Middle Eastern food."

"It is not a place you go for food, my dear. I didn't want to take Elizabeth there either."

"Yes, she told me she had never seen it."

"Right."

"Well, I'm sorry for your loss, Ray. If you need help with anything, don't hesitate to call me. Elizabeth—Lizzie—was a dear friend. Thank you for giving me her folks' number."

We said goodbye, and I immediately called the number Ray had given me. I recognized from the area code that it was an Arizona number. A woman answered, and it was indeed Lizzie's mom. I told her who I was and how long I had known her daughter. She was inconsolable and sobbed through our entire conversation.

"Poor Lizzie," she sobbed. "I loved her so much. I can't believe she's gone. My life will never be the same. And poor Ray too. He's devastated too, of course."

"I'll do my best to find out exactly what happened, Mrs. Wurtz," I said as firmly as I could. "Did Lizzie tell you about any medications she was taking? You know, she was trying to lose weight."

"Yes, I know." She was desperately trying to regain her composure. "Ray may have given her something, but she didn't tell me."

"Is Lizzie's dad still around?"

"Yes, he's here, and he's devastated too."

"If you, or both of you, decide you want to drive out here, you can stay with me, Mrs. Wurtz. I have plenty of room. Lizzie and Ray's house is still surrounded by police tape."

"Police tape?" Her high-pitched voice sounded shrill. "But it was an accident."

"Yes, most likely, but the sheriff has to cover all the bases."

"I see. Well, thank you."

"I'll get in touch with one of our other friends too. You might like to talk to her as well."

"Thank you," she sobbed. "I'm so confused I can't think straight. I don't know what to do. I want to support Ray, of course."

"That's okay. There's nothing to do right now, and I'll stay in touch."

After we said goodbye, I just sat there looking at my phone, deleting ads that constantly appeared in my emails. Lizzie's mom seemed to care just as much about Ray as the loss of her daughter. She evidently didn't know anything about Lizzie and Ray's deteriorating relationship. Maybe it wasn't that bad. Maybe I was overreacting. But I really wanted to see the restaurant or bar that Ray was in the habit of absconding to. I Googled Middle Eastern bars and clubs in San Bernardino. Only two came up. One was called Al Sheikh. I noted the address and called the phone number that came up on the screen. A woman with a foreign accent answered and told me that the club opened at five pm and closed at two am. I asked her if she knew someone by the name of Dr. Ray Khazin.

"Yes, He's the owner." Bingo!

"Oh, I see. Thank you." I tried to think of something to say without sounding inquisitive. "Actually, I have a party of foreign businessmen here, and they wanted to see some of the local night spots. Thank you again. What's your name?"

"Fatima," she said simply

"Thank you, Fatima." I hung up and waited for a few moments before I went into the bedroom to see if Ed was awake. His eyes were open so I lay down in the crook of his arm. "Our morning hike wore you out, didn't it?" I gave him a peck on his cheek.

"Well, I was really tired. It's been a rough week." He pulled me closer. "I heard you talking to someone. Who was that?"

"Lizzie's mom. I called Ray first, and he gave me her number. She's naturally inconsolable, and I promised to find out exactly what happened to her daughter. I also called Ray's restaurant down the hill in San Bernardino where Lizzie said he spent most evenings after work. It's a Middle Eastern bar or nightclub or something. I'd like to go down and see what it's like, but when I talked to Ray, he didn't seem too eager for me to see it, which makes me want to see it even more." I turned my face toward Ed to see if he'd get the hint, but his face showed no emotion. "Since it's evidently a night club, I don't think it's appropriate for me to go by myself," I continued. "It's too late to call Maria to stay with JP tonight, but maybe tomorrow. Can you take off tomorrow night and come with me if Maria can stay with JP?"

"Okay. What time?"

"How about seven o'clock? And out of uniform, obviously."

"Obviously," he said with a bit of his usual sarcasm.

"Ed, you really are an okay guy."

"Okay? That's the best you can do?"

"Okay, wonderful, and I love you."

———

Maria came over a little before seven o'clock that evening, and I left soon afterwards to meet Ed at the station. The drive down the hill was quick. Most of the traffic was going the other way—uphill. Ed was at the wheel as he was most of the time when we went some place together. He wore a white golf shirt and a blue sports coat over gray slacks. His close-cropped military-style haircut suited him. I had put on a dark blue fitted dress and blue heels. We were, after all, going to a nightclub.

It was already dark by the time we saw the neon sign with the name Al Sheikh Hookah Lounge. The building was well maintained and bathed in a red glow. A smell of shisha wood met us at the entrance where a man sat smoking a hookah pipe. It brought back memories of a different time. Inside were more hubble-bubble pipes ready for customers. A woman in a flowing white chiffon gown with a black hair band across her forehead that partially held back her long black hair met us. "Care for a pipe, sir?" she asked Ed.

Before he could answer, I told him he should try.

"What am I supposed to do?" he asked with a laugh.

"Okay," I said patiently. "It's a water pipe. They light a little shisha wood in this cup at the top here to heat some tobacco. Sometimes there's no tobacco." I pointed to the little metal cup at the top of the wooden stand. "The smoke comes through this hose, and you just smoke. It's not strong, but maybe you shouldn't inhale."

"So you've tried it then?" he asked a bit doubtfully.

"Yes, but women in the Middle East don't usually smoke it. I just tried it for fun."

Ed was fortunately game for trying something foreign and unfamiliar.

"Are you Fatima?" I asked the young woman.

"No, Fatima is off tonight. My name is Rosie."

She had no accent that I could discern. She lit Ed's pipe, and I heard the water gurgling in the hose. While Ed smoked, Rosie showed me into the dark lounge.

"Are you expecting Dr. Khazin tonight?" I asked.

"No, he'll not be here tonight as far as I know."

I repeated my story about the foreign businessmen who were in town, and she smiled seductively.

"Most nights, we also have belly-dancing shows here," she said proudly. "We'll have a show tonight."

My jaw dropped, at least a little. I had no idea belly dancing would go over in San Bernardino, although I knew that quite a few Middle Easterners had settled in the area, and I remembered hearing that they were even planning to build a mosque out here. Rosie bent down to pick up a piece of trash. Her movements were graceful.

"Oh, and do you dance, too?" I asked after she had put the trash in a small trashcan.

"No, not yet, but Dr. Khazin wants me to take lessons. It's difficult."

"Yes, I know. I tried it."

"You did?"

I was about to tell her that I had lived in Africa and had often visited and stayed in places around the Middle East. However, I was afraid that she would tell Ray, and I wanted to remain incognito. "And what if the men want to get to know the dancers a little better? Do you have a place for them to be more private and intimate?"

"No, they'll have to go somewhere else. Only Dr. Khazin has a room here."

"Oh, I see," I said, trying to keep a neutral tone. "I guess it's more convenient for him to stay down here instead of driving up the mountain if it's late."

She smiled and looked at me, her head askance. "He meets with a group of friends here. They all like to hang around and smoke. Dr. Khazin's used to that. He still has family over in Jordan and Lebanon, I think. His friends are from over there too, and they all seem to have a lot to talk about. They talk in Arabic. At least I think it's Arabic. I can't understand a word of what they're saying."

"Really?" I said and tried not to sound too surprised.

"Have you met him? He hasn't been here for a few days," Rosie continued.

I mumbled something, but she didn't seem to pay any attention. I didn't want her to alert Ray that I had been here snooping around. She probably didn't know that he had a wife who had just died in an accident.

By now, a few other patrons had wandered in. They were all standing by the bar, and Rosie went behind the counter to serve them. I ordered a glass of red wine and carried it over to join Ed.

"How was the smoke, Ed?"

"Not for me, honey. It smells good, but it really doesn't have much taste."

"I guess you're more of a cigar kind of guy." We both laughed.

"Have you even seen me smoke cigars or even cigarettes? I don't smoke. Period. It's a disgusting habit. I'm glad you don't smoke either. This…" he held up the water pipe, "is for investigation purposes"

I offered him my wine, but he shook his head and rose to go back to inspect the rest of the club. All was quiet and seemed above board. However, I felt certain that Ray was far from a straight-up guy. He most likely had some of these girls on the side. I wished Lizzie could have had more time to tell me her story. Even from the little she had said and the way she had looked, I knew she was not happy.

In the car, I told Ed how I felt about Ray. "I'm more and more convinced that Lizzie's death was more than an accident," I said. "There's more to this case than meets the eye, Ed."

"I'll see if the place has a proper permit," Ed said.

"I'm sure it does. They've got belly-dancing shows there most nights too. And Ray has a room in the back where he spends the night when he *works* late." I made quotation marks around *works* with my fingers.

"Do you think prostitution goes on there?"

"No. Ray is the only one who has a room there, according to Rosie. She showed me around when I told her I was just there to scout out the place for my foreign business associates."

Ed glanced over quickly and laughed. "You and your imagination!"

"But why would he stay there if he had a wife at home?"

"You mean motive? Your friend was in the way, so the wayward husband killed her?" He shook his head. "The doctor has an airtight alibi. He was at the hospital performing surgery at the time of her death. His first surgery appointment was at nine o'clock and his second one at ten. There's no way he could have scrubbed down after the first surgery, gone home, killed his wife and returned for his second surgery by ten. The medical examiner put the time of death at nine am and no later than nine forty-five."

"Even so, can you let me into the house tomorrow? I want to have a look at the marks on the bathroom wall. I wonder if they could mean anything. And why would someone try to wipe them off? And what about that strange bloodstained handprint?" I looked at him pleadingly, but he kept his eyes on the road. "Ray is not at the house. Maybe I could go over with one of your detectives. I cannot shake the feeling that something is wrong here."

Ed sighed. "Megan, let the department handle this. I know you think we're slow, but we have our procedure. Yes, it could be a coincidence that the doctor came home and found her dead. And yes, he could have hired someone to do the deed."

I remained silent for a few moments. "I just want to help you dig for evidence, Ed, and I will only go with a deputy if you can spare one."

Ed just muttered something. "Okay. I know I won't have any peace until I let you have your way. I'll see what I can do."

"Thank you, Ed. You won't regret it." I leaned over and squeezed his arm. I could see from his furrowed brow that he was in deep thought, maybe suspicious himself. Otherwise, he would not have been so willing to humor me. "I promised Lizzie's mom to do everything I could to find out what exactly happened to her daughter, and I intend to keep that promise."

––––––

A sheriff's deputy from San Bernardino was waiting at Ray and Lizzie's house when I arrived the next morning. Well-built, he was of medium height, not much taller than I am, no more than forty, I guessed. As I came closer, I noticed his large brown eyes that matched his brown sheriff's uniform. His eyelids drooped a little, giving him a sad look as if he had seen too much for his age. I introduced myself and explained that I had permission to go into the house.

He held out his hand. "José Garcia," he said as he shook my hand firmly. "But you can call me Joe, Ms. Viets."

He didn't ask for any ID, so I assumed he was expecting me. He led me through the hallway and into the bathroom. The blood had been wiped off the tiled floor but not very well. The bloodstained wall did not appear to have been tampered with. A handprint and red lines that someone seemingly tried to wipe off remained. I took a few pictures with my cell phone.

"Does it look to you as if someone tried to wipe off the bloodstains?" I asked Officer Garcia.

Garcia looked closer. "I see what you mean. Could be."

"And what do these strange marks mean? Doesn't it look like someone tried to write something? Leave a message?" I shot Garcia a quick glance and pointed to something that looked like the letter P or possibly an F as the circle was not completely closed.

"Yes, it could be a P as the lines are curved." He looked at me with his sad eyes. "We can send it in for DNA testing."

"You mean by cutting out a square of the wall?" I was surprised Garcia made the suggestion.

"I can't see any other way, can you?" He bent down and used his hands to do an informal type of measurement around the blood.

"It is most certainly the victim's blood." I didn't want to get too excited but feared that blood was Lizzie's after all.

"Well, it could be, but if you think of this as a crime scene, it could be a message from the killer written in the victim's blood. Some criminals have bizarre ways of making their marks. It's as if they want to draw attention to themselves, especially serial killers."

"True," I said. "Good point. And the killer would most likely have worn gloves, so no DNA from him." I paused. "But why should a killer try to wipe the stains off?"

"Who knows how these people think?"

"I wonder if you could apply some Luminol around the bloodstains. Maybe the bloodstains that were wiped away would become more visible."

"I'd have to go back to the station to get some," he said. "I agree that something doesn't look quite right here."

"The victim was a good friend from school," I commented. "And I owe it to her and her family to find out what really happened to her. My intuition tells me that something doesn't add up here."

Deputy Garcia smiled indulgently as if he wanted to say, "Women and their instincts and intuitions."

"What made you want to go into law enforcement?" I asked as we stared at the wall.

"I took criminal justice courses at San Bernardino Valley College, and it got me interested in police work."

"I used to teach at Pacifica Community College."

His eyebrows rose slightly. He nodded, and I sensed that his respect for me rose a notch.

"Okay," he said. "Something is odd about this scene, and I agree that there are grounds for further investigation. We'll try Luminol to see if we can make anything of the strange marks. What's that ancient Egyptian writing called again?"

"Hieroglyphics?"

"Yeah, that's right."

"I'll give you a call when I get back from the station. And I have to fill in the sheriff on what's going on."

I gave him my phone number, and he locked the door before we each went to our cars.

I went home to see what Maria was up to and to take Duchess for a walk. I made sure Maria was all set to pick up JP from nursery school.

In the early afternoon, Deputy Garcia called to tell me that he was on his way back to the Khazin home, so I drove over to meet him once again. He carefully sprayed Luminol on the stained wall, and the blood that someone had tried to wipe away became more visible. I went closer and knelt on the cool tiles that someone had cleaned. Lizzie and Ray most likely had a cleaning woman who came whether they were home or not. The letter now showed as a clear P. Then, slowly, before my naked eyes, appeared a faint slanted line from the straight stick of the P. It was not a P but an R. My blood froze for a second, and I had goosebumps.

"Look," I said with excitement and pointed. "It's an R."

Garcia frowned, and his face showed bewilderment. "So, does that mean anything to you?"

"Yes, my friend's husband's name is Ray, Dr. Raymond Khazin."

"Well, this may take the investigation in a different direction. But Dr. Khazin has an iron-clad alibi."

"I understand that, but he could have hired someone to do the job for him."

"Possibly." He scratched his chin.

"At least now we have reason to believe that this was not just an accident," I continued. "And I think we should cut out a piece of the wall and send it in for DNA testing. It will surely show that it's my friend's blood and that she or the killer tried to leave a message." I looked at Garcia to see how he was taking all of this. "You guys dusted for fingerprints, so Dr. Khazin's fingerprints and DNA will show too. He lives here."

Garcia was quiet but nodded in agreement.

"Good," I said. "Let's get to work."

"I have to have clearance from my supervisor."

"Naturally," I agreed. "Can you ask Ed to have forensics hire a local man to do the job? My father-in-law is a contractor and can arrange for a drywaller to cut out a piece, then replace the drywall and paint it. We don't want to spread suspicion that anyone is treating this case as anything other than an accident."

"Shall we meet here tomorrow, then?"

"Can we get it done today?" I asked eagerly. "I'm afraid Dr. Khazin is going to return and clean it all up."

"How are we gonna get a drywaller to come out so quickly?"

"I have my ways," I said and smiled coyly.

———

As soon as Garcia left, I went straight to work to procure a drywaller. I called Joe, my father-in-law. He had retired from the family contracting business he had started but had stepped back in after Chris died.

"Joe, Megan here. How are you and Sandy?"

"We're good, Megan. What's going on?"

"Everything is fine, but I'll come straight to the point."

"Okay." Joe spoke with hesitation, knowing my imagination, probably wondering if I was causing trouble.

"How fast can you get hold of a really good drywaller? It's a small job, just cutting out a 12x12 square from a bathroom wall and then patching the hole up again so that the cut doesn't show."

"What's the rush?"

I took a deep breath. "It's a long story. My friend from school died suddenly, supposedly from an accidental fall on her bathroom floor as there's no physical evidence of anything else so far. But I now know for sure that she was deliberately killed, and the evidence is on that small square of the bathroom wall. The deputy I'm working with is getting permission to extract a piece of wall and send it for DNA testing."

"Is Ed in on this?"

"Yes, he's been on the scene, but another sheriff's deputy, one José Garcia, is the official investigator. Do you know him?"

"No, I don't think so."

"He needs the job done quickly so as not to arouse suspicion that anyone is treating it as anything other than an accident. Most of all, he doesn't want the husband to think so."

"Do you think the husband did it, then?"

"It's possible."

"Well, I could come up myself and look at it," Joe offered.

"Oh, no, Joe. Don't you have someone who's already up here who could do it on overtime or something? He would be paid extra."

"Well, Ben is close. You remember Ben, right? He did some work for you once as I recall."

"Yes, I remember him. Can you call him?" I could hear my own worried tone and made myself calm down. What if Ray showed up before we could get that piece of drywall out for testing?

"Okay, Megan, I'll get back to you." Joe was always so self-possessed. Maybe that comes with age.

"Thanks, my dear father-in-law and my son's favorite grandfather."

I could hear Joe chuckle.

Ben called a little later, and I explained what I needed him to do and gave him the address. Then I called Garcia and once again, he and I met at the house.

"You called the sheriff?" I said.

"Yes, and he was a little reluctant to give me a go ahead, but he finally okayed it."

"And it's okay to use a local contractor to do the job?"

"The guy will be paid but has to keep his mouth shut about what he's doing. Could get in trouble otherwise."

"I already have a man lined up, and he'll keep quiet." If Garcia was surprised, he didn't show it.

"I'll talk to the sheriff and explain why we wanted to act so quickly."

Ben joined us shortly afterwards in his white contractors' truck and set to work. Ben is in his forties. He's originally from Mexico but speaks good English. A little bowlegged, maybe from riding horses as a boy, but he's small and agile. Deftly he removed the bloodstained square, which Garcia wrapped in a special bag so as not to damage any possible evidence.

"I'll take it with me to the station. This will go in our evidence collection box in case the bathroom becomes a crime scene," Garcia declared.

He turned to Ben who was preparing to patch up the square hole. "Let's not patch the hole or the towel rack holes until the official cause of death is determined, in case the death is not an accident." He looked at me as if he wanted my approval, and I nodded.

"I'll pay you later, Ben," I said as he was leaving.

"It's okay, Miss Megan. The sheriff's department will take care of it."

On the way home, I called Ed and left a message for him to call me back. At the house, Maria and JP were eating supper in the kitchen, and I joined them.

Instead of calling back, Ed came over just in time to say goodbye to Maria and goodnight to JP. He had driven straight from a meeting down in San Bernardino and was still in his uniform. As usual, he went into the bedroom to change into his usual T-shirt and jeans before he joined me in the kitchen and fixed himself a cup of coffee.

"Have some supper, Ed. There's just enough left for you."

"Okay, thanks," he said and sat down at the kitchen table. While Ed relaxed with his coffee, I heated the leftover tuna casserole in the microwave

"So, I hear you had an exciting day," Ed said and looked at me with his glittering blue-green eyes, his head tilted to the side.

"Yes, while you were sitting in meetings all day, one of your deputies and I were hard at work, and I believe I can say with a high degree of certainty that my friend was deliberately killed. Murdered."

"And who's the killer?" Ed asked, looking at the food I set in front of him.

"I don't know yet, but can you use your influence to have deputy José Garcia assigned to the case?"

"And you're sure there is a case?"

"Absolutely. I have no doubt whatsoever."

"And why Garcia if I may ask?" he said in his characteristically sardonic tone. "I suppose he's good looking. Is that why?"

"Ed, stop fooling around. It's really irritating and disrespectful. My friend just died, and I want to make sure justice is done here. I'm serious."

"I was just curious. Why Garcia?"

"Well, as a matter of fact, he is handsome," I said teasingly. "But more to the point, he listens and pays serious attention to what I have to say." I went over to him and pinched his cheek, and he pulled me down on his lap.

"I'm sorry, honey. I'm just tired of all the crime we have around here. And now another murder case." He sighed and looked dejected. "What's happening to this area? I know you have a nose for this stuff, and I agree that something doesn't smell right here, but..." He didn't finish the sentence but looked at me with a sad expression.

"I'll do my best to get Garcia on the case."

"I knew you'd come around, Ed. You're a smart guy."

"Did I hear a slight reproach in that remark?" He scraped his plate and seemed to savor the last bite of tuna casserole.

"No. No reproach, Ed. You know I adore you."

# 4

---

# THE OBSERVANT NEIGHBOR

I n the days that followed Lizzie's mysterious death, I had neglected my own mystery novel. I returned to it now as a way to help me mentally and emotionally process Lizzie's death and see where the investigation would go.

*Nabila Brown, a successful young black lawyer, had been found brutally murdered in her upscale condo in Redondo Beach. She had suffered four stab wounds to the chest, all of them fatal. There had been a struggle, and in her clenched fist was a clump of black hair. My sleuth Jule McCormick had offered her assistance to the police, as she often did, and suggested that the hair most probably came from a woman, indicating that the perpetrator was a female. McCormick had talked to the lawyer's sister Pamela Brown, who worked as a paralegal in her sister's office as well as Nabila when she worked at home. As was her MO, McCormick focused on the lifestyle and psychology of the victim.*

I was out on the deck in the still morning hours one day, pondering possible clues when I heard Maria bustling about in the kitchen getting JP fed and ready for nursery school. I closed my laptop and came in to make myself some buttered toast and pour a glass of orange juice. After JP and

Maria said goodbye and drove off, I sat down at the piano and went through some scales and Hanon exercises. I was in the middle of a meditative nocturne by Chopin when the phone rang.

"Hi, Megan. It's Cheryl. Ed just told me that Dr. Khazin's wife was an old friend of yours. I'm so sorry." Cheryl was Ed's sister-in-law through his deceased wife and a nurse at the hospital.

"Yes, we had just reconnected. She came over for lunch one day, and the next day we went out on a hike around the lake. Well, not all the way around. Only part way. She had gained a lot of weight and was trying to lose some. She was really quite heavy. Do you think she could have had a stroke or a heart attack?"

"Possibly." She paused for a moment. "How well do you know her husband, Dr. Khazin? He's a very good-looking man. Many of the young nurses here are crazy about him. Heidi Hillstrom was particularly smitten and didn't seem a bit sorry to see your friend out of the picture. She's new. Blond, cute, late twenties She's told a couple of her co-workers that she and Dr. Khazin were having an affair and that he would soon divorce his wife."

"Really?" I pretended to be surprised but wasn't really. The man had always struck me as a wolf in sheep's clothing. "Do you think this Heidi could have had anything to do with my friend's death?"

"Oh, no. No, not at all. It was an accident, wasn't it?"

"Maybe. But some things don't add up here."

"You mean his affair?"

"Was that common knowledge?"

"I don't think he made any effort to conceal it."

"Did you know he owned a restaurant down the hill, more like a Middle-Eastern nightclub really, with belly dancers and shisha pipes?"

"Shisha pipes? What's that?"

"Water pipes that are popular in Arabian countries." I had to stop and take a deep breath as I was feeling more and more agitated over Lizzie's fate. "He was hardly ever home and had a room in the same building where he sometimes spent the night. I wonder with whom."

"You mean with Heidi or any of the other nurses?"

"Maybe. Or with one of the belly dancers."

"Megan, are you making up a story for another of your mystery novels?"

"No," I said emphatically. "But I promised my friend's mother that I would do my best to find out exactly what happened to her daughter. She was only in her thirties."

"Sorry, Megan," she said in a conciliatory tone. "Is there anything I can do to help?"

"No, I don't think so. Wait…" I thought for a moment. "Actually, do you think you could find out Heidi's work schedule? I think I might want to come over and talk to her."

"Yes, of course." She paused and cleared her throat. "Meanwhile, how are you and Ed coming along? Any news?" I could hear her chuckle.

"No. No news. We're doing just fine the way we are. I think Ed's waiting for James to return home from London."

"Yes, I know. Any updates from James?"

"An email arrives now and then. He seems to be doing fine, but I think he's ready to come home too."

"I'm so sorry his mother doesn't get to see him grow up. She'd be so proud."

"Yes, he's a good kid. Smart too."

"I agree. And thank you, Megan. We all appreciate your hand in this. Ed appreciates it too."

"Yes, I think so. At least I hope so. And thank you for checking on Heidi's schedule. Maybe I'll see you when I come over."

———

I was too restless to write. I finished my Chopin nocturne and then took Duchess for a walk along the lake. As always, Duchess was game. As soon as we reached the path, I let her loose so she could chase gophers, squirrels and anything else that moved. We walked all the way over to Lizzie's house and just hung around. An elderly man of ample girth, with wisps of gray hair and gold-rimmed glasses, stopped to chat.

"You are Mrs. Khazin's friend, are you not?" he said. His speech was slow and deliberate as if he was reciting a line in a play. "I saw you the other day, and I recognize your dog. I live next door." He pointed to the large yellow house in the midst of an expansive property that reached down to the shoreline.

"Yes," I said. "My name is Megan Viets. Mrs. Khazin—Lizzie—and I were in graduate school together, and we also taught together for a while."

He smiled benevolently, showing a row of big white teeth, unusually white for a man his age. "I am so sorry. She was not very old, was she?"

"No, she was still in her thirties. She had served in the Foreign Service before graduate school." I looked at him. He was a big man who obviously liked to eat and drink, but I could see that he might have been a handsome man in his day. "Were you around on the day they found her?"

"Yes, I was here all day and saw the ambulance, the firetruck, and the sheriff's cars around noon."

"The time of death is estimated to be between nine and nine forty-five am, according to the medical examiner," I said. "Did you see anyone around the house at that time?"

He kept his eyes fixed on the house and shifted his weight from one foot to the other. "Yes, actually, I saw a small green SUV pull up in front of the house as I was finishing my breakfast. I went into my bedroom to get dressed and when I came outside, the car was gone."

"You're very observant." I wanted to ask him if he was retired and if so, what he had retired from, but I restrained myself. "You didn't see anyone go into the house then?"

"No. Sorry. I wish I had paid more attention. But I did see the car around that time, although it could also have been a little earlier."

"Do you live here full time?" I asked.

"No. Only half the year. I have a house in West Hollywood where I spend the winters." He moved a little closer as if he wanted to take a better look at me. "My wife died two years ago, but I visit her almost every day when I am down there. Her urn stands in a crypt in a mausoleum near our house."

"I'm so sorry."

"Oh, thank you. She was old and suffered from Alzheimer's. It was distressing to see her slowly lose her mind. We had a long and happy life together." He paused for a moment and looked over at the tall trees as if in deep thought. "I have a companion who stays with me now."

I whistled for Duchess to come back and bent down to put her leash back on. "You look familiar," I said and stood up straight.

He smiled, once more showing his very white teeth. "My wife and I were both actors. My name is Basil Rutherford, but you're too young to remember the films and plays we appeared in."

"Maybe, but I know I've seen you before. I used to be a teacher at Pacifica Community College," I said for no particular reason other than to keep the conversation going. "I taught literature and writing, but I've taken a leave of absence to write mystery novels."

"Oh, really. That sounds interesting. I'm also trying to write. I am working on a movie script right now and a play, but it's hard work. Maybe you could help me with the editing."

"Oh, I don't know anything about scriptwriting. I'm sure you'll do fine on your own."

Duchess was tugging at the leash, but I bent over, held her collar and kept scratching her head to calm her. "I'd better be going," I said. "So glad to have run into you. And keep writing." I waved as Duchess tried to pull me along. "Thanks for the information. I'm anxious to find out what really happened to my friend. Falling on the bathroom floor shouldn't kill you, should it? She was too young."

"No. It is strange," he said thoughtfully and nodded in agreement. "I'll try to remember the time that I saw the car." He waved too,

"Oh, you're really quite sharp. Thanks again."

When we were well out of sight, I removed Duchess's leash once more and called Cheryl back. She picked up right away.

"Cheryl, do you know what kind of car your nurse friend Heidi drives?"

"I don't know exactly, but I think it's a light green SUV, either a Toyota or a Honda. Something like that. Why?"

I told her about Lizzie's very observant neighbor who had seen a green SUV pull into the driveway on the morning of Mrs. Khazin's death. "But he didn't see anyone get out of the car and go into the house. I know it may not mean anything, but you have to admit that it's a strange coincidence." I looked around for Duchess. She was just a little ahead of me, digging up something by a tree. "Did you find out when Heidi is on duty?"

"Yes. She's off today but comes on tomorrow morning at 7 o'clock. Do you want me to mention that you'd like to talk to her?"

"Yes. Maybe I could take her to lunch or something."

"That sounds like a good idea. We usually break for lunch sometime between 11:30 and 1:30. I'll let her know."

"If I come over around noon, maybe I'd catch her," I said hopefully.

"Sounds good. I take it that Ed's in the midst of all this too."

"Yes, of course, but one of the deputies from San Bernardino will be assigned to the case if there is a case. Do you know José Garcia, a good-looking guy, pushing forty maybe?"

"No, sorry. Got to go. Maybe I'll see you tomorrow."

———

The next day, I called the hospital and asked for Heidi Hillstrom.

"Just a moment. I'll connect you."

I waited several minutes and finally Heidi answered. I introduced myself, said I was a friend of Mrs. Khazin and would like to talk to her.

"I'm sorry. I really didn't know Mrs. Khazin at all," Heidi replied curtly.

"I'm a friend of her husband, Dr. Khazin too."

"Well, I know him, of course. He works here at the hospital."

"Yes, I know." I took a deep breath. "Could I take you to lunch today? I live really close." I tried to sound as upbeat and cheerful as possible.

"I usually have lunch here at the hospital."

"That'll be fine. In the cafeteria? How's twelve o'clock?"

"Okay."

The hospital sits tucked away on a hill above the highway, overlooking the water, surrounded by tall cedars, sugar pines, and majestic oak trees. The parking lot was newly paved, and I easily found a spot. A young receptionist with long black hair and large brown eyes sat at her desk in the small vestibule, checking IDs and answering questions. I told her I was here to see Heidi Hillstrom.

"Do you have an appointment?"

"Yes, I do."

"I'll call her for you." She printed out a name tag that I stuck on the T-shirt that I wore with my short denim skirt. I sat down on a chair at the opposite wall and waited.

Heidi was tall with long blonde hair, mid to late twenties, just the type that I thought Ray would go for. Lizzie, too, had been blonde and shapely. It didn't seem that long ago.

"Hi," she said as we shook hands.

"The cafeteria is upstairs in this building, right?" I said. "Lead on to the elevator." I gestured for her to go ahead of me.

There was an awkward silence in the elevator, and we both pretended to study the numbers above the door that lit up on each floor. The cafeteria was bright and airy, filled with hospital workers wearing blue, green, or black scrubs.

"They actually have pretty good food here," Heidi commented and ordered the day's special: meatballs and pasta. I ordered the same and paid while Heidi carried her tray over to a table by a window that had a view of the lake's east side.

"So, you didn't actually meet my friend Elizabeth then," I said after we had situated ourselves at the table.

"Oh, we met a couple of times. She was really overweight, wasn't she?"

"Yes, but she didn't used to be."

"Really?" She looked at me with raised eyebrows. "I think that weight may have caused her to fall."

"Possibly."

"You think it could have been something else?"

"Oh, I don't think anything," I said quickly. "I don't know. Slipping and falling on the bathroom floor like that will hurt you, but it shouldn't kill you."

"It could if you fell the wrong way."

"I suppose."

We took a few bites. The meatballs were delicious. I finished chewing before I continued. "Were you there on the morning of the accident?"

"There where?" She flushed slightly.

"At Dr. Khazin's house."

"Who told you that?"

"A neighbor saw a green SUV like yours in the driveway that morning. You do have a green SUV, don't you?"

"I have a small Honda CRV, yes."

"Were you there?"

"What day was it?"

"Friday morning."

"No, I don't think so though I was at the house now and then, picking up stuff for Ray."

Oh, so she referred to him as Ray now? I mulled over that slip for a moment while finishing my meatballs.

"Did your friend tell you that she and Dr. Khazin were getting a divorce?" Heidi asked as she took a drink of water.

Even though Cheryl had mentioned something like that in jest, my jaw dropped, and I looked at the young, pretty nurse. "No. Were they?"

"Yes. Ray and I are in love, and we are planning to get married," she chirped. "That's what you heard, and that's why you're here, isn't it? To find out if it's true." She smiled curiously before she continued. "And, yes, it is true."

Her story shouldn't have surprised me. Heidi was just the type Ray would lead on. "No, that's not at all why I'm here. I hadn't heard that."

"She didn't confide in you, then?"

I shook my head. "No, we had just reconnected. I hadn't seen her for a few years. Did Elizabeth, Mrs. Khazin, know about all of this?"

"I assume Ray had told her. He said he had."

"Well, Ray flirted with a lot of women," I said firmly. "We never took him seriously."

"That's a pretty mean thing to say."

"Sorry. But that's just the way he is."

"No, it's not. People don't understand him. His wife didn't. He's a serious man and a brilliant doctor."

Putting *Ray* and *brilliant* in the same sentence seemed a bit far-fetched, I thought to myself as I chewed on an unbuttered roll. *Average* would have been a better description. "What about the other nurses? Don't all the young and pretty ones have a crush on him?"

"What are you saying? Are you trying to insult me?" She looked at me with pale menacing eyes, and a flushed face.

"No, not at all. I'm sorry. I'm just a little confused. He and my friend Elizabeth were getting a divorce, and now she's dead? That's very convenient, isn't it?"

"What are you saying? That her death wasn't an accident?"

"No, that's not what I'm saying. It's just a strange coincidence, isn't it?"

"Well, it happens."

"Yes, it does." I paused. "Would you like a cup of coffee?"

"Sure. I'll take one to go."

"Okay. And I'm sorry if I sound a little bewildered. It was probably an accident, but I promised her mother I'd find out. If you were at the house, be sure to tell the investigating officer. His name is José—Joe—Garcia. Maybe you know him."

"Never heard of him."

"Or tell the sheriff. It could help to establish a more accurate time of death. Think about it. Maybe you saw something. Even if it's something trivial and meaningless to you, it might help. It may tie up some loose ends."

"What loose ends?" She now sounded belligerent. "The woman had an accident, okay? She fell, and the fall killed her."

"Yes, it's probably as simple as that." I looked at her calmly, an attempt to quell her unexpected and uncalled for belligerence. "No need to get upset. Let's have some coffee."

We both got our coffee in to-go cups.

"Thank you for coming, Heidi. And don't mind me. It was most likely an accident, but she was an old friend, and I want to make sure."

"Thank you for lunch," she said in a more conciliatory tone as she looked around her to check that she had everything. She deftly balanced her coffee cup as she hurried to the elevator.

Divorce! I couldn't imagine Ray leaving Lizzie for this girl. Pretty and sexy? Yes. But marriage?

Cheryl and another nurse came through the door as I was leaving, and we all stopped and said hello. "Why don't you have your coffee with us before you go?" Cheryl suggested when she spotted my cup. Her eyes looked tired, but as always, she had a ready smile on her face and seemed as upbeat and buoyant as ever. She introduced her colleague as Judy. I remembered Judy being the nurse on duty the night Chris died. She was stout and in her forties, a little older than Cheryl with a pleasant round face framed by short brown hair. Both looked professional and competent, the kind of nurses who could handle the most difficult patients. They ordered the daily special too, and I followed them to their table.

"How did your lunch with Heidi go?" Cheryl asked.

I hesitated a little before I answered. "She told me that Dr. Khazin was going to divorce his wife. And she sounded serious when she told me that he was going to marry her."

Both Cheryl and Judy looked at me and broke out laughing. "Is that what she told you?" Cheryl asked.

"Yes, that's what she said." I looked at both of them. "You're laughing. Any truth to that?"

"I doubt it," Cheryl said, and kept chuckling in between bites of meatballs.

"We all have a crush on Dr. Khazin," Judy continued, and looked up at me. "You have to admit, he's gorgeous."

"He's too much of a skirt chaser for my taste," I countered.

"You like the steadier type, don't you? Like Ed," Cheryl said jokingly and winked at me.

"Oh, yes, I heard you're dating the sheriff now," Judy interjected. She stuck a meatball on her fork and brought it to her mouth.

"We're actually engaged," I said firmly. "But in no hurry to get married again."

"Maybe when our nephew returns from London," Cheryl proffered. The term *our nephew* threw me off momentarily, but Cheryl was, of course, James's aunt.

"So, was that Heidi's car at Dr. Khazin's house on Friday morning?" Cheryl continued.

"Possibly. But Heidi said she couldn't remember specifically. She often went to the house to pick up stuff for Dr. Khazin, or Ray, as she calls him." I sighed. "I'm sorry, but this whole sordid affair is so confusing. You don't die from slipping and falling on the bathroom floor when you're only in your thirties and have a lot of padding to mitigate the fall."

"You could if you hit your head just so," Judy said, and pointed with her finger to a certain spot on the side of the head.

"Did you know that Dr. Khazin had a Middle Eastern club, a nightclub sort of, down in San Bernardino, with shisha pipes and belly dancers and the whole schtick?" I asked Judy.

"Yes, Cheryl just told me."

"Well, Ed and I went down there and met a couple of the girls. He has a room there too where he often spends the night when it's too late to drive back up the hill."

"That's doctors for you," Cheryl said with a slight sneer.

Cheryl and Judy were not particularly interested in Dr. Khazin's escapades and when they started to talk shop, I excused myself and left.

On my way home, I stopped by the sheriff's station to see if Ed was in. I found him in his office, legs on his desk, leaning back in his chair and talking on the phone. He sat up straight when I entered, and I sat down on a chair across the desk from him.

"What's up?" he asked as he hung up the phone.

"Oh, nothing much. I took Heidi, one of the nurses at the hospital, to lunch at the hospital cafeteria. She told me that Dr. Khazin, Ray, was about to leave his wife and marry her. Heidi, I mean."

"Whoa!" Ed leaned forward, his arms on his desk and his hands folded.

"Yes, that was my reaction too. His wife had an accident and died. Quite convenient, wouldn't you say? Saved him a whole lot of trouble."

"Did you see Cheryl?"

"Yes, I had coffee with her and Judy."

"Did they know about it?"

"No, not really. They thought it was just the pretty nurse's fantasy. According to Judy, all the young nurses have a crush on the handsome doctor."

"Yes, it's possible that the good doctor killed his wife. Garcia is following up on it. But the doctor has an airtight alibi."

"He could have hired someone."

"Megan, come on. Just because he's a scheming womanizer and a lousy husband doesn't mean he's a killer."

"I know, but I haven't heard of anyone, except maybe an elderly person, who has died from falling on the bathroom floor either, especially considering all the padding she had. And she was only in her thirties."

"That's true, but she hit her head."

I sighed and shifted in my chair. "I may have another call to make to see if he has more skeletons in his closer."

# 5

## THE DOCTOR'S SECRET LIFE

B ack at home, I remembered from my research that an investigator follows the money to find clues. Having a private practice in our small resort was not as lucrative as having a practice in Los Angeles. As the only surgeon at our hospital, Ray Khazin was fully booked, but I still wondered why he had decided to bury himself up here. And what about Lizzie? Did she want to live here? She had told me she didn't have a job but was hoping to find one.

I opened my laptop and used Google to pull up the history of their property in the public records. Both Ray and Lizzie were listed as the owners. The purchase price was nine hundred thousand dollars; they had paid only the minimum down and had assumed a large mortgage. Four months earlier, they had also taken out a second loan, possibly a revolving equity loan, for one hundred thousand, maybe to use as the down payment on the restaurant. I searched the site and found that El Sheikh Restaurant and Bar in San Bernardino had been purchased four months ago. I paid a fee to access his credit report and found another interesting tidbit of information: Ray had filed for bankruptcy six years ago. Even so, with a doctor's salary, procuring a business loan would probably not pose a problem.

I Googled Dr. Raymond Khazin's bio and website and found several complaints against him and read an article in a Torrance newspaper about an investigation of Medicare fraud he had been involved in. I decided the time had come to call Carrie Jensen, my friend at the FBI office in Long Beach. Last year Ed had brought her and another FBI agent, Andrew Wells, to my house to ask me if I could identify a mafia boss from photos they spread out on my kitchen table. After that, I worked with them for weeks, and they said I was instrumental in catching the guy who had been on the FBI Most Wanted list for seven years. Afterwards, Carrie came up to our mountain resort for some R&R a couple of times. We were both musicians, but she only had a keyboard in her apartment. She loved my Steinway grand, and we had played some duets together.

"Oh, hi Megan," she said after I had identified myself. "What's going on? Are you in Long Beach?"

"No, I'm home. I haven't heard from you for a while and wanted to touch base, check up on you. Are you in your office?"

"No, I'm in my car."

"When are you coming up to the mountains for some R&R again?"

"Soon, I hope, but I'm buried in work right now."

"Well, we have another suspicious death up here." I said and told her about Lizzie's accident and my suspicions that it was not an accident. "I'm working with a San Bernardino detective named José Garcia. Do you know him?"

"No, I don't believe so."

"Cute guy."

"Oh, yeah? Are you going to introduce me?"

"I thought you were busy."

"Not that busy." Her laugh resonated through the car's Bluetooth system.

"I can't help feeling that my friend's husband had something to do with his wife's death, but he has an airtight alibi. He's a physician, Dr. Raymond Khazin. He has a private practice at our hospital. I looked him up in the public records and Googled his bio. He seems strapped financially, although he's a doctor and makes good money. I also read that he had been investigated for Medicare Fraud. That's your department, as I understand it."

"That's right."

I told her about the cryptic scrawls in blood on the wall and how we had cut a piece of the wall out so that the bloodstains could be tested for DNA.

"So, you're not the only suspicious one, then?"

"No, the sheriff, Ed—you remember Ed, don't you?"

"Yes, of course. I'm sorry he's taken, Megan."

I laughed. "Okay, but joking aside, Carrie." I cleared my throat and took on a more serious tone. "As usual the sheriff's department here complains that they're understaffed and cannot follow every crazy lead and notion I have, but I want justice for my friend. Ed too says that something doesn't smell right, but he's tied up with political stuff and major changes in the department right now. That's why I've gotten myself involved again." It was quiet at the other end of the line. "Are you still there, Carrie?"

"Yes, I'm listening."

"Ray, or Dr. Khazin, appears to have had affairs with other women. One young and pretty nurse told me he was about to divorce his wife and marry *her*, but Ed's sister-in-law, who's also a nurse at the hospital, believes that's just a fantasy. 'All the young nurses at the hospital have a crush on him,' she said. He's really good-looking. He owns a kind of Middle Eastern men's club down the hill in San Bernardino, with belly dancers, Middle Eastern water pipes, and who knows what else. He keeps a room in the back of the building and often spends the night down there."

"He's a busy man."

"Yes, and I'd like to know if he's straight up, not only with Medicare, but also with medical and private healthcare companies. Isn't this all FBI business?"

"Yes, that's right. We're the agency investigating and exposing healthcare fraud. We have special agents who deal with all of that as well as kickbacks to physicians from the pharmaceuticals. It's hard to believe all the shenanigans that go on in the medical industry."

"Can you check more thoroughly whether or not there are any more suspicions about his dealings with Medicare? With medical and pharmaceutical companies? His full name is Dr. Raymond Khazin." I gave her the name of our hospital as well as Ray and Lizzie's home address.

"I'll see what I can do, Megan," she said. "But I'm in my car. Can you text all that information to me?" She paused for a moment. "There's a reward for you if you qualify as a whistleblower. I'm on a case with the IRS right now. That's another agency you might want to check out. Find out who this doctor's CPA or accountant is."

"Good idea."

"In the meantime, I can do some checking with one of the special agents."

Since she was driving, I didn't want to continue with a lot of small talk. I thanked her and again invited her up for some hiking and for playing some duets together before we said goodbye.

I took out some of the pieces Carrie and I had played last time she was here and practiced my parts. Then I limbered up my hands with some scales and finger exercises before I played a few of Beethoven's beautiful etudes. I often did my best thinking when I played the piano. Music makes my brain cells more alert.

There was still time before Maria went to pick up JP, so I took my laptop out on the deck and began to peck away at my novel.

*The clump of black hair found in Nabila Brown's clenched fist clearly came from a woman. The hair was sent to the lab for DNA testing. Professor McCormick discovered that there had been a disagreement between Brown and two female clients who reportedly were in a relationship with each other. My sleuth had paid a visit to the two women and surmised that jealousy might have been involved. Nabila Brown's murder was clearly a crime of passion, and my sleuth suspected that one of the women had tried to initiate a relationship with Nabila.*

JP brought me back from fantasy to the real world again with his chatter when he and Maria returned from nursery school. After a quick snack, he went out on the deck to play with his toys and talk to his imaginary friends until supper time. Then it was *Mommy Time*. I found comfort in the daily routine of reading, singing, and interacting with JP, a routine followed by bath time and bedtime.

Ed came by after all was quiet and Maria had left. He removed his tie and unbuttoned his shirt before he embraced me.

"How was your day?" I asked mechanically.

"Oh, the usual. But I may have some news for you."

My eyes widened, and I looked at him expectantly.

"Garcia told me that your friend and the doctor had bought life insurance policies on each other a few months ago."

"For how much?"

"A million dollars each. It could mean a financial motive, I suppose."

"Good work, Ed, but a million dollars in California today isn't really that much."

"That's true, but it's something."

"But surely not enough to kill for, and had he taken out more, he would certainly have raised the insurance agent's eyebrows."

By now, we were in the kitchen, and Ed sat down at the table. "I pulled up the public records," I continued, "and found that they have close to a couple of million in real estate debt."

Ed whistled. "Damn, this case is looking more like a murder every day. Is that debt only the house?"

"That's including his restaurant. The Middle-Eastern club is in Ray's name, but both are listed as owners of their house. Another little detail I learned is that Ray filed for bankruptcy six years ago."

"Bankruptcy? On a doctor's salary? That's hard to believe." He headed to the refrigerator and rummaged.

"Want something to eat?"

"No, I'm good. I'll have a beer, though." He swung the 'fridge door closed as he twisted the cap off a beer bottle.

"I also called my friend Carrie Jensen at the FBI office in Long Beach," I continued.

"Why would you do that?" Ed looked at me curiously.

"You remember that we became friends after we worked together last year, don't you? I invited her to come up and play the piano again." I cocked my head a little and smiled innocently. "Since Ray appears to be strapped for money, I also wanted to find out if he has tried some shenanigans with Medicare, medical and private health insurance companies. Just a little unofficial probing, of course."

Ed sighed and sat down again with his beer. "I talked to the District Attorney. He agreed that a second and more thorough autopsy is warranted. This death may not be as simple as a fall."

"That's good, but I'm sorry a thorough one wasn't done right away. Hopefully, the medical examiner took blood samples and samples of the contents of her stomach."

"I sure hope so," he said and paused. "Another autopsy will take a few days. Dr. Khazin is not too happy. He wants the body cremated as soon as possible. That's the custom where he comes from, I understand."

"That's not true in his case and, more importantly, it's not true for Lizzie. It's the tradition among Muslims, but Ray is a Christian. Catholic, I believe. That may be why a divorce was not an option for him."

"And murder was?"

"Yes, I know. Nothing makes any sense."

"If the autopsy is clean, Megan, we have no case." He cleared his throat. "Don't be like the badger," he said, and looked at me seriously. "Don't grab onto your prey with your whole body and soul. Sometimes we have to let things go."

"I understand that, Ed. But be sure to keep me updated, okay?"

"I will. I promise. Officer Garcia is a smart guy. Oh, and you can work with him too. I'm sorry about your friend, and I realize you want to know the truth."

"And I'll let you and Garcia know what Carrie learns from the special agents who deal with healthcare fraud."

———

I was in the kitchen when Carrie Jensen, my FBI friend, called. I didn't immediately recognize the number and let the phone ring a few times before I realized it could be her.

"Your instinct, or intuition or whatever you call it, proved right once again, Megan."

"Really? What have you found out?"

"Your wily doctor friend's office in Torrance has been under investigation for fraud for some time. Our agents found several items listed in the office computer under *consulting fees*—the code name for *kickbacks*."

"Interesting. How much money are we talking about?"

"Millions."

"Wow!" I had to take a deep breath to absorb this piece of news. "I wonder where all the money is going. He paid only the minimum amount down on the house he and Lizzie purchased up here in our resort, and the same is the case with his restaurant or club down in San Bernardino. Any signs that he over-prescribed opioids, too?"

"I don't know."

"What about Medicare fraud?"

"I'll put you in contact with an agent who works that department. She said she was interested in talking to you."

"That's awesome, Carrie." I paused for a moment. "I wonder if he paid his taxes due to the IRS?"

"That too you can ask my colleague about. Her name is Sally Ferguson."

"Can I call her? Do you have her phone number or email or something?"

Carrie gave me Sally Ferguson's contact information. "But why don't you wait until she calls you," she suggested.

"Okay. Maybe I can come down and meet her in her office."

"Well, arrange that with her."

"Okay. When are you going to take some time off and come up for another hike and piano hour?"

"Maybe when I finish with this case."

"Okay. Don't work too hard."

We said goodbye and hung up.

I wanted to text Sally Ferguson's cell phone number, announcing that I would call her office later in the afternoon. Then I realized that would be presumptive, and I should follow Carrie's advice of waiting for the agent to contact me. Besides, I needed to think these last few days through first. Fortunately, it did not take long for Sally Ferguson to call me. She introduced herself very formally, and I thanked her for calling.

"I understand you have some information for me on a Dr. Raymond Khazin."

"Well, I know Dr. Khazin. He was married to a good friend who fell and died only a few days ago. I'm suspicious that it wasn't an accident, as some think. I have a weird feeling that Dr. Khazin had something to do with his wife's untimely death."

"I see."

"I'd like to make an appointment to meet with you in your office or somewhere to talk to you if you have time."

"If you like. Dr. Khazin has been on our radar for a while as Carrie may have told you."

"Yes, I'd like to know about these *consulting fees* at his Torrance practice and also who his accountant is. He took out a life insurance policy on my friend for a million dollars, but he was in debt for double that amount. If he has defrauded Medicare and received so-called consultant fees from pharmaceuticals, I wonder where the money is going."

"Good point." She paused. "Let me ask you something. Are you connected with the police up there?"

"I guess you could say that," I said and laughed. "I'm engaged to our town's sheriff, Ed Cronin. Last year, your colleague Carrie Jensen and I worked with Ed on a case together."

"Yes, so I heard."

"Now I'm looking to see if Dr. Khazin had a motive for killing my friend—if she was, in fact, murdered."

"There's a little coffee shop just a few doors down from my office. How about we meet there at eleven o'clock tomorrow? That way, you don't have to go through all the security we have around here these days."

"That works for me. Thank you. I assume there's parking around there."

"Yes, plenty of street parking."

"Great! See you tomorrow at eleven."

After I hung up, I sat there thinking, bending and stretching my hands like a real pianist, speculating. What on earth could Ray be involved in?

———

Ed arrived soon after JP and Maria returned from nursery school. "I have a new contact in the FBI's Long Beach office," I told Ed while we were all playing with JP out on the deck.

He looked at me with raised eyebrows. "Oh, yeah? I thought you were engaged to me. What's his name?"

"It's a she, and her name is Sally Ferguson. Do you know her?"

"No, I don't think so." He shook his head. "I guess there are more and more females working in the Agency these days."

"That's right. And you need to hire some women too, Ed."

He looked at me but remained silent.

"Yes, Ed. Many women can actually be very good at police work, especially detective work." I shot him a quick glance and smiled mischievously. "Maybe if we had more women of the right kind in police forces all over the country, we wouldn't have so many unjustified shootings."

"You think so?"

"Yes, I do. And I don't mean that all women have the personality or demeanor to be street cops. Clearly not every man is all that suited for street policing either. Quite frankly, the biggest advantage I can see is that creative women will not resort to gunfire right away in a *situation*, as you call it."

"You may be right." He concentrated on playing with JP's little truck for a while. Maria had gone back into the kitchen.

I told him that my new FBI contact and I planned to meet the next day and that I wanted to see how much of Ray's shenanigans she would share with me. "I guess I'm looking for a possible motive Ray may have for killing Lizzie."

"It sounds like this is going to be a bigger case than our small department can handle, Megan. As you know, we're more into stolen golf carts, intoxicated tourists that yell and scream in front of businesses, scaring customers away, lost hikers, controlled substances, a couple of petty thefts." He paused. "And I'm just listing a few of the things that have happened in the past twenty-four hours. And in a week or two, the fire season starts."

"I know. You don't have an easy job, Ed, but think about how important your work really is. Doesn't that make you feel good? Besides, you can forward cases like Lizzie's to the San Bernardino office."

―――――

The next morning, Ed was gone before I woke up, and after the morning routine, I drove down to Long Beach to meet my new contact, Sally Ferguson. I sat at a table outside the old-fashioned coffee shop, which gave me a good view of the street. Only a low planter with colorful petunias separated me from the sidewalk. It was a nice day with a cool breeze from the ocean that was only a block or so away.

A young black woman in sunglasses and short-cropped hair stopped and glanced over the tables. She was petite and shapely, formally dressed in dark dressy slacks and a white long-sleeved shirt. She looked very much the part of an FBI agent. Early thirties, I guessed. Without knowing for sure, I waved. She smiled and came over. We shook hands as we introduced ourselves.

"It's actually nice to get out of the office for a while," she said and sat down opposite me. "We spend so much time sitting in front of a computer."

"Same here," I said. "I like to get out too. I'm a writer, and it sometimes gets lonely."

"Oh, yeah? I like to write too. What do you write?"

"Murder mysteries."

"Oh, that's really interesting," she said. "So, what do you have for me?"

I was taken slightly aback since I thought *she* might have something for *me*. "Well, I guess now I'm working on a real-life mystery," I said. "My good friend from grad school, Elizabeth or Lizzie Wurtz, was killed. Well, not officially killed. She fell on the bathroom floor, and her death appears to be an accident. But I have a strong hunch that her husband, Dr. Raymond Khazin—Carrie Jensen told me you would know his name—had something to do with her death."

"And that's Dr. Raymond Khazin who used to have a practice in Torrance?" She looked at me inquisitively. "What makes you suspicious?"

"I'm not sure. He has an alibi. He was in surgery at the hospital at the time of her death, but he could have hired someone. He is having an affair with a young nurse whose car was spotted at the house around the time of my friend's death. He conveniently showed up at the house to find her dead and had taken out a large life insurance policy on her a short time earlier. My friend also said he spent little time at the house, preferring to stay at his restaurant most nights. And Lizzie never mentioned him coming home during the day."

A young, preppy waiter who looked like he could have been one of my students—after all, Long Beach State University was located nearby—came with cups and a pot of coffee. "Coffee for the ladies?" he asked.

"Yes, please," we both chimed in together and nodded vigorously. He poured the coffee and brought over cream and sugar.

"But there are several other things," I continued, and took a sip. "First of all, Lizzie was only in her thirties. A fall on the bathroom floor should not have killed a woman that young. True, she may have hit her head, but there were also some cryptic marks on the wall, as if my friend or the killer wanted to leave a message of some sort. I was able to see her briefly before the coroner took her to the morgue and detected a strange odor."

"Poison?"

"Lizzie said her husband prescribed weight loss pills for her, but she often pretended to take them then pocket the pill. The initial investigation never mentioned the odor or pills, but poison could still be possible—at least the way I see it."

"You mean a poison that dissipates fast?"

"Exactly. And furthermore, the doctor seems to be strapped for cash," I added.

"Well, evidently he wasn't."

"You mean he had money obtained by illegal means?"

"We believe so but have no proof."

"But where has that money gone? Do you know who his accountant is?"

"Yes, Phillips & Zorovitsz in Torrance."

"Wow! That's a big firm."

"Yes, and you won't find anything there."

I looked at her a bit bewildered.

"That firm no doubt keeps everything above board and in line with the IRS and the tax laws," Ferguson said. "They're not stupid."

"I see." I scratched my chin and paused. Ms. Ferguson was holding her cup with both hands as if she wanted to warm her hands. Her elbows were on the table. I didn't feel the physical cold but did feel a chill from the lack of evidence that could connect Ray Khazin with his wife's death.

"But where's the money?" I asked.

"Well, that's the big question."

"He wouldn't have time to gamble."

"Right. But we have heard through our CIA operatives in Beirut that weapons from a clandestine gun running ring in the Los Angeles and Long Beach harbor areas are coming into Lebanon. The name Dr. Raymond Khazin showed up unexpectedly on a document."

My jaw dropped, and I sat there speechless for a while. "Surely not to the Hezbollah or any of the other radical Muslim groups," I said finally. "They get enough weapons from the other Arab countries."

"Right. According to the CIA, the weapons appear to be destined for an opposition group that wants to throw out Hezbollah." She put her coffee down and looked me straight in the face. "I hear from Carrie that you lived in the Middle East some years ago and know something about the culture over there."

"Yeess." I said hesitatingly, needing a few moments to take in all this. I took a few long sips of coffee before I asked, "Do you think my friend might have gotten wind of these activities?"

"It's possible."

I was thinking of Lizzie. She had served in the Foreign Service in Lebanon and was no dummy. "Maybe she smelled something rotten," I said slowly. "And it may have cost her her life?" I shook my head, at a loss as to how to continue our conversation. "So, we have two or three cases going here," I said finally. "Possible kickbacks from pharmaceuticals, Medicare and Medicaid fraud, gun running, and possibly a murder or aiding and abetting a killer."

"That's right."

I made a whistling sound and threw up my arms in exasperation. "I always thought Khazin was a jerk, a handsome devil who bewitched women, and a lousy husband. But gun running and murder? That never entered my mind." I had to stop to take a deep breath. "He has a Middle Eastern restaurant and club in San Bernardino for men mostly, I think, with shisha pipes and belly dancers. He keeps a room in the club that he uses, maybe with his favorite dancers."

"Yes, I saw that. Have you been there then?"

"Yes, our sheriff, Ed Cronin, is my fiancé. He and I visited the club to check it out under the pretense that I was scouting out night spots for some visiting businessmen. Have you seen it?"

"No, I haven't."

"But you know about it. You've had the doctor under surveillance for some time. Am I right?"

"Yes, he's been on our radar, but mainly for fraud. That's my department's job."

"I see. So where do we go from here?"

"Well, the murder case is not ours, but it all hangs together, of course, and we might involve ourselves."

"Do you think the restaurant or club or whatever it is could be a money laundering outfit? When Ed and I visited, we talked to a couple of the girls working there. I don't think any of them know anything, but they told me that a group of men would meet there, smoke their pipes and talk loudly and animatedly in Arabic."

"Hm, that's interesting. I don't know. The restaurant is in his name, and the permits are in order. He has a brother who lives in the Los Angeles area too. The brother may also be involved in this alliance."

"Holy crap! Excuse my language. This is a lot bigger than I bargained for."

"I know, and we'll handle it. But you might be of help. Carrie says that you have a nose for detective work. She and you worked on a big case together last year, right?"

"Yes, but she and the sheriff really made it all fall into place."

"Maybe, but Carrie gives you credit too."

"Thank you. That's nice."

"She also told me about your relationship with the sheriff. Seems like a good match."

"Yes. We're engaged. We were in Paris last year when he proposed out of the blue. He's a nice guy but in no hurry to actually tie the knot. How about you?"

"Not married and no children. I have a boyfriend on and off."

"I have a little boy. I was married to the sheriff's brother, but he died as the result of an accident. Ed and I came together after that."

We finished our coffee, and Sally put four one-dollar bills on the table.

"I guess you come here often," I said and smiled. "Is that what they charge for coffee here?"

I put a five-dollar bill down, and Sally insisted I take one of her singles back.

"We don't want to spoil them," she said, and we both laughed.

I had planned to do a little shopping on my way back, but I had so much on my mind that I drove straight home. To contact the CPA office would be fruitless, as Sally had said. CPAs have their privacy obligations. The FBI could get what they wanted, and everything there would be above board, anyway. Ray was no rocket scientist, but smart enough to cover his tracks.

I also wanted to talk to Joe and Ed. It was probably time for them to call in the FBI officially to help with Lizzie's death. I had no doubt it had something to do with Ray's other schemes. Even if the autopsy didn't show anything other than a head wound, there was surely enough circumstantial evidence to warrant a serious investigation, if not an indictment. I stopped at El Pollo Loco in Fontana for a bite to eat and then went to JP's nursery school to pick him up early. I made it home before Maria left to pick him up. I remembered that Ed had a meeting that evening, so I decided I'd call him in the morning.

# 6

## FAMILY TIME

The week had flown by so quickly that I had lost track of the days. Ed called from his car while he was out on his rounds. The first forest fire had broken out farther east, but no one was hurt, no structures damaged or even close to the fire. The fire trucks were on site, but the fire department decided to let it burn itself out. Of course, the forest needs a fire now and then to renew itself, and the animals know better than to hang around. However, the distance from one end of the county to the other is enormous, and Ed was busy. Except for two domestic violence incidents during the night, everything else had fortunately been quiet, Ed said, but the weekend was coming up with short-term renters and boisterous parties.

"How do you feel about Mexican food tonight? I'll come over later this evening and bring dinner from Papagayos," he suggested. "That way, Maria can go home early."

"That sounds like a good plan," I agreed. "She's been around a lot this week while I've been here and there. How about those chicken *flautas?* JP really likes those. And I really haven't done any grocery shopping these last few days either."

"*Flautas* it is. I think that's their specialty, anyway."

To my surprise, Maria had some reservations about going home early."What about dinner?" she said. "It's Friday, and Ed will come and expect to eat something."

She had raised both Chris and Ed like her own children after their mother died. They both referred to her as *mamita* or sometimes to tease her *mamacita*—little mother. She had three sons of her own, and I suspected the youngest one might be my father-in-law's son, maybe a product of an affair Maria and Joe may have had. The son looked so much like Chris and Ed. The possible affair was strictly a rumor, I thought. However, when I mentioned as much to Chris one day, I was quickly silenced. I never brought it up again, but I knew Maria was a beneficiary on the family trust. To me it was also clear that Maria still carried a torch for my father-in-law, a handsome older man, many years her senior. I had no doubt that Maria had been paid well, and she'd been a good mother to all of them.

"Ed is bringing dinner tonight, Maria," I said. "Chicken *flautas*. He wanted you to have some time off. Of course, the *flautas* will not be as good as yours, but we'll manage."

She smiled and nodded with an air of satisfaction, her big brown eyes sparkling. Despite a few extra pounds around her tummy, she was light on her feet in the white nurses' shoes she liked to wear. "Okay," she said. She grabbed her bag and started for the door.

"I'll see you Monday morning unless Ed has something for you over the weekend," I said and waved.

"Are you sure you be okay?"

"Yes. I need to spend some time with JP too. I've hardly seen him all week. *Hasta la vista*."

*"Hasta luego."*

There was a message from James on my phone. Final exams were around the corner at his college in London. Afterward, he planned a trip to Italy and Greece with some friends before returning home. College funding and the trip, of course, courtesy of his grandfather, Joe, the money being part of the family trust fund.

He wondered what I thought of that idea and what I might suggest he should be sure to see.

Ed would be disappointed that James was delaying his homecoming, but he'd get used to the idea. I started to work out an itinerary for James in my head as I drove to pick up JP. On the way home, we stopped to buy ice cream. JP talked non-stop about all the naughty things his little friend Arden had said and done. I wasn't sure whether Arden was a boy or a girl, but he or she had apparently kicked the teacher, pushed the other children, and bit little Shawna. I remembered a book by Shirley Jackson called *Life among the Savages*, in which the author wrote that her son transferred all his bad behavior to an imaginary friend named Charles. I hoped JP was not the one kicking the teacher and biting his friends. His teacher always pointed out what a good boy he was.

JP and I were at the piano playing a little *duet* when we heard Ed's signal. JP jumped down and ran to the door. He helped Ed carry the plastic bags with the food to the kitchen before Ed went into the bedroom to change. He knew better than to wear his uniform around a rambunctious boy eating Mexican food.

The *flautas* were delicious, shredded cheese and chicken rolled up in a flour tortilla and lightly fried with plenty of homemade guacamole and sour cream. When we finished, JP went straight from the table to the bathtub.

Ed was a stricter disciplinarian than I was, and bedtime was rigorously observed. Ed cleaned up the kitchen while I put JP to bed, then he joined me on the couch. I showed him James's email. "Did you get the same message, Ed?"

"I don't know. I didn't check." He pulled out his phone. "No, I don't see it. How come he tells you and not me?"

"He probably expects me to soften the blow," I said mockingly. "So, he's not coming directly home after school is out and needs more money."

Ed just groaned.

"He wants to see more of Europe while he's over there. I think it's a good idea, and you and his grandfather can afford it."

While Ed pouted, I gave him a kiss on his cheek, then continued more seriously. "Actually, what he wants is for me to figure out an itinerary for him and his friends since I've been there."

"And when do I get to see all those places?" Ed said and feigned a fake sigh and a crestfallen expression.

"Well, you've seen Paris and London, and we could go over to meet James and travel to Italy and Greece, but we're in the middle of a baffling case."

"I'll keep that suggestion about Europe in mind. Now, what did you learn from your FBI friend?"

"It's hard to believe, and it sure took me by surprise, but Ray has been on the FBI's radar for a while. He may have defrauded Medicare and possible other Medical practices for millions. But there's no record of where the money is going."

"Gambling debts?"

"It doesn't look like it." I told him about the suspicions that there was an illegal gun running operation in the Long Beach/Los Angeles harbor area, shipping weapons to an opposition group in Lebanon. "Ray's name has allegedly cropped up on some document or other."

Ed's face looked like a living exclamation mark. "Holy cow!"

"That was my reaction too."

"What stories are you telling these people to get them to share all their secrets with you?"

"I have my ways." I gave him my most innocent smile. "Carrie and I are close, and she trusts me. And she considers me an informant."

Ed shook his head. "How could the doctor be so stupid as to use his own name in a business like this?"

"I don't know. Maybe it came up accidentally in certain money transfers." I paused to give Ed a chance to process the information. "And I wonder how the restaurant figures into all of this."

"And what does it have to do with your friend's death?"

"I don't know," I said. "Maybe she was too nosy. She was a pretty smart and perceptive woman."

"I have no doubt about that."

I had let go of his hand, and we sat there in silence, thinking all this through. At least I did.

"Do you want a drink?" I asked.

"Yeah. I'll fix you something. I'll just have a beer." He rose and went back into the kitchen to find something in the wine cabinet. He returned with a glass of rosé for me and a can of cold beer for himself.

"In any case, this case is too big for our small department. This is FBI stuff. I'll call them and tell Garcia to take care of the formalities on Monday."

"I'll call Ray to see how he is and if I can help in some way. I should update Lizzie's mother too. She thinks Ray is such a fine man. She'll be shocked to learn the truth about him."

"Are you gonna tell her everything?"

"No. Not my place. At least, not yet."

———

After we finished the coffee and bagels that Ed and JP brought from the village the next morning, we put Duchess on a leash and took a walk along the lake. The sun was already warm and the air still.

"I wonder what I would have learned if Lizzie and I could have taken one more hike together as we had planned," I said as I let Duchess loose to chase the squirrels. As expected, Ed frowned at me for letting the dog run off leash.

"There's no one here, Ed," I said.

"I know, but if everyone who came here let their dogs run off leash, we'd have a problem, wouldn't we?"

"Relax, Ed."

He remained quiet as he watched JP run after Duchess. JP was not afraid of the dog but feared the squirrels.

"Has anyone heard from Ray or seen him around this week?" I asked. "I assume he had surgeries scheduled and had to work."

"I've gone by the hospital a few times, but I haven't noticed his car although I haven't particularly looked for it either."

"Have you driven by his house?"

"Of course. His car hasn't been in the driveway."

"I haven't been to the house since Ben cut and drywalled the holes in the bathroom." Ed was ahead of me but stopped and waited. I looked at him, and he took my hand and squeezed it. "There's no more police tape around the entrance, is there?"

"No."

"I'd like to go inside again," I said. "Maybe I'll call Ray and offer to help him take care of Lizzie's belongings, her clothes and stuff. Maybe I could make use of some of it. Maybe Lizzie's mother would like some of her things too."

"I assume they had a housekeeper. She would probably need the clothes more than you."

"It's not that I want her clothes, Ed. I want to see if there could be some clues among her personal things. I want to take a look at those diet pills too." I looked up at him. "What diet pills give you headaches and problems with balance? Maybe she took other pills too. What could cause her to have an accident on a straight road with no traffic?"

"Well, I could get a warrant," Ed suggested.

"Maybe. But let me talk to Ray first and see how he reacts to me taking some of Lizzie's clothes and belongings for myself and her mother. He may still be at his brother's house."

"I don't know what you expect to find," Ed said doubtfully.

———

On Monday morning, I called Ray at the hospital. I wondered if he would find it strange that I wanted to go through Lizzie's belongings. However, I didn't think he would object.

"He's not in yet," the receptionist said, "but I can leave him a message to return your call."

"Thank you. Do you know if he was at the hospital last week?"

"I'm not sure. I'm not here every day. His wife died a little over a week ago."

"Yes, I know." I left my name, number and a message for Ray to contact me. Then I asked if nurse Cheryl Day was on duty, but it was her day off. I called Cheryl at home and asked if she had seen Dr. Khazin at the hospital since my friend's death.

"No," she said, "I don't think he was in at all last week. His surgeries were either rescheduled, or patients were referred to the Colton Medical Center."

"What about Heidi?"

"Heidi was here on the days she was supposed to be here. You don't think she and Dr. Khazin would elope right after his wife's death, do you? That would be absurd."

"I know, but I wonder where he is. I want to ask if he needs help sorting through Lizzie's belongings."

"I see. I guess you're not going to accept that your friend died of an accidental fall."

I sighed and cleared my throat. "Did you know that she had a mysterious car accident on a straight road in broad daylight with no other cars around?"

"No. When was that?"

"A couple of weeks ago."

"I had no idea. Do you think she was suffering from some kind of illness?"

"I don't know. But I need to talk to Ray. I'll keep you updated."

After I hung up, I called Lizzie's mom again. She seemed calmer and more resigned to what had happened. She had not heard from Ray since he called to tell her about her daughter's death. "Have you talked to him?" she asked me.

"No, I'm trying to contact him. If you hear from him, could you tell him I'm trying to reach him? I want to see if he needs any help sorting through Lizzie's things." I paused for just a moment. "Is there anything of hers you'd like to have, Mrs. Wurtz?"

"I don't know. I guess I should come out there myself."

"It's okay. I can do it. And if you don't want anything, I'll donate it to a church out here that helps recent immigrants."

"Yes, I'd like that," she whispered, and I heard a soft sob.

"I'm so sorry, Mrs. Wurtz. I'll call you again soon."

"Thank you."

I called the hospital again and asked for nurse Heidi Hillstrom. She was on duty but didn't pick up her phone. I told the receptionist I would stay on the line until she was free. It took only a few minutes of canned piano music before I heard Heidi's voice, more subdued now. No, she had not seen Ray.

"When did you see him last?" I asked.

"I don't remember. Maybe the day before the accident. Why?"

"When you see him, could you please ask him to call me? I want to help him sort through his wife's clothes. Her mother would like to have a few items."

"Okay," she said. Perhaps she was resigned to the fact that the wily doctor wasn't quite as close to marrying her as she might have imagined.

I called Al Sheikh, Ray's restaurant, and talked to Rosie, but Ray had not been there for several days. She had heard about his wife but had not seen him since. "What about the group of friends that usually came to smoke and hang out with him?"

"No, they haven't been here this week either."

I pulled up the public records to look for Ray's brother. I remembered Lizzie telling me that his brother lived in Rancho Cucamonga, but I didn't know his first name, and there were several Khazins in that city. Close relatives appeared under each last name and under Richard Khazin, a brother named Raymond Khazin was listed. Bingo! I had to pay $1.99 to access the telephone number. No problem. I called, and Ray's brother picked up. I introduced myself and asked if Ray was there, but he told me that Ray was not available.

"I'm sorry. Ray told me he was staying with you for a few days. He's still not back at his house and hasn't been at the hospital all week. His friends are starting to worry about him."

"Well, he does have some important business to take care of. I'll let him know that you called. Megan Viets, you said?"

"Yes." I gave him my phone number.

I had now exhausted my list of people to call. I'd have to wait to see if Ray would call back before I called my contact at the FBI. Maybe I could go over to Lizzie's house without his permission. After all, I was just going to look at her clothes and jewelry. I sat down at the piano and played some spirited Scott Joplin pieces to release some of my excess energy. I told Maria I'd pick up JP.

Ed stopped by later on one of his rounds. I told him about my fruitless telephone conversations.

"It doesn't sound like he wants to see or talk to anyone right now," Ed said. "I'm sure he'll call you back at some point."

"I want to go over to Lizzie's house and look through her things," I said. "If Ray doesn't contact me and give me permission, I'll just go over to the house, anyway."

"Megan, just wait until we have the autopsy results. If there's anything there, we'll get a search warrant. You could jeopardize the case, if there is one, and you could put yourself in jeopardy."

"And if the autopsy comes back clean?"

"Then we don't have a case, Megan."

"The poison I'm thinking of dissipates a few hours after the victim's death."

"You're making too much out of this, Megan. Let it go. The FBI is onboard now. Let them do their job."

I said nothing further, a sneaky way of letting Ed think I wouldn't go to Lizzie's house. But my hunch was too strong—I'd risk jail time to prove Lizzie was murdered and her husband did it.

Perhaps Ed thought he'd won because of my silence. In any case, he had a meeting and had to leave.

I remembered that Chris's crazy wife had been a whiz at picking locks and had left a lock pick that I had put away in the mudroom. I found it and studied it before I tried it on the locked side door in the kitchen. It worked, and I put it in my purse. Tomorrow I'd go over to Lizzie's house with or without Ray's permission.

———

After the morning rush at our house, I drove over to Lizzie and Ray's lakefront home. I parked a little down the road and stopped by Mr. Basil Rutherford's house to see their observant neighbor. I used the big brass knocker to announce myself as I didn't see a doorbell. A stranger opened the heavy oak door. I introduced myself.

"I'm Jack, Mr. Rutherford's driver and companion." He was younger than his boss, but his hair was graying too. "Come in," he said with an inviting smile. "Basil will be down momentarily."

"Hello, Ms. Viets," Mr. Rutherford said as he came up behind me. "So nice to see you again."

"Good to see you too, Mr. Rutherford. You have a good memory."

"Thank you. Comes from working in plays for decades."

Jack excused himself and walked toward the back of the house.

"I wondered if you had seen anyone next door since we spoke last. Have you seen Dr. Khazin's car at all?"

"No, I don't think the good doctor or his car has been there. The maid, Linda, was there one day, but she didn't stay very long. We use the same gal, and she came here afterwards."

"Otherwise, no activity?"

"No, I don't think so, but of course I can't be sure. I go to bed early, and someone could have been there in the evening."

I had my doubt that someone could have escaped this man's watchful eye. "I talked to my friend's mother. She wanted me to pick up some of Lizzie's belongings. She lives in Arizona and hasn't been able to reach her son-in-law, so I offered to go over and take a look."

"Do you have a key?"

"Yes, I hope it works." I wasn't entirely confident that I would be able to pick the lock as I had planned. "Did Lizzie give you a spare key by any chance?" I asked hopefully and started to walk back toward the door. "I know neighbors often do that around here in case of an emergency?"

"No, she never gave me one," he answered as he followed me outside. "But I think she hid a spare under that rock over there on the side." He pointed. "I saw her remove it one day to open her door. I assumed she had forgotten her regular key. Good luck!"

I thanked the gracious gentleman and walked over to Lizzie's front door. The lock pick didn't work as easily as it did on my kitchen door, so I went over to the rock Mr. Rutherford pointed out and found the key. I looked behind me but saw no one, although I had no doubt the neighbor had me under observation.

Once inside, I went straight to the kitchen and started looking through the shelves and cupboards. I thought Lizzie's vitamins and other pills would be there, but I found none. Her diet pills would have to be somewhere in the house. Maybe in the bathroom.

The bathroom was adjacent to the master bedroom on the first floor, and I stopped in the bedroom first. The bed was neatly made, and everything looked clean and orderly. I opened the drawers of Lizzie's lingerie chest and picked up her jewelry in the top drawer. Some of it was expensive, and I weighed it all in my hand before putting it back. Robbery was obviously not a motive in Lizzie's death. I opened the door to the walk-in closet. Lizzie's dresses, coats and pants hung neatly on one side. Her shoes and boots stood on a shelf below. Ray's slacks, shirts and suits hung on the other wall. I checked for pockets in Lizzie's pants. It irritated me that so few women's garments even had pockets. Nothing there.

The dining room was across the hall from the bedroom and held only a table with dining chairs neatly placed around it. Lizzie's black purse sat on one of the chairs. I opened it and found her keys, which I quickly put in my pocket. I left her wallet and her hairbrush alone. There were no pill bottles in her purse, and I wondered where her phone could be. I called the number Ray had given me, hoping it was her cell number, but I heard no ringing anywhere.

Suddenly, I heard a car engine and a car door slam right outside. I froze for a moment, but then quickly retreated back into the bedroom and into the closet, closing the door. It didn't sound like Ed's car. Could it be Ray? But why would Ray show up here now when no one seemed to have heard from him? Maybe someone told him that I was looking for him, and he decided to check the house. I could hear the front door open and close, followed by light footsteps. I tried desperately to think of a good story, in case it was Ray. I couldn't imagine how it could be anyone else.

After a few minutes, I heard water running in the pipes somewhere, and I thought someone must have turned on a faucet in the kitchen. I opened the door a little and saw a tall, heavyset woman pull a vacuum cleaner into the living room. It must be Linda, the maid. I stepped out from my hiding place. "Hi Linda," I called out as I walked through the bedroom and stopped in the hallway. "I didn't know you'd be here today."

"Who are you?" she said gruffly and looked at me suspiciously. "I come here every Tuesday."

"Oh, I see. I'm Megan, Mrs. Khazin's friend. Her mother wanted me to come over and look through her daughter's belongings. You know, of course, what happened here the other day, right?"

"Yes, Mrs. Khazin had an accident and died."

"Yes, that's right. Did you see Dr. Khazin last week?"

"No, but I figured he'd want his house cleaned, so I came. He didn't leave any money for me—they usually leave cash in the kitchen—but I just cleaned a little bit and went next door to clean. The doctor hasn't left any money for me today either, and it doesn't look like anyone's been here at all. I'll just do a light dusting and vacuuming."

"No problem, Linda. I'll pay you for both days. How much does he owe you?"

"Miss Elizabeth usually pays me eighty dollars a week, but I didn't stay long so fifty will be okay."

"I'll pay you one hundred and fifty dollars for both weeks since you had to come all the way out here. How's that?"

"Thank you, but I clean for the neighbors too, so a hundred is okay." She looked at me carefully as she fidgeted with the vacuum cleaner cord. "I'll probably be out of a job now," she said. "Do you need anyone to clean for you, ma'am?"

"Thank you, Linda, but I have someone who's been working for my husband's family—the Cronins—for many years."

"You were married to Chris Cronin, right?"

"Yes. Did you know him?" Of course, this was life in a small town. Everybody knew everything about everyone's business. Naturally, everyone knew Chris and Ed.

"Yes, I grew up here," she said. "I remember him from high school."

"I see. So you know the sheriff too?"

"Yes, I know him. I heard that you're seeing him now."

"Yes, you heard right." I didn't want to say any more since Ed and I had not made our engagement public, although that was probably all over town too. I looked at her rough hands. Maybe she wouldn't have to do any scrubbing today. "I wonder if you could help me fold some of Mrs. Khazin's clothes," I said.

"Sure."

"I'll ask her mother and Dr. Khazin if it's alright for you to take some to your church or somewhere. My friend had many nice things that someone ought to be able to use." Linda might want a few items for herself, I thought. She was a big woman too. "Be sure to shake out the dust and check all pockets," I said. "Turn them inside out. We can put it all on the bed until I talk to Dr. Khazin."

We started on one side with the coats, turned the pockets out, and picked up coins, paper clips, short library pencils, candy wrappers, and receipts.

"So, do you have a family, Linda?" I asked.

"Yes, a husband and two sons," she said with a smile, as if mentioning her husband and sons gave her pleasure. "They're both in high school." She chatted about her family while we continued with Lizzie's pants. I let Linda do most of the folding, as she did a better job than I did. When we finished, she checked the laundry hamper for more clothes.

Suddenly, something other than a coin or paper clip fell on the floor and rolled over to the side. It was a pill, more like a capsule. I picked it up with a Kleenex, held it up against the light, and turned it around. "Do you know where Mrs. Khazin kept her pills, Linda?"

"Some are in the kitchen, I think, and some in the bathroom."

"I didn't see any in the kitchen," I said. "I'll look in the bathroom."

I hesitated entering the master bathroom where Lizzie had fallen and died, but I took a deep breath and pulled myself together. Everything seemed to sparkle. Linda had probably cleaned there the week before. I looked on the counter, on the shelves and in the medicine cabinet but found nothing except a bottle of aspirin, two bottles of Tylenol PM, some Neosporin and Cortaid. I met Linda in the kitchen.

"Nothing left in the kitchen except for some multivitamins and Caltrex," she announced.

"Any capsules that look like this one?" I held up the one that had fallen on the floor. "It came from the pair of pants you took from the hamper, didn't it?"

"Yes, it was one of her khaki pair."

I went back and picked up the pants to examine them more closely, but I didn't think it was the pair she had worn on our hike. I scrutinized the capsule again and thought I saw some scratches on one side. "I'll take this pill with me," I said. "If she took pills, it could help determine the cause of death."

While Linda finished vacuuming, I called Officer Garcia. I told him what Linda had found and asked him if he could come over.

Linda was soon ready to leave, but I asked her to wait as a sort of alibi for my being in the house and also because she had found the capsule when she shook out the pants pockets.

Garcia must have been close because he arrived within half an hour. "How did you get in?" he wanted to know.

"I have a key," Linda replied hurriedly. "I'm the housekeeper and come here every Tuesday whether someone is here or not. They just put my money under a bowl in the kitchen."

Garcia looked at me, but I ignored him. "Linda has found something interesting," I said in order to distract him from my entry and to get this visit back on track. "Actually, Joe, I'm here to help Dr. Khazin sort some of his wife's clothes, and Linda found this in one of Mrs. Khazin's pockets." I held the capsule up to show him. "We didn't find any prescription medications, but if she took pills, it could help determine if the cause of death was something other than just a simple fall. It's just a hunch, but I'd like for you to send it to the lab for analysis."

"Okay, I'll do that. What else did you find?"

"Nothing of interest. Linda has done a good job cleaning. Come, and take a look."

Garcia hesitated.

"It's okay. You can come in and look. It's all cleaned up as if nothing has ever happened in this house."

Garcia walked around while I wrote a check for Linda and gave it to her.

Outside, Linda locked the door. "I usually leave my car in the driveway since I'm just going next door, okay?"

"Sure. And thank you Linda."

"Thank you for the check," she said and left.

As Linda went into the house next door and Garcia headed to his car, I saw Mr. Rutherford and Jack leave.

# 7

# SUSPICIONS ABOUT DR. KHAZIN'S WHEREABOUTS

The next day, I called Sally Ferguson and left a message asking her to contact me. I didn't feel like working on my book, so I took Duchess for a walk. I was down by the dock when Sally returned my call, and I sat down on a bench overlooking the water.

"So, what do you have for me today?" she said. I was again taken aback by her question. I didn't feel like an informer; I wanted information from her, but I played along.

"Well, I can't locate Dr. Khazin anywhere. He hasn't been at the hospital. His patients have been rescheduled or referred to other clinics. I called the Al Sheikh Hookah Lounge in San Bernardino and his brother Richard's home in Rancho Cucamonga, but no one has seen him or heard from him. His brother did say Ray has important business to take care of and he would let Ray know I called. Do you know where else he could be hanging out?"

"No, we're looking into whether or not he has left the country. In addition to his American passport, he has both a Jordanian and a Lebanese passport."

"Wow! I didn't know that," I said in amazement.

"Yes, many immigrants want to hold on to their own nationalities, which is usually not a problem."

"I guess they don't want to burn all bridges." I paused to clear my throat. "My friend Lizzie met Dr. Khazin when she worked in his medical office. They married rather quickly, and we always thought he married her to qualify for American citizenship. Lizzie had worked in the Foreign Service and he may have thought she knew some shortcuts. To tell you the truth, I don't know why that was important to him. He already worked here as a licensed physician, but I suppose he had his reasons."

"I see," she said flatly. She didn't appear interested in how Ray had become an American citizen.

"Any specific clues that he's flown the coop?"

"We're checking."

"That's good," I said slowly, wondering what to do if Ray had left the country. "May I call you again in a few days for updates?"

"Sure. How's your homicide investigation going? I know there's no evidence linking him to the murder."

"I know, but we'll have another piece of evidence when the results of the second autopsy come back," I said with confidence. "I wish they'd done a more advanced autopsy right away. As you know, some poisons can only be traced for a few hours after the victim's death."

Duchess was trying to dig up something near the water. I looked at the expansive lake that lay there dark and silent and sighed. "Duchess, get away from there." I made shooing motions that the dog ignored.

"Her husband, the wily doctor, found her and supposedly examined her," I continued. "I think the medics and the medical examiner took his word that it was an accident, but I distinctly smelled a strange odor."

Sally just mumbled something. I wouldn't be surprised if she thought I was a bit deranged, me thinking that I knew more than the medical examiner and the doctor.

"I wonder if he could be in Lebanon," I said just as much to myself as to Sally.

"Yeah, I've been thinking the same."

"Does Lebanon have an extradition agreement with the United States?"

"No, although Jordan does. And other countries in the region, but not Lebanon."

"Interesting." If he was in Lebanon, I realized that he could very well get away with murder.

"We have alerted the authorities at LAX and Orange County airports. They are the only airports around here with direct flights to Europe, but he might have gone through Chicago or New York or a slew of other airports that have nonstop flights across the Atlantic. It's a real cat-and-mouse game."

"I can see that," I said. I didn't mention anything about finding the mysterious capsule. I'd keep that tidbit of information until it had been analyzed. What the lab technicians would find—if they'd find anything at all—I did not know.

"And even if we locate him," Sally continued, "we don't have enough evidence to bring him back, anyway."

"So why are you looking for him, then?"

"He's still under surveillance, and we want to know where he is."

"That's good. And if we find enough evidence for the San Bernardino District Attorney to indict him for murder, we'd have a reason for wanting him back in this country."

"True."

"Maybe we could set up a ruse to lure him out of Lebanon, if that's where he is. Lebanon would be the most likely country he would flee to, don't you agree?"

"Yes, I do," she said with a sigh that signaled the end of our conversation. "Keep up the good work. And let us know if you hear anything."

"Will do," I said. "And you'll do the same, right?"

"Will do."

I looked around for Duchess. She had just found a spot to relieve herself and was back on the chase. I called Deputy Garcia and told him about Dr. Khazin's multiple passports, in addition to his American one.

"I know some people from England who have both British and American passports. Canadians too. I wouldn't mind having a Canadian passport myself if the politicians make a mess of this country," he said with a snort and paused before he went on: "So, you think the doctor's marriage to your friend was one of convenience?"

"Well, no. Oh, I don't know," I said. "But it's a thought. I'm not sure if marrying an American makes the partner a citizen or not. Maybe Ray Khazin took the test and became a citizen that way. But now that he's a citizen, he may have felt that he didn't need her any more. And it's possible he has other women that he entertains in his private room down at the Al Sheikh Hookah Lounge."

"You mean that would be his motive?"

"I don't know." I'm sure Garcia could hear my frustration over the phone.

"He could have just divorced her."

"Yes, it doesn't make sense. He's Catholic, and divorce is frowned upon. That would raise a red flag for sure. Maybe he thought he had devised a plan for a perfect murder and could pick up the one million in insurance."

"Yeah. That's a nice little sum."

I saw Duchess coming toward me. She seemed to think it was time to go home. I rose, and we started up the path just as a red-tailed hawk circled overhead. What a sight! The hawk was probably looking for a small duck or a coot. What great hunters they were! I wish I had the same skill.

I heard only static on the phone. "Are you still there, Joe?"

"Yes, I'm here."

"I'm moving around, and the connection may go in and out," I explained and then continued, "The fact of the matter is that we don't have any hard evidence until we have the result of the second autopsy. Then again, that autopsy may prove nothing criminal. When do you think the results will come back?"

"This week, they said, but I'm not holding my breath."

"I don't know what should take them so long. On TV, the results come back the next day. Then again, this isn't TV. It's reality."

"Who knows? They always say they don't have enough manpower."

I hurried up the path to catch up with Duchess and was a little out of breath. "We know that Dr. Khazin has contributed substantial sums to this organization of Lebanese expatriates. A group of Lebanese compatriots meet regularly at his club to talk and smoke shisha pipes. It's the latest trend among men in the Middle East, I understand."

"Really? You seem to know a lot about what's happening over in the Middle East. I'm impressed."

"Well, it's a different world. I know. I lived there for a while. You'll let me know when you hear something?"

"That I will."

————

Later, I told Ed the same story I'd told Officer Garcia.

"The doctor seems to have a busy life," Ed chuckled. We were in the kitchen, and he was rummaging around making a cup of coffee. I had the feeling he wasn't all that interested in Dr. Khazin and his antics, and it irritated me. "The autopsy should be in soon," Ed finally disclosed. "We'll see what happens then."

"I'm not expecting much, Ed. Not unless they take samples from the bones and other tissue, which I hope they'll do. Ray knows how to avoid leaving evidence that can show up in a simple autopsy. What I'm more interested in is what the capsule we found in Lizzie's pocket will reveal. I'm sure it's one of the diet pills that Ray prescribed. Lizzie told me they gave her a headache and made her feel dizzy. She told me that she sometimes didn't take the pills and instead put them in her pockets. The one we found may have been one she had forgotten about."

"I grant you that it's an interesting thought, Megan." He took a deep breath and blew the heat from his coffee. "I wonder how many husbands and wives kill each other without ever being detected."

"More than we'll ever know. But I bet that's harder to do than we think," I quipped.

————

A couple of days later, I stopped by the sheriff's station. I wanted to talk to Ed about an invitation we received that needed an RSVP as soon as possible. Ed wasn't in, but I literally bumped into Detective Garcia who was on his way out the door as I entered. Garcia had come up from San Bernardino for a meeting unrelated to our investigation, he told me.

"I was just about to call you," he said as I gave a deputy a note to put on Ed's desk. "The autopsy report came in yesterday."

"Well, what did it say?"

"Not much."

He followed me out to my car

"So, what specifically does the report reveal?" I turned around to face him.

"The results are inconclusive," he said. "There were traces of potassium cyanide in the bones, but the amount was so small that it could have come from eating mushrooms. Did your friend liked mushrooms?"

I shook my head. "I have no idea. We had just reconnected. I can't remember eating mushrooms back when we were in school."

"There was also an irregularity in the esophagus, a small tear that could be attributed to poison, but again inconclusive."

"That's interesting." I said. I looked across the road at the small outdoor café. "You're a coffee addict like all the other deputies around here, aren't you?" I said. "I see deputies in the doughnut shop almost every day." I tried my best to flash him an inviting smile. "Can I offer you a cup, Joe?" I pointed to the café. "I want to hear all the details and your thoughts."

"Okay," he said, and I led the way across the road

We sat down at a rough-hewn wooden table, and a waiter, a middle-aged man with a white apron tied around his waist, came right over with two mugs that he set in front of us. I took a sip of the lukewarm liquid while Garcia doctored his with both cream and sugar.

"Sooo…" I looked at him expectantly as I played with my cup of cooling coffee.

"Well, the coroner did change the cause of death from *accidental* to *undetermined*."

"So, doesn't that raise enough questions to pursue the case further?"

The waiter came over to offer us a refill. "The coffee is cold," I said, and the man took both our cups and poured them out in a planter next to our table before refilling the mugs with fresh, hot brew.

"I'm with you. The sheriff and the department agree," Garcia said. "The FBI is now officially involved in the investigation. Sheriff Cronin will handle most of it at our end, but I'll be assisting."

"Good. As I told you, the Bureau is already investigating Dr. Khazin for defrauding Medicare and taking kickbacks from pharmaceutical companies, although they have no real evidence. That's probably why they were so willing to cooperate with us from the beginning. They wanted to see if we could come up with physical evidence that would link Khazin to Lizzie's death." I took a few sips again before I went on. "So far, the evidence against him is circumstantial. We're acting on a hunch, suspicion, intuition and instinct." I gave Garcia a bright smile. "Yes, I know," I said a bit sarcastically. "Men don't want to hear about women's instinct and intuition."

"Well, it's not that," he said defensively. "In police work, we have to have physical proof."

I sighed and took another sip of coffee. "Yes, physical proof," I said and stopped to clear my throat. "You sent the capsule in for analysis, didn't you? The capsule that Linda, the housekeeper, found in one of Lizzie's pockets while she was over at the house cleaning?"

"Yes, and the results of that one should come back soon." He gulped down some coffee and shot a quick glance over at the station. "The DNA testing of blood stains takes longer—probably several weeks—not that the test itself takes that long, but there's a backlog."

"You mean the blood stains on the square that we cut out of the bathroom wall?"

"Yeah."

"I'm not expecting anything new from that one. It's Lizzie's blood. Who else's could it be?"

"Well, it's one more piece in the puzzle and one more piece of evidence that would show we have a case and can get a warrant for Khazin's arrest."

I was thinking of all the problems with detecting potassium cyanide. "Are you familiar with potassium cyanide?"

"Yeah. It's a killer."

"In large amounts, yes. But, according to my research, if ingested in small amounts, it shows up in a routine autopsy for only a few hours after the victim's death. But if ingested in small amounts over time, it may build up in the bones. That may be why the second more advanced autopsy showed small amounts. The poison, together with a secondary cause, could then decrease the chances for survival. See what I mean?"

"Yeah, I get it," Garcia agreed. "We'll see what that capsule tells us."

"It's, of course, also possible that Lizzie could have fallen many times before the last fatal fall. She crashed her car for no apparent reason too. Another crash may have been more deadly."

Garcia finished his coffee just as a thought struck me. "The Russians dispense their poisons in tea. And some are killed by putting antifreeze in their favorite drink, but have you ever heard of killing someone with poison inside a pill, Joe?"

"No, I don't believe I have. And it sounds unlikely. It also sounds like a writer's over-active imagination." He gave me a sympathetic grin then rose and took out his wallet ready to pay.

"No, I invited you, Joe," I said. "I'll pay." I put a five-dollar bill on the table. "Thanks for your information. At least we're making some progress."

"Yeah, no problem." We walked back to the station together. Ed's car wasn't in the parking lot, so I assumed he was still out, and I went on home.

———

Ed came by after work and told me he had read the autopsy report.

"What do you think?" I asked.

"Well, it was inconclusive."

I followed him into the bedroom and sat down on the bed to watch him change and do a little touch up with his razor.

"Yes, but it surely raised enough questions for further investigation, don't you agree?"

"Yeah, I agree," he said decisively. He put away his razor and looked at me with a frown. "And if it hadn't been for you, this case would have been dismissed by now." He came over to give me a quick kiss on the cheek. "Where's JP?"

"He had a play date and will stay for dinner at his friend's house so Maria left early. I have steaks ready for the grill. If you take care of the grill, I'll do the baked potato and salad." We had become a good team. I had long been amazed at how tough and unapproachable he could be when he was on the job, yet how gentle he was at home, a real homebody who grilled steaks to perfection.

"So, what exciting stuff did you have to deal with today?" I asked as we sat down to dinner on the deck.

Ed had brought a bottle of Cabernet, and he poured two glasses. He took a big chunk of steak and chewed it carefully before he answered. "Another death investigation," he said. "But the woman was ninety-seven years old. It's possible she died of old age. But that's for the coroner to determine. Most of the day I spent in meetings about emergency and preparedness response."

"That sounds good. Being prepared for emergencies in a small mountain resort place like here is wise. It takes too long for services to get here. Best we take care of it on our own, if possible."

"Exactly. And what about you? Are you prepared and ready for a disaster?"

"Well, I try to follow all the recommendations."

We concentrated on the food for a few moments, washing down chunks of great steaks with delicious wine.

"But here's another case for you," Ed said suddenly. "Someone reported a vehicle that had been driven off the highway and fallen down a cliff. When the deputies and fire department arrived on the scene, they found a decomposed female inside. She had probably been dead for months. It's very steep where they found the vehicle with a lot of brush so it was hard to see."

"Hadn't anyone reported her missing?"

"No. No one apparently had."

"Well, who was she? They must have found some ID. A driver's license or something."

"The driver's license was so damaged that they couldn't read anything on it, and there were no credit cards or bank cards," he said between bites of steak, potato and sliced tomatoes. "It looked like the car had been in a collision. The license plates were completely destroyed."

"That's terrible." I took my last bite of steak and sipped my Cabernet. "I hate to admit it, but that sounds like the making for a great novel." I chuckled but ducked my head, a little embarrassed that I could find something creative in a person's death.

"And unlike your friend," Ed continued, "this woman evidently doesn't have anyone to speak for her, so her case will soon be filed away with the other cold cases in a dusty cabinet in an archive somewhere." He looked out at the lake with a distant expression. "In one sense, your friend was lucky," he said thoughtfully. "If someone did her in, he—or she—will be held accountable."

"I wonder if Lizzie had been involved in accidents before the one you told me about," I said.

"I didn't hear of any."

"She could have fallen many times before too. You should have seen how unsteady she was, and, as far as I know, she didn't drink."

JP came running through the house and out on the deck. I rose, and with JP in tow, I went out to the driveway to thank the mother while the two friends gave each other big hugs. That was the end of our adult conversation until it was time to get ready for bed.

"I wonder how long it will take to have Lizzie's mysterious capsule analyzed?"

Ed sighed. "It should have been here by now. Everyone is short on manpower. Backlogs everywhere. But I'll check on it tomorrow," he said firmly with his can-do attitude.

# 8

# THE ANALYSIS OF THE MYSTERIOUS CAPSULE

A few days, later Officer Garcia came over with the news I had been waiting for.

"Sheriff Cronin thinks the result of the analysis is important enough for me to tell you in person," Garcia said with a smile as I held the door for him to enter. "The sheriff said that this removes all doubt. Your friend's death was no accident."

"Okay. So, what was it?"

Garcia apparently wanted to savor the moment. He smiled secretively as we walked out on the deck. "What's the matter?" I said. "Stop beating around the bush. Let's hear it."

"Great view you have," he said.

I stared at him, not knowing if I should be irritated or humor him.

"Thank you. But enough of the chit-chat." I pointed to a chair, but he remained standing by the rail.

"The capsule is some kind of a prescription pill, but it contains more than medicine. A small amount of potassium cyanide had been added. The lab technician evidently found a small pinprick on the side of the capsule, maybe from a hypodermic needle that was most likely used to infuse the cyanide."

"I knew it," I exclaimed. "Lizzie told me that her husband gave her these pills one by one, which to me sounded really strange to start with. She said he told her they were diet pills. Because they made her feel ill, she sometimes just pretended to take them but instead stuck them in one of her pockets. She may have forgotten about the one in the pair of pants Linda and I found in the laundry hamper. If those pants had been washed, the capsule would probably have dissolved in the water." I sank back in my chair, relief at having solid evidence for Lizzie's death, making me weak but jubilant. "What a stroke of luck!"

"Yes, your friend may have taken several of these capsules over time until one finally killed her."

"Poor Lizzie! If I could have had a few more days with her, I might have talked her out of taking these so-called diet pills and she would have lived." I shook my head.

Garcia looked at me with his sad eyes. He clearly wanted to give me some time to collect my thoughts before he continued. "But what luck that you remembered that she faked taking these pills and instead hid them in her clothing. I imagine that's why you searched the pockets."

"Linda searched the pockets."

"Yes, that's what you said. And if all the laundry had been done, no one would have found out. It could have been the perfect crime."

"I know."

Garcia's eyes seemed fixed on the lake. "The fact that she didn't die sooner may have puzzled the doctor," he said, as he turned toward me in amazement.

"Yes. It scares me to think about it. She could have died before we reconnected. Have you ever heard anything like this, Joe? I know I haven't. It's so simple yet so ingenious. And I almost missed it. How easy it really is to do away with someone."

"The way I understand it, the poison was stored in the bones and fatty cells of her body," Garcia said, looking as if he were pondering the issue deeply. "Maybe the dose was finally big enough for her to die or at least big enough to cause her to collapse and fall."

"You may be right. This is as close to a perfect crime as I've ever seen and probably ever will see." I shuddered to think how easily I could have missed the most crucial evidence we had so far.

"As a skilled surgeon, it was a piece of cake for Ray to handle the hypodermic needle and inject the right amount of potassium cyanide, a poison he had access to in the hospital or could simply have ordered online. And just because of one forgotten pill, it didn't work the way Ray had planned it."

Garcia shook his head in bafflement. "Yes, the perfect crime—almost," he said and gave me a high-five.

"And the doctor found her and told the paramedics that she had accidentally fallen and hit her head," I said. "Of course, no one questioned the doctor, so there was no need for any further examination or an advanced autopsy."

"It doesn't look good for the department," Garcia commented slowly.

"Sloppy police work all around." I took a deep breath. "Ed told me plainly to stay out of it. Good thing I didn't listen."

Garcia gave a shrug and got ready to leave. "I guess I'll be on my way."

I thanked him again and walked him to the door.

To clear my head, I sat down at the piano and played a few random pieces that came to mind. I needed to think everything through. I decided not to call Lizzie's mother. What would be the purpose? Ray's poisoning her daughter would not provide any consolation. Instead, I called Sally Ferguson and told her the whole story about the forgotten pill in Lizzie's pocket and the potassium cyanide injected into the capsule, most likely with a hypodermic needle.

"What a bizarre story!" Sally exclaimed. "Never heard anything like it. Congratulations!"

"Well, I can't really take credit for it," I said. "The housekeeper found the pill, and the sheriff deemed it important enough to have it analyzed."

I could hear Sally chuckle. "I'm sure you had something to do with it too."

I remembered the old joke around our house back on the farm in Wisconsin about Scandinavians not knowing how to accept compliments. "What a nice dress," we would tell our Norwegian grandmother. "Oh, this old rag? It's at least twenty years old, and I probably got it on sale because it was out of style even then..." She would make a whole story out of it. Our uncle would then interrupt her and say, "A simple thank you will do, Mom." We would all laugh, and Grandma would smile indulgently.

―――――

Ed already knew about the poisoned pill and grinned overbearingly as he came through the door after JP was in bed and asleep. "So, we have a real case now, honey. And all thanks to you."

"You sound as if you disapprove."

"What are you saying?" he objected. "Of course, I approve. I'm proud of you. The whole department is proud of you. Although technically, you shouldn't have been involved at all. Still..." He put his arm around my shoulder and gave me a hug.

"I'm proud of you too, Ed," I said and took his hand. "You too knew there was something wrong and decided to team up with me finally." I knew I was pandering or at least indulging him, but he had a lot going on up here with fires, some set by an arsonist, and petty thefts. Even so, the department had been sloppy in their handling of the case.

I took a deep breath before I continued. "Of course, it's not entirely straight forward from here on."

"What do you mean?" he said gruffly.

"Well, Dr. Khazin was not the only one who could have injected the poison."

"You mean one of the nurses?"

"Maybe it was just a joke around the hospital, but according to Cheryl, they all seemed to have a crush on the handsome doctor. Maybe someone wanted to get rid of Lizzie."

Ed nodded and looked at me. "You mean Heidi, for example?"

"Yes. According to the neighbor, Mr. Rutherford, Heidi may have been at the house that morning."

"And injected the poison?"

"I don't know. Maybe it's time for another lunch date with Nurse Hillstrom."

Ed frowned but nodded in agreement.

"You look tired, Ed. We'll deal with all that tomorrow. Let's talk about something else."

Ed was very much looking forward to his son James's homecoming from London. We hadn't seen him since we left him there last August. I kept trying my best to prepare Ed for the changes James would have gone through. I remember how my own students had matured after even one short semester abroad.

"I'm sorry his mother doesn't get to see her son grow up, Ed," I said. "I'll try to fill in the best I can."

"I know, honey. And James has really taken to you."

"Yes, we'll have a real family, Ed, with two sons—once we—I mean you— finally decide we should tie the knot and officially get married."

"How about after James gets settled back home and has a plan for the future?" He paused. "I'm sure he'll approve."

―――――

A couple of days later, I was running errands in our little resort town when I caught a glimpse of a young woman with long blond hair and green scrubs. I saw only her back, but she looked like Heidi, so I ran up behind her. "Heidi," I called. She turned around and looked surprised to see me.

"Hi," she said.

"What are you doing down here in your hospital scrubs?"

"I'm on my lunch hour and needed some new shampoo and hair conditioner and a couple of other things."

"Same here." We walked together along the parking lot. "How are you doing?"

"Okay, I guess."

"Have you heard from Dr. Khazin yet? Ray?"

"No, not a word. I don't understand it." She gave me a sad look.

"Forget about Ray, Heidi. He's not the straight-up guy you think he is."

"You keep saying that, but I can't believe it."

"Believe it." I felt sorry for her. She looked so young and seemed so naïve. "The FBI is investigating him for possible fraud and irregularities."

"How do you know that?"

"I have friends who work for the FBI."

"Oh yeah? And I'm supposed to take your word for it?"

"Heidi, please listen to me. Ray may have had something to do with his wife's death."

"That's crazy. You're just jealous, like the rest of them."

"What? Who? The other nurses?" I asked in amazement.

"Yes."

"Heidi, you were at the Khazins' house on the morning of Mrs. Khazin's death. You'd better come clean about that visit or you may be indicted for murder or as an accessory to murder."

Her mouth fell open, and she stopped abruptly. She looked me straight in the face, seemingly at a loss for words.

"Heidi, Dr. Khazin's neighbor saw your car in the Khazins' driveway on the morning of Mrs. Khazin's death. What were you doing there?"

Heidi had turned pale, her eyes wide, and she stood there as if frozen to the ground.

"Tell the truth, Heidi."

"Okay," she said finally. "So I was there, and Ray's fat wife was there too, but very much alive."

"What were you doing there?"

"Ray asked me to go over to the house and pick up a prescription pad he had left on the kitchen counter."

My eyebrows rose. "Did he normally leave stuff at the house?"

"Yes, I often went over to pick up something he forgot."

"Did you have a key?"

"Yes, Ray gave me his because he said his wife might not be up yet. I returned it when I got back to the hospital."

"And was Mrs. Khazin still in bed?"

"No, she had just gotten up, I think. At least she was still in her robe."

"Oh, was it the red silk robe that I know she liked to wear?" I asked, knowing that Linda and I had not seen a red robe among her clothes, only a blue one.

"No, a light blue one that was too small for her. She couldn't close it, and she was in her underwear."

"Did you say hello?"

"Yes. I briefly told her what I had come for. I grabbed the pad from the kitchen counter and left."

Heidi was calmer now and told the story in such a straightforward manner that I felt she was speaking the truth. "I see," I said. "And what time was that?"

"It must have been a little after eight o'clock. I returned to the hospital and gave Ray the pad and his key back before his first surgery. His surgery was scheduled at nine o'clock, I think."

"This is very important information, Heidi. It helps confirm the time of death."

"And when was that?" she asked, and her question sounded genuine.

I told her and continued, "Be sure to tell the story to the detective, Heidi. It's important."

She nodded. We had now reached her light green Honda SUV. She looked at her phone and said she had to rush back to her shift at the hospital, while I continued my errands. I believed her simple story. She was not sophisticated enough to have gone to the house surreptitiously with a hypodermic needle filled with just the right amount of potassium cyanide and injected it into a pill or capsule. As older more experienced nurses, maybe Cheryl or Judy could have done it, but that would be absurd.

I called Garcia on the way home and suggested he obtain an official statement from Heidi. If this case ever went to trial, she could be a potential witness. "I don't think she had anything to do with Mrs. Khazin's death, Joe," I said. "Her story is so simple that she's believable. She is or was in love with Dr. Khazin, and in that sense, she could have a motive. But I don't think she's that hateful or evil. She may be a schemer, but she's too young and naïve for that kind of a murder."

"I'll talk to her and let you know what my assessment of her is."

"Good," I said. "Anything else new? Any sign of Dr. Khazin's whereabouts?"

"No, nothing so far. I wouldn't be surprised if he's left the country."

"Hmm, yes. Maybe," I said.

Once at home, I put my purchases away, then I sat down to work on my novel, but I could not concentrate. I told Maria I'd pick up JP, and I decided to go early to observe the children play and interact. I was happy to see that JP could hold his own.

———

The DNA test of the bloodstained bathroom wall showed no surprises. Ed brought the news when he came over. He had taken off early, and we all—JP, Duchess, Ed, and I—took a long walk along the lake.

"The results of the DNA test on that drywall came back today," he said casually

"Oh," I said. "Did it reveal anything we don't already know?" I took the leash off Duchess so she and JP could chase a chipmunk.

"No, the only DNA was from your friend. It was her finger that had made the scrawling marks."

"Yes, that's what I thought. To me it was clear from the start that Lizzie tried to leave a message."

"The handprint was also hers," Ed continued. "There were a few fibers from the cloth that had been used to wipe it away. That was on the floor."

We walked along the path. "I guess that was a waste of time and money," I said with a sigh and pointed to another hawk circling overhead.

Ed stopped and looked at mc. "No. Not at all," he said seriously. "A jury wants to see DNA—that is, if this case ever goes to trial."

"How much more does the District Attorney need for a grand jury hearing?"

"He needs physical evidence, something that ties the doctor more firmly to the case." He whistled for Duchess as she was nowhere in sight. She came bolting back, followed by JP. Ed gave her a good rub on her head before she ran off again.

"Oh, I almost forgot to tell you that I talked to Lizzie's mom," I said. "Mrs. Wurtz. Ray had called her. He told her he was ready to bury Lizzie —or rather cremate her—as she had stated in her will." I looked at Ed to make sure he was listening. "Have you ever heard of anyone our age having a will, Ed?" I waited a couple of moments before I went on. "Maybe when they took out the life insurance on each other, they also made a will." I paused. "Do you have a will, Ed?"

"No. Everything is in the family trust. My personal assets will go to James."

"But do you have a will stating how you want to be buried? A living will and advance directives for medical and burial decisions or whatever they call it?"

"No, I don't."

"I know I don't. Robert, my first husband, didn't either. When he was killed in Africa, I brought what was left of him home. His parents were already dead, and I had him cremated. Later I hired a small plane and had his ashes strewn over the Pacific Ocean where he so often practiced flying." I kicked a small rock as if it were a soccer ball. "So why would Lizzie have a will like that?"

Ed didn't answer but waited for me and took my hand. We continued walking hand in hand.

"Anyway, when Mrs. Wurtz suggested she wanted to come out, Ray told her it was unnecessary. He told her that he was staying with his brother, and he said that staying with me would be an imposition since Lizzie and I were not that close."

"Well, you hadn't seen her for a few years," Ed interjected. "Didn't you offer Lizzie's mom a place to stay here if she came to California?"

"I did. Lizzie and I were study buddies in the past. We took the same classes and shared everything. When we reconnected, we picked up right where we had left off."

"Dr. Khazin may not have been aware of that."

"Maybe, but still. I knew Lizzie before Ray met her, which he ought to remember. And to go ahead and cremate Lizzie without letting her mother come out and see her daughter one last time! And not letting me know either for that matter." My throat felt constricted, and my voice quivered a little. "He also told Mrs. Wurtz that he was very busy right now. He said he had some important business to take care of and that he would hold a memorial service later." I hesitated. "I can't believe this guy."

Ed put his arm around my shoulder as if to calm me down, and I put my arm around his waist.

"Try not to let him get you all riled up. We'll get him. One step at a time," he said reassuringly.

"I know you will, Ed." I leaned into his side. "I also told Mrs. Wurtz very cautiously and unemotionally that Ray might not have been such a good husband the last few years. I don't want to tell her my suspicions." I took a deep breath and cleared my throat. "Sooner or later, she will learn the truth somehow. Not from me, I hope, as I don't want to be the bearer of bad news." I took a few steps in silence and then continued. "Although she didn't protest, she didn't sing Ray's praises like she first did."

We ambled along, enjoying the fresh mountain air and each other's company. "So, next week James will be here," I said after a while. "Who's going to pick him up at LAX?"

"I'll take the day off and drive down there," Ed said quietly. "Wanna come along?"

"Since the traffic is so horrendous and we don't know exactly when the plane will land, why don't we call a limousine service?" I suggested.

"I can follow the plane on my phone," Ed protested.

"I know, but it takes two hours to drive there, and I know this limo driver, Jimmy, that I used to refer people to when Robert flew dignitaries to the States. I'd like to see him again, anyway."

Ed's eyebrows rose, and he looked at me. "But James will expect to see me as soon as he gets off the plane."

"I don't think so, Ed." I shook my head and pushed myself a little away from him. "You want to see him right away, and I understand that. You haven't seen your son for a year, but he'll be tired. And you've got to be prepared for a big change in James," I said seriously. "He's an independent young man now. He will not want to be babied and told what to do anymore. Certainly not by you."

"Well, I'm still paying his bills." He let go of me and started to walk ahead.

"It's not about money, Ed. Say the wrong thing, and he'll be gone."

"How do you know?" Irritation showed in his tone of voice.

"Because I had students who went abroad. They were babies when they left and young men and women when they returned." By now, I had adopted my teaching tone.

"James was not a baby when we left him in London last fall."

"No, he had already had a taste of freedom and independence during the few weeks he studied in Oslo over the summer."

"Maybe I shouldn't have let him go. He's all I've got." He kicked some dirt with his hiking boots.

I waited a while before I continued. "He's not all you've got, Ed. And in any case, you can't hold on to your children as if they're some prized possessions."

Ed started tossing flat rocks in the lake. They skipped and created ripples on the water. Duchess thought he was playing a game with her, and she and JP ran wildly back and forth between Ed and the lake.

Since there was no point in pursuing the topic further, I tried a more upbeat approach. "The first thing he'll want is a big, juicy American steak," I said. "That's something you can't find easily in Europe. You'll grill, and I'll fix the rest. For dessert, we'll have an ice cream sundae. If he wants a cold American beer or a glass of wine, he can have that too."

Ed looked at me with a frown as if I was trying to sabotage him or undermine his authority, maybe ruin James. "He's only nineteen."

"Since the legal drinking age all over Europe is eighteen, I'm sure he's had his share of beer over there, Ed, and maybe stronger stuff too. And, as you know, he can legally have alcohol here too under his parents' guidance."

Ed frowned even more, while I smiled innocently. I knew it was not going to be easy for Ed—or for James.

"We'll invite his friend Thomas over too, and after we've finished eating, James and Thomas will want to leave, get in their cars and hang out with friends." I was merciless. "And Ed, I won't allow you to tell him he can't go," I said firmly. I could see battles ahead. I caught up with him and took his hand. "It's not easy being the father of a teenager, Ed," I said in a more conciliatory tone. "It's like walking on thin ice, but I saw my share of *helicopter parents* hovering over their adult students when I taught at Pacifica College, and it didn't do anyone any good. I'll subtly remind James to get a late admit to a college around here, although he may already have received counseling from an advisor at his college in London and turned in an application to USC too."

A hike by the lake clears the mind, and talking with Ed about his son made me forget about Lizzie for a while.

# 9

## THE FBI HAS A PLAN

I called my FBI contact Sally Ferguson in Long Beach near midday. She was in her car, so I tried to be brief. She had no major news, she said. Raymond Khazin was the name on all his passports.

"I thought Raymond might have been an adopted American name that he took when he became an American citizen," Ferguson said. "Many foreign nationals do that, but Raymond is apparently not an uncommon name in the Middle East."

"Well, Lebanon was ruled by the French, and it is vastly different from the other Middle Eastern countries," I said. "Many Lebanese are Christian and speak French as their native language, in addition to Arabic. Many are trilingual. A friend of mine who was raised in Beirut and still lives there went to French schools and speaks both French and Arabic fluently in addition to English. You may know this, Sally, but when the Muslim majority revolted and took over, many Lebanese fled the country and ended up in Europe, Canada or the US."

"Yes, I know." Sally said, and I could hear her chuckle. "But thank you for that cultural geography lesson, Megan."

"You're welcome! Any luck finding this elusive physician?" I asked.
"No."

"He is apparently still around," I continued. "He called his mother-in-law in Arizona a few days ago to tell her that he was about to have her daughter cremated. He told her it was unnecessary for her to come out to California to visit and see her deceased daughter first."

"I see."

"He also told her that there would be a memorial service sometime in the future. Right now, he said, he had some important business to take care of." I cleared my throat several times before I continued. "I haven't told Mrs. Wurtz anything other than that her daughter had an accident. She has enough sorrow for now. But she sounded a little less enthusiastic about her son-in-law."

Sally muttered something. Maybe she was preoccupied with something else she was working on.

"When you find him, you'll let me know, right?" I asked. "I have some questions I'd like to ask him too, if you'll let me."

"We will."

"Oh, the DNA from the bloodstains on the bathroom wall came back but nothing surprising there," I said. "Only the victim's blood showed up. Her finger made the scrawling marks, and her hand made the bloody handprint. The fibers from the cloth used to wipe the marks off showed nothing."

"Thank you, Megan. We already heard, but good job. We've got to catch this sucker, don't we? I'm at my destination, and I've got to go, but we appreciate your help and will let you know as soon as something comes up."

After we ended the call, I sat down at the piano and played some pieces by Beethoven to clear my mind. Then I worked on my own mystery story about the murder of the young Nabila Brown. She was a smart lawyer but had poor taste in men. The focus was now on her boyfriend, a fitness instructor at a nearby gym.

———

A couple of days, later Ed told me that two FBI agents would be at his office the next day. "You should be there too. Can you be in my office at eleven?"

"Sure. What's up?"

"Major developments, I understand. We'll hear about it tomorrow."

"They could come over here too," I said. "A little more comfortable perhaps."

"Okay, but let's meet in my office first."

"Fine. I'll be there."

The next day, I drove over at the appointed time. Sally Ferguson and Carrie Jensen were already in Ed's office. Both women were in dark blue slacks and white long-sleeved shirts. It was a warm day, and I had shed my sweats for designer jeans and a tank top. Ed was sitting in his chair, and after greetings, the rest of us sat down opposite him.

"So, what's up?" I asked. Just then, a deputy came in with a message for Ed, and everyone remained silent until he left.

"Dr. Khazin has left the country," Carrie blurted out.

"Wow!" I exclaimed. "I guess I'm not terribly surprised. For the past couple of days, I've had a nagging feeling that he'd gone somewhere. How did he slip through security without your knowledge? Do you have any idea where he went?"

"He had reservations on a nonstop flight to Paris, but we learned too late that he checked in early on a flight to Chicago and later showed up on a manifest from JFK to Paris," Carrie continued. "He's a slick customer."

Another deputy came into Ed's office. After he left, I suggested we drive over to my place to avoid interruptions. I knew Ed could have closed the door; he was, after all, the sheriff.

"I live really close," I said. "That way, we can avoid all these interruptions."

"Great, if that's okay with you," Carrie said to me and then turned to Ed. "What do you think, Sheriff? You okay with that?"

"Sounds like a good plan," Ed said. "I'll catch up with you later."

The two agents followed me in their white, unmarked sedan and parked next to me. I quickly got out and went over to open the door for them. Once inside the house, I led them over to the couch. "Can I bring you a cup of coffee?" I offered.

"That would be lovely," Carrie said and came with me into the kitchen. She carried the first cup over to Sally before she returned for her own. I brought in milk and sugar with my own cup.

"Lovely house," Sally commented. "So isolated. A good place for writing, I imagine."

"Thank you. And, yes, I love it here." I sat down on a chair facing them.

"So, how can I help?" I proffered.

"Well, by now our elusive doctor is in Paris," Carrie said. She looked at me but didn't continue.

"So you want me to go over there to bring him back to the States?" I said jokingly.

"No, it's not that simple," Sally said and took a sip of her coffee. "We don't have an extradition agreement with France, and in any case, we have no indictment."

I too took a sip of coffee before I responded. "At least now, with the information revealed by the second autopsy and the pill injected with the same poison, the San Bernardino District Attorney will surely issue a warrant for his arrest."

"You'd think so, but there is no firm physical evidence. It's all circumstantial," Carrie lamented.

"I know," I said. "But we have a husband, a physician, with at least one extra-marital affair who may have married my friend because he thought that a foreign service officer could clear his path to American citizenship. He recently bought a life insurance policy on his wife for a million dollars, a wife that he's had no intimate relationship with for months, according to her. We have an autopsy that shows traces of potassium cyanide in the victim's system, albeit insufficient to conclusively determine the cause of death. But we also have a prescription pill, a capsule, prescribed by her husband and injected with the same potassium cyanide, a feat that could only have been performed by a skilled medical professional." I paused to take a deep breath. "We have a message scrawled on the wall with the victim's blood, and now this physician husband has fled the country." I had to clear my throat several times as I looked from one agent to the other. "Maybe he felt the heat of being on the watchlists of both the FBI and the local sheriff's department." I was on a roll and kept going. "I'll ask the sheriff," I said and then changed my tone as I smiled mischievously. "No, I'll *tell* him to demand an indictment."

We all laughed. They both knew that Ed and I were in a relationship together.

"We all know being in a relationship with law enforcement means nothing to the DA," Carrie said. Again we laughed, but Carrie added more seriously, "And like I said earlier, we have no physical evidence tying him to the crime scene. Even if the DA agreed on the basis of circumstantial evidence, how are we going to get Dr. Khazin back here?" She paused, and I looked at her expectantly. "Also, I don't think Paris is his final destination."

"I agree," I said. "He's going on to Beirut."

"Yes. We have the CIA monitoring the situation over there, but we do not have an extradition agreement with Lebanon either."

"So, we need a ruse," I suggested.

"That's right." Carrie said.

They both looked at me, but I shook my head. "I don't have any suggestions right off the top of my head."

"That's okay, but we're wondering if you're still in touch with people you knew over there," Carrie said

"Well, yes, I'm on Facebook with my old friend Hoda. She's Jordanian but grew up in Beirut where she still lives. I'll message her to see if I could call her." I looked at my phone. "It's almost midnight over there now, so maybe I can call tonight or early tomorrow morning." I looked at the two agents who sat there with expectant expressions. "Hoda is part of the elite in Lebanon," I explained. "She counts members of the Jordanian royal family among her friends. The old king was married to an American actress, and the children, including the present king, speak perfect American English and look like regular Americans. Hoda knows everything that goes on over there." I pulled up some of Hoda's Facebook posts and showed the agents pictures of Hoda with royals and other dignitaries.

"She's quite attractive," Sally commented.

"Yes," I agreed. "And smart. Fluent in English, French, and Arabic. She knows everybody and may know one or two of the CIA operatives too. I know that she would be a good contact and source of information for them."

"And maybe for us too," Carrie said. "Do you think she might know our good doctor and his family?"

"Possibly," I nodded. "I feel certain Ray's family would be among the upper class there. Hoda would be as good a bet or even better than the CIA." I bit my lip, wondering how much of my story the agents believed and wanted to hear, then decided to continue. "When my first husband and I lived in Africa and traveled around the Middle East, I wasn't all that impressed with our CIA agents. They seemed to be overly occupied with going to cocktail parties with other international diplomats. Maybe that was the way they gathered information—a nice lifestyle—but they often missed what was brewing among the local people, the grassroots. I'm sure it's difficult work and with new technology, their operations have hopefully improved."

"Yes, we have good people over there now," Carrie said, a little defensively.

"That's good. So, do you want me to contact Hoda? I guess I could go over there too. I'm dying to visit again. The Middle East grows on you, but it's a dangerous place right now."

"Yes, we know. But for now, contacting your friend would be a good start."

"Sure."

"Well," Carrie said and looked at me. "We'd also like to put you in contact with Interpol on Cypress. I might go over there myself.

"Really? When?"

"Well, first we have to have an indictment," Carrie explained. "Then we have to come up with a ruse to get the good doctor out of Lebanon. We have an extradition agreement with Cypress."

I remained silent for a few moments and took a sip of my coffee, which was by now cold. "Maybe I should go with you," I suggested. I was often homesick for Beirut, the *Paris of the Middle East,* as it was once called. But that was many years ago.

"You have a small child, and it's not a good place to travel for pleasure," Carrie said thoughtfully. "But if all else fails, maybe we'll take you up on your offer. We'd take all the necessary safety precautions, and we would have Interpol agents with us." She looked at me. "You know people over there, and you're familiar with some of the culture. You also speak French and know how to handle yourself internationally."

I smiled. "Well, thank you for that endorsement. Wow!"

"Hopefully, it won't come to that, but keep the thought."

"Let me talk to Hoda and find out firsthand how the situation is over there." I paused for a moment. "Next week, the sheriff's son is returning from London after a year abroad, and I want to be around to help him adjust."

"Of course. Let's talk after next week. First, we have to have the indictment."

We all finished our cold coffee. With all that we had discussed, I had forgotten to offer them seconds. Carrie rose and walked over to the piano. She needed little encouragement to play, and soon she and I played some of our old duets. Sally had to try too. She played the guitar, she said, and tried out some e-flat chords. Then, to her own accompaniment, she sang Gershwin's *The Man I Love* to our wild applause.

After they left, I had a lot to think about.

———

Ed came over in the evening. "So, what plans did the FBI agents have for you this time?" he said. There was a bit of sarcasm in his tone.

"Oh, no plans, really. We talked about how to get an indictment, mostly." I wasn't ready to talk about the FBI's plans yet and switched the subject.

Ed grabbed a beer from the fridge, and we went out on the deck. "Isn't it time for you to demand action from the District Attorney?" I shot him a quick glance as we leaned over the rail, watching the sailboats in the waning sunlight.

"I'm in the process of preparing a request even as we speak," Ed replied confidently. "It will be delivered tomorrow or the next day." He took a deep breath and looked out at the darkening lake. "Maybe some physical evidence is lacking, but the circumstantial evidence is overwhelming. It should be more than enough for a grand jury to indict, in my opinion."

"So, are you okay with me calling my old friend Jimmy to pick up James on Wednesday, then?" We sat down in the comfortable deck chairs, and Ed downed a couple of gulps of beer.

"I guess it makes sense."

"It really does, Ed. He'll be tired and will probably fall asleep in the limo. The flight comes in late in the afternoon, and by the time they drive up here, it will be time to go to bed. Maybe you could take the following day off. We'll all have a big breakfast and listen to his stories. It will take him a day to recover from the jetlag."

"I see you have it all figured out." His tone was melancholy, and he finished the beer.

"I've traveled that route many times."

"Yeah, I know. And I'm just a simple country sheriff." He shifted restlessly in his chair.

I bit my lip and watched him for a moment. "Relax, Ed. We'll have a great time."

"Yes, I know."

The next day, I called Jimmy. We reminisced about the good old days, and he promised to take care of the sheriff's son. Then I emailed James and told him whom to look for after he went through customs at LAX.

———

The days went slowly for Ed, but, luckily, he had a busy week. On Wednesday, he stayed at work all day and had barely gotten home before I heard Jimmy drive up to my front door. I ran out to greet both him and James. James looked older. His cheeks had filled out.

"Hi, Megan," he said with a wide grin as he embraced me. Ed stood in the doorway, and I watched the two of them give each other an awkward *bro-hug*. I helped Jimmy carry the bags inside and settled his fee. We talked for a while, and after he had something to drink and used the bathroom, he took off again.

JP was already asleep, but James went into the bedroom to look in on him. "He sure looks big," he commented.

"So do you, James," I whispered from the doorway. I didn't want to wake up JP. "We'll all have breakfast here tomorrow before he goes to school. Maria will be here too."

Ed was unusually quiet and walked around uneasily. "You ready to sleep in your own bed tonight, son?" he said finally.

James smiled. "Sure am, Pop."

We agreed on breakfast the next day, and they left for Ed's house.

———

Maria was excited to see James. She treated Ed as her son, and James was like her grandson. JP was shy at first, but soon warmed up to his long-lost cousin. We all sat down at the kitchen table together and enjoyed a big breakfast of scrambled eggs and Maria's homemade rolls. JP's eyes followed James's every move, and James decided to go with Maria and JP to the nursery school.

"I can't believe how much JP talks," he said over and over again, shaking his head. "I guess he wants to show me off to his friends."

"Are you happy, Ed?" I asked after they left.

"He sure has changed."

"Yes. The boy in him is gone. He looks more like a man now and probably thinks like one too." I looked at Ed's unsmiling face and made myself another cup of coffee. "You want another cup, Ed?"

"No, I'm good."

"I wonder if he has a girlfriend over there," I said musingly. "I'll have to remember to ask him later."

"What if she's European?" Ed said with a worried look on his face. "He may want to go back there."

"Or she could come here."

"Hmm, yes, I guess."

I remained silent for a while before I brought up the subject I'd wanted to talk about all morning. "When are we going to tell James about our wedding plans, Ed?"

"I thought we agreed to wait until he had settled down a little."

"Don't you think he'll figure it out when he realizes that you practically live here now?"

"Well, now that I have my son home, I may stay at my house more." He said as he cocked his head a little mischievously.

"What am I supposed to make out of that?" I asked accusingly.

"Well, I didn't particularly want to go home to an empty house, you know, especially when you, Maria and JP were here having a party."

"James will soon be gone again, Ed."

Ed sighed. "Yes, I know, so shouldn't I enjoy him while he's around?"

"His mother is not there, Ed, and he always liked to be around Maria and JP."

"And you," Ed added as an afterthought.

"Right," I said firmly. "So we should tell him that this house will be his as well now."

Ed shifted uneasily in his chair.

"No rush, Ed. And I will not stoop to arguing with you about this. But I'd like to have everything out in the open. I feel uncomfortable pretending we're just brother-in-law and sister-in-law and that he's just my nephew."

"Really?"

"Yes, really! You two can still spend time in *his* childhood home, but I bet he'll be over here just as much as you are." I rose and took some dishes over to the sink.

"Before our big lunch today, I want to sit down with the three of us so you and I can tell him how it all happened." I paused and took a deep breath. "And we'll ask how he feels about his father and his Aunt Megan making our relationship more formal."

Ed was still sitting at the kitchen table. He rose and started pacing. He walked into the living room and then the gym. I sat down at the piano and played Mendelssohn's Wedding March for fun. "You know this one, Ed?"

"Yes, of course I do." He chuckled. "You little vixen." His mood had lightened.

We both stopped talking and listened as the van pulled up in the driveway. I continued playing a few more strands of the lively march. Maria went straight to the kitchen and started rattling the pots and pans.

"Let's all go out on the deck," I said to James. We went outside and stood by the rail. "I guess our little lake looks small to you now, James," I said. "But you have to admit it's pretty."

"Yes, maybe we can take the boat out today," he suggested.

"Good idea," I said. "But first, your dad and I have something to talk to you about." I shot a quick glance at Ed, who looked first at James and then at me.

"Oh, you're finally gonna tell me that you got married," James laughed, not at all surprised if that was the big news.

Ed and I looked at each other and started laughing too.

"I figured that out a long time ago, although you never wrote anything specifically about it."

"Well, you had so much else on your mind, son, that we wanted to wait until you came home," Ed said sheepishly. His cheeks were visibly flushed. "And the thing is, we aren't married yet," he added.

"Why not? What's the big deal? Or if you want to live together without getting married, that's okay too." He paused and looked from me to Ed. "I knew you were living together when we met in Paris, Dad. Megan told me."

Ed's jaw dropped at least a little, and he glared at me.

"Oh, no, Ed. I didn't say *that*." I turned to James. "I just asked if you were surprised that your dad and I would share a room."

"That's right. I remember," James admitted. "And I said I wasn't surprised." He had adopted a new air of worldliness. "In Europe marriage is so last millennium, Dad."

I knew we would often hear about how they did everything so much more avant-garde in Europe. "I guess your dad would like to make it more formal," I said. "He being the sheriff and all, and this being a small conservative community. Your dad is old-fashioned, you see." I glanced at Ed and smiled indulgently. "Isn't that right, dear?"

Ed stared at his shoes and didn't say anything.

"Oh, come on, Dad. Don't be so behind the times. Megan is so much more with it than you are."

That assessment made Ed finally chuckle, and we all started laughing. At forty, Ed was naturally over-the-hill in James's eyes.

"I don't care what you two do," James continued, feigning exasperation. "But I'm glad Megan will take care of you, Dad. I wouldn't want you to live alone in this Puritan, out-of-touch place."

I nodded in agreement. "I'm glad you look at it that way, James," I said. "I've been trying to explain to your dad that you've seen some of the world now and won't want to be tied down here for the rest of your life."

"I don't know what's wrong with staying around here." Ed commented. "I grew up here and stayed, and so did my brother. But I don't suppose anyone listens to me anymore." He tried to feign indignation, but I don't think he really convinced anyone.

I cleared my throat several times and walked close to James. "I don't ever want to try to take your mother's place, James," I said and put my arm around his waist. "But I'll try to be the best stepmother I know how." Out of nowhere, tears welled up in my eyes. With a Kleenex, I wiped two drops that had escaped down my cheeks and put on a happy grin. I didn't dare look at Ed. I knew he didn't want to show any emotion in front of his son. I took a moment to compose myself before I continued. "But first, I need to make sure you get settled into a good university. That's what your mother would have wanted too."

"I know," James agreed. "But give me a few days to adjust to this place again."

"Sure," I said. "We've invited Thomas and his family for lunch. We'll have good ol' American steaks. How's that?"

"Good. I haven't had that for a long time," James said with a sigh.

"I know. And for dessert, we'll have ice cream sundaes."

"Yummy, yum."

"You said something about taking the boat out, James. Why don't you and your dad go for a spin around the lake while I help Maria prepare everything? When you return, you can help your dad with the grill."

"Megan is an organizer, isn't she, son? Just like Mom."

I nodded and looked at Ed with approval.

Ed took Duchess out of the pen, and the three of them disappeared down the path to the dock. When Thomas and his family arrived, we all sat down at the big table in the dining room. Maria helped me serve, but Ed insisted that Maria sit down and eat with us too. James soon announced our upcoming wedding plans, and we drank toasts to everyone we knew.

# 10

## THE CEDARS OF LEBANON

A s my FBI contacts and I had discussed after they told me that Ray was most likely in Lebanon, I messaged my old friend Hoda, whom I had known when Robert and I lived in Africa. Robert often flew dignitaries to Beirut, and when space permitted, I went along. On one of our trips, I met Hoda, an elegant woman originally from Jordan. She knew everybody, and we now kept in touch on Facebook.

I asked her if I could call her and what time would be convenient. I had a question I wanted to discuss with her on the phone, I said, not via text. She messaged me back late in the evening and reminded me of the time change between Beirut and California. Beirut was ten hours ahead of us.

I called Hoda the next day as soon as Maria and JP were off to school. After a few minutes of small talk, I came to the point. "Hoda, you know everybody that is anybody over there. Do you know the Khazin family?"

"Yes, I know a Khazin family. They're in the pharmaceutical business, at least many of them are. A couple of them are physicians. They're also into real-estate development."

"Yes, I think they are the right Khazins. Do you by any chance know a Dr. Raymond Khazin?"

There was a long silence, as if she were thinking. "Yes," she said finally. "I think he's the one who just returned from the States because his father is ill."

"Wow, Hoda! You're a treasure trove of information." I remembered how the small upper echelon of well-to-do Lebanese knew everything about everybody. It was just like a small town. "Are you also aware that a group of expatriate Lebanese are working to overthrow the current government?"

"No, Megan. You may remember that I don't get involved in politics, but I may have heard that there's a warehouse near the harbor full of weapons, supposedly from the United States. But I don't know that for sure."

"Do you know if the Khazins are involved in getting these weapons into Lebanon?"

"I would think that would be unlikely, but there's a lot of buzz around here that it's time the current government steps down. If they don't step down, some are threatening that they'll be forced out."

I paused for a moment or two and cleared my throat. I did recall that Hoda didn't like to talk about government intrigues, so I left it there. "Do you know if Dr. Khazin has a wife waiting for him in Beirut?" I continued.

"A wife? No, I don't think so. I think I would have heard about that. He was married to an American woman in California."

"Does he have any children in Lebanon as far as you know?"

"No. I would have heard about that for sure, even though it is a big family."

"Dr. Khazin has a brother in California. Did you know that?"

"Yes. I have heard that, but I can't remember his name."

"Richard?" I suggested.

"Possibly."

"Well, that's not important."

"As I said, it's a big family."

"Do you know where Raymond Khazin hangs out?"

"Oh, the usual places, probably. You know, bars where the young crowds go to smoke shisha pipes are trendy now."

"Yes, Raymond bought a restaurant in San Bernardino near Los

Angeles and transformed it into a Middle Eastern club with shisha pipes, belly dancers and the whole set-up. He kept a room in the building and often spent the night there—who knows with whom?"

"And why are you so interested in this guy? He's a handsome man, as I recall, as are all the men in that family, but not especially your type." She started laughing, and her laugh was infectious.

"He was actually married to a good friend of mine from school," I said.

"Really? You said *was*? You mean he's no longer married to her?"

"She died," I said slowly and took a deep breath again. "Lizzie met him while they both worked in the same medical office when we were in grad school. They married rather quickly. Perhaps he thought he could get US citizenship more quickly that way. Not that I know how that would benefit him, as he was already a practicing physician here. I did some research on that marriage thing, and you have to be married three years to the same person before you can apply for citizenship. So..." Megan shrugged, though she knew Hoda couldn't see it.

"Oh, I can understand that completely. With all the instability around here, anything but Lebanese citizenship—or any other Middle Eastern citizenship, for that matter."

"How are the conditions over there now?"

"Okay—not as bad as the international media wants you to believe. But corruption is everywhere. You have to know how to navigate around it and go on with life."

"What about tourism?"

"Oh, yes, we still have tourists, mostly Germans and Swedes. There's no stopping them." She cleared her throat. "Are you thinking of coming over for a visit?" I could hear a deep sigh. "We had some fun times when you were here last, didn't we?"

"Yes, I'll never forget," I agreed. "And I'm dying to come for a visit. But I have too much going on here right now. As you have seen on Facebook, I have a little son now."

"I've seen his pictures. He's really cute."

"Thank you." I leaned back in my chair. I was still out on the deck.

"You have to come over here for a visit instead, Hoda. I have plenty of room for you to stay."

"I might just take you up on that."

I looked out at the lake. "Actually, Dr. Khazin's wife, Lizzie, died rather mysteriously. She fell on the bathroom floor and evidently hit her head and died just like that."

"Oh, my goodness. How old was she?"

"Thirty-eight or nine. Too young to die from a simple fall on the floor."

"I'm sorry."

"The truth is, Hoda, I think Dr. Khazin may have had something to do with her death. He had grown tired of her and had at least one serious affair and probably more that we don't know about."

"Are you serious?"

"Dead serious, Hoda. A couple of FBI agents also have their eyes on Dr. Khazin for other irregularities, but they cannot prove anything illegal." I took a deep breath. "Hoda, here's my question. Can you surreptitiously find out Dr. Khazin's whereabouts? Obtain his contact information, his address or email? I don't suppose there's a way to obtain his telephone number?"

"So, you want me to snoop?"

I laughed. "How about a little sleuthing? Does that sound better?"

"It sounds dangerous."

"No more dangerous than flying around with Robert in his little corporate jet. Remember?"

"Yes, that was a lot of fun."

"So, what prince or sheikh are you seeing these days?"

"I'm slowing down, Megan."

"How about using your contacts to connect with Dr. Raymond Khazin?"

"And what should I tell him?"

"Nothing. You're a master at small talk. Just get his phone number and email or something. You're his type, Hoda. He'd be flattered if you asked him for his number."

"You're crazy, Megan. As always."

"We're both a little crazy, Hoda. Don't you remember?" I could hear her chuckle. "Can I call you again in a few days?" Without waiting for an answer, I continued. "And is this a good time? It's morning here and evening in Beirut. Or maybe this is the time you're out in high society?"

She chuckled again. "No, it's fine. I carry my phone in my purse."

I told her how I missed her before we reminisced about our good times in Beirut.

———

Later, I told Ed about my friend Hoda in Lebanon and our telephone conversation.

"So, she knows Dr. Khazin, eh? Interesting. But what good is it gonna to do us?" He flopped down on the couch in the living room and crossed his legs.

"I know, but it does tell you that today, for the most part, no one can escape the law by traveling to another country." I sat on the other end of the couch. I was shoeless and put my legs up on the seat cushions.

"That's true, but you know that we can't go into another country and arrest people. We have no jurisdiction in the Middle East."

I sighed and shook my head. "But there are other ways," I said pensively.

"We can't go in and kidnap him either. You know better than that. That's against the law in our country, and it's against international law too." He paused. "I guess the Russians do it, anyway. They just send in spies and put poison in their tea." He grinned and moved closer. "So, is your Lebanese friend a spy?" he continued and started to rub my feet.

"She's as good as anyone at finding out what's going on."

"You're putting people in danger, Megan."

"Not really if we're smart. We have to think of a way to lure him out of Lebanon to another country, a country that we have an extradition agreement with. Greece maybe or Italy."

"He'd have to go willingly."

"I understand that. But maybe by using psychology we can get him. We need to find a soft spot in his character, a weakness, and have agents ready when he willingly walks into our trap. As Shakespeare shows us in many of his plays, we all have a tragic flaw, and Dr. Raymond Khazin has one too. We need to figure out what it is."

"Megan, this is the real world, not one of Shakespeare's plays." He shook his head and looked at me seriously.

"I know that, Ed, but Shakespeare deals with human nature, and human nature is pretty much the same today as it was back then. Under the right circumstances, we all have the capacity for evil." I pulled my feet up, folded my hands around my knees, and stayed silent while Ed leaned back and closed his eyes.

JP had a play date, and just as the friend's mother brought JP home, James drove up in his old Range Rover. James spent most of his time catching up with his old friends, but he regularly came over to show us the latest gadgets he had purchased and often stayed for dinner. Maria had left early, but the rest of us sat down at the kitchen table and helped ourselves to her fried chicken and mashed potatoes.

While Ed sat next to me in bed reading a report later that night, I thought about my conversation with Hoda. I wondered what life was like in that part of the world right now. I thought about my many walks along the beautiful Corniche, the road that overlooked the blue Mediterranean Sea. What did the country look like after the various civil wars and all the destruction that followed? What would Hoda come up with? She would surely find a way to obtain Ray's email or telephone number. What an amazing woman she was! How could we lure Ray out of Lebanon?

————

If Ray had other affairs besides the one with Heidi the local nurse, I wondered if any of them had produced a child. Ray was a medical doctor and had probably supplied his paramours with birth-control pills. But what if one of the women wanted to have a child with Ray? She might have neglected to take her pill.

Lizzie and Ray never had any children, but I remembered Lizzie telling me that she had seen a gynecologist who said she was healthy. Were there other reasons why they didn't have children? Were these other reasons why Ray wanted to have sex with Heidi and his other mistresses? I felt sure that Ray wanted children—most Arabs I had known adored their little boys and girls.

But if Ray left children in the wake of any affairs, then where were they? Who cared for them? Was that where Ray's money ended up? Could possible children be used to trap Ray? Maybe Heidi could provide some insight here. What was her sex life with Ray like? Maybe with the right incentive, she would talk. I didn't want to invite her to lunch again. I'd have to run into her surreptitiously.

Before noon the next day, I drove out to the hospital. Maybe I could catch her when she left for lunch. The lush green oaks surrounding the buildings bore testimony that summer was here. It was a gorgeous property. I parked my Subaru in the shade where I had a good view of the entrance. People entered and exited the building, but no sign of Heidi. No one had mentioned it if she had left her job, but I realized that was a possibility. She was young and could easily get another job and start over in a new place. I decided to go in to ask the receptionist.

"No," the middle-aged woman said after checking the schedule for nurses on duty that day. "Nurse Hillstrom is not here today."

"But she still works here, right?"

"Oh, yes." The receptionist looked at a piece of paper taped on the wall next to her phone. "She'll be in tomorrow at 7 o'clock."

"In the morning?"

"Yes, A.M."

"Thank you. I'll try tomorrow."

"Do you want to leave a message?"

"No, thank you. No message."

———

The next day I again parked in a shady spot under a big oak tree with an unobstructed view of the hospital entrance, but where I wouldn't be easily spotted by people walking in and out of the building. The lunch hour had started, and people in blue or green scrubs began exiting the building. Almost immediately, I spotted Heidi with another nurse. Her long blond hair and brisk walk gave her away. I left my Subaru and called to her a couple of times until she turned around and saw me.

"I was just thinking about you, Heidi," I said, and she stopped and faced me. "What a stroke of luck to see you."

Fortunately, she didn't ask what I was doing there at this time, although if she had, I'd have made up a story to tell her. The other nurse kept walking over to another car.

"Are you going home for the day, or are you on your lunch break?"

"Lunch," she said and held up a small cooler for me to see. "I actually brought lunch today, but I left an apple in my car." We were standing by her small green Honda SUV. She opened the door and retrieved her apple. Then she started walking toward some benches and picnic tables near a little glen of trees overlooking the water.

"Do you mind if I join you for a few minutes?" I said and followed her over to a heavy stone picnic table. "I have something I'd like to talk to you about."

She nodded and looked at me skeptically as we sat down opposite each other.

"How are your patients?" I asked. "Do you have a lot of them to care for?"

"I usually have four or five, but today I have six."

"Are some of them difficult?"

"Only one is," she said as she unwrapped her sandwich. "An older woman who refuses to do anything for herself. She keeps saying that she was an only child, and I think that's the problem. Everything was probably done for her and handed to her."

I was happy hearing Heidi talk in full sentences instead of giving me one-word answers. I waited until she had taken a few bites of the sandwich before I continued. "Heidi, you know I am helping investigate my friend's death," I started cautiously. "I'm working with the sheriff as well as the FBI."

Her big blue eyes widened.

"And I'm trying to find Dr. Khazin. Do you know where he is?"

"No, I don't have a clue. Do *you* know where he is?"

"I don't know, but he may have left the country and could be in Lebanon."

Heidi looked out on the lake. "That's where he's from," she said in a dreamy voice.

"He never contacted you then?"

"No, not a word. I cannot understand it. And after all we had been through."

"How long had you been seeing him?"

"Since he came here. I was assigned to be his nurse." She kept nibbling on her sandwich and took several sips of her water.

"That's almost a year, isn't it?"

"Yes. First, we took walks together. Between surgeries or after. We talked about our backgrounds, where we were from. He was interested in my last name Hillstrom. It's Swedish, you know."

"Yes, I know. I'm half Norwegian."

"Oh, really?"

"On my mother's side." I looked at her and smiled. "We might be cousins." We both laughed, and she drank some of her water. I thought maybe she would be ready for my more personal questions by now. "And soon he asked you to have sex with him."

"He wasn't that direct," she said and looked down as if trying to concentrate on the rest of her sandwich. "He had a little studio just down the hill from the hospital." She pointed in the direction of a house beyond the oak trees. "He said that he stayed there when he had a patient he needed to check on during the night. He invited me over one night. I went to that little house with him many times, and that's where we usually slept together. It was so wonderful." She paused and looked over at a house shaded by trees. "And all the promises he made and the plans that we made. I can't believe he just left like that without telling me."

"I'm so sorry, Heidi." We sat there quietly, looking out at the water. I motioned to the sandwich, apple and water. "Go ahead, and finish your lunch."

She finished her sandwich and started on her apple.

"Did he give you any birth-control pills, or did he take any precautions himself?" I knew I was skating on thin ice here, and in an effort to show that I cared, I put my hand on her arm. However, Heidi was cool. She was a nurse, after all.

"No," she said in a neutral tone. "He said if I got pregnant, he'd take care of it."

"I see." Her forthrightness baffled me.

"He examined me and wanted to have sex right after I ovulated. I was to tell him immediately."

"And did you find that strange?"

"Yes. But he said that would be the most satisfying for me."

I had to make an effort to retain my composure. She still seemed so naïve and innocent.

She packed up the apple core and crushed her sandwich wrapper as she continued. "But of course I knew that, being that I am a nurse."

"It sounds to me as if he wanted to have a child with you, Heidi."

"Yes, that's what I thought. But I loved him, so why not?"

"I guess." I paused for a moment. "Will you continue to work at the hospital after all this?"

"I don't know. I talked to Cheryl one day."

"Oh, yes. Good. She'll give you some sound advice."

"Yes, she's smart and nice. I think that some of the other nurses were jealous of me. You know, being with Ray and all."

"Maybe." I shifted a little in my seat. "Do you think Ray had affairs with some of them too?"

"Cheryl thinks so, but why? Why would he tell me all these things then? It makes no sense."

"I know." I sighed. This was not an easy conversation. "When all this is over, Heidi, you'll be a stronger woman. I know it's hard right now, but eventually you'll be glad you had this experience. Not only will you be stronger, but you'll also be a better judge of character."

"I *am* strong," she said firmly. "I'm stronger than I look, you know."

"Maybe. And maybe if we work together, we can find this guy and bring him to justice."

She grabbed her bag as if ready to go back to work.

"Heidi, I told you that Ray had a Middle Eastern club down the hill, right?"

"I heard, but he never told me or took me there."

"I know. Mrs. Khazin hadn't seen it either."

Her eyebrows rose, and I cleared my throat.

"Heidi, this is going to come as a shock to you, but the sheriff and I went down there. It was a hangout for men. It seems that some of Ray's compatriots meet there to smoke and discuss issues in their homeland. And there is something else. They had belly dancers perform on weekends. Ray had a room in the building where he sometimes spent the night instead of going up the winding mountain highway in the dark. His wife spent most nights alone."

"Are you going to tell me that he spent the night with the dancers? Is that what you're saying?"

I nodded. "Yes, that's what a couple of girls who work there told me."

"What a frickin' pig!" She rose and held the water bottle upside down above her mouth and drank the rest of the water as if to wash away the whole sordid affair.

"I agree," I said.

"I hate him. How can I ever trust anyone again?"

"You will, Heidi. But you'll certainly be less gullible." I stopped to think about what would drive a man to this kind of behavior. He obviously had a psychological problem, maybe a deep-seated pain, something that had hurt him for a while. I had never liked Raymond Khazin from the moment I met him. He was arrogant, but I now realized the arrogance covered up something. Lizzie fell for him though, and he screwed her over big time too. "Fortunately, most men are not like that, Heidi, and don't hate my friend," I said. "You and she were in the same boat, smitten by a deceptive snake. I for one want to see him brought back here to face the music, as they say. Are you with me, Heidi?" I looked at her hopefully.

"You bet," Heidi said firmly. She looked at her phone. "Oh, time to go back to my patients. But I feel better already."

"I'll be in touch, Heidi." We stood and walked toward the hospital entrance together. "Do you want to come over to my house one day, maybe on your day off? Then we can lay plans."

"But he's in Lebanon. I've heard there's a lot of unrest over there right now."

"I know, but I'm starting to think of a trap to get him out of there. Although there's no physical evidence that he had anything to do with my friend's death, there's a lot of circumstantial evidence, maybe enough, to petition the District Attorney to indict Ray for murder. What do you think of that?"

"Really?"

"I'm thinking of a plan if you'll help me." I followed her over to the trash can so she could toss her trash from lunch

"Okay. Count me in."

———

I ran some errands in the resort, and on my way home, I saw the van with Maria and JP in front of me. I pulled into the driveway right behind them. We enjoyed a snack together before Maria left. When Ed and James came over for dinner, I told Ed about my meeting with Heidi.

"Doesn't it sound as if Ray wanted to have a child with Heidi?" I said as James took JP outside.

"I suppose. And she was okay with that?"

"That's how I understood it. Now I wonder if Ray had children with any of his other mistresses. Maybe a sick child could bring the doctor out of Lebanon. What do you think?"

"Hm. Maybe." He seemed distracted.

"Any indictment yet?"

"Everything has been submitted. It should be here any day now."

We made ourselves cups of coffee and joined JP and James on the deck. The sun was setting, and the lake looked like glittering gold. How could there be so many deception points in such a beautiful and peaceful place?

# 11

## AN UPDATE FROM LEBANON

The weekend brought more warm weather, so on Saturday morning we packed a picnic basket and took the boat out. The water was still too cold to swim, but James had brought his fishing rod and soon caught a rainbow trout. JP tried to mimic everything James did and created much laughter. The local movie theater was showing a rerun of the *Lion King*. Ed and I took the two boys to the afternoon show because James had plans with friends that evening.

Ray's flight to Lebanon after Lizzie's death seemed to belong to another world. Hoda, my Lebanese friend, was most likely out at various social events for the weekend, so I waited until Monday morning to call her. I brought my phone out to the deck where the connection was better.

"Hello, Hoda. It's Megan," I announced as soon as she answered. "Am I lucky enough to catch you at home?"

"Yes. I've been out all weekend, so today has been a day of rest. How's everything?"

"Good."

"I met an old friend of yours yesterday, Dr. Risq, who used to work for UNICEF. You remember him, don't you?"

"Of course I remember him. We were going to write a book on UNICEF and the organization's work in the Middle East, but there was never enough time. He drove like a maniac. I don't know how I survived riding around the streets of Beirut in his car."

"I told him I'd talked to you and updated him on your life in California. I believe he still carries a torch for you, Megan."

"Don't be ridiculous, Hoda. He married an Egyptian woman after I left."

"Well, the Egyptian woman is history, so now is your second chance."

We both laughed, and I leaned back in my chair.

"Hoda, do you know if Dr. Khazin brought a child or children with him when he returned from the States?"

"No, I don't think so. Is it important?"

"It could be."

"I could find out for sure, but I think I would have heard about it if he had brought someone with him."

"It would be awesome if you could find out for sure, Hoda. I'll call you again in a few days if that's alright."

"Sure. And how are things over in California?"

"Well, my fiancé's son came home last week after spending a year in London, so we've all had some catching up to do."

"Sounds exciting. I've had a niece staying with me for a few days. She keeps me busy."

"Maybe we should bring your niece and my nephew together sometime."

We chuckled as we discussed impossible futures for a few minutes.

"I'm also cleaning out some of my deceased friend's things, mostly clothes, to help out her mother, who's devastated, as you can imagine."

"Sounds sad. I'm so sorry, Megan."

"Thank you." I agreed, knowing this was evening for Hoda, and she needed downtime. "Listen, Hoda. I'll let you go so you can spend time with your niece and get some rest. I'll call you in a few days."

I walked over to the rail to watch sail boats bobbing along all over the lake. I thought about Heidi's bizarre story and my old friends in Beirut. I decided to call Cheryl at home. I knew she had worked all weekend so I assumed she might have a day off today.

"Cheryl, do you know for sure that Dr. Khazin carried on with other nurses at the hospital besides Heidi?" I asked, coming straight to the point.

"No, not for sure. Why?"

"I just wonder. Heidi told me that she and Dr. Khazin had unprotected sex, and she seemed to think he wanted her to get pregnant."

"That sounds too weird."

"I know. He hasn't been here long enough to have a baby, but I wonder if there's a pattern. Before coming up here, Lizzie told me he had practiced in Torrance. He and Lizzie didn't have any children. I wonder if he had children with any of his other mistresses."

"Boy, you are nosy, aren't you? How are you going to work that into a conversation?" She laughed aloud. "And what are you trying to do, anyway?"

"We have to figure out a way to lure Ray out of Lebanon because we have no extradition agreement with that country. A sick child could serve as bait."

"I see. Well, I'll give you the names and addresses of the places he worked before coming to our hospital."

"Cheryl, you're so amazing."

"We have that information at the hospital. I'll swing by with a copy after work today or tomorrow."

"Let me know, so I'm home."

"No problem. Talk to you later."

"Okay, and thanks."

Cheryl came by the following afternoon still in her scrubs. I made coffee for us and brought our cups out on the deck. She gave me three addresses. I recognized one.

"The first address is the place he practiced when he met my friend," I said. "I know where the two others are in Torrance."

"And how are you going to bring the conversation around to the nurses' sex lives?" she asked jokingly. She walked over to the rail and marveled at the view. "We don't always appreciate the beauty that surrounds us up here."

I joined her and took a sip of the hot coffee.

"I don't plan to," I said. "I want to find out if he had any children with anyone around there. He didn't have any with his wife."

"And you think he wanted to have a child with Heidi?" Cheryl turned toward me. "How did you bring that up with her?"

"Well, she is a nurse, and it didn't seem to be a big deal to her." I chuckled a little and took another sip of coffee. "Besides, we're pals now."

"Really? That was fast."

"I recognized that her last name, Hillstrom, was Swedish, and she told me that her father was indeed from Sweden. I told her that I was half-Norwegian on my mother's side, so we connected. She realizes Ray led her on, then betrayed her. She's mad. Hell knows no fury than a woman scorned, according to Shakespeare."

"Yes, I seem to have heard that one before." She held her cup up to her mouth with both hands, took a slow sip, then set the cup on top of the rail.

"Anyway, she now wants to capture the bastard and bring him to justice just as much as I do. We're trying to hatch a plan together."

"Amazing." She looked into her cup and remained silent. Cheryl and Jonathan didn't have any children either. She had told me that it was by choice, but I wondered if they regretted it now that they were past forty. I switched the subject and asked about her work. I always enjoyed hearing stories about her eccentric patients.

After she left, I called Sally Ferguson at the FBI, but she had left for the day. The waiting game was constantly on. I caught her early the next morning, though, and told her about our plan so far. She liked it immediately.

"Can you call the two Torrance offices and tell them someone will call on them?" I asked. "Or do you want to go yourself? How do you want to handle it, Sally?"

"The murder case is not mine, but I can still call and tell them you're coming."

"Okay. That will make it more official." I paused. "Any news about the Medicare fraud case? Or Dr. Khazin's kickback scheme?"

"No, but we're still on it. And the indictment is approved, I understand."

"I haven't seen it or heard it officially, but the sheriff told me that the request has been submitted, hand delivered, I heard."

"Yes, it's official. I just heard this morning, as a matter of fact."

"Good. So now we need to outfox the scoundrel and put him on trial."

"We need to keep it out of the media, though. We don't want the elusive doctor to suspect anything yet. If AP or Reuter or any of the other international news agencies start reporting on it, it will be all over Lebanon the next day."

"Believe me, I know."

"I'll make appointments for tomorrow. Is anytime okay?"

"No problem. Late morning or early afternoon would be good because of the traffic, but I'll adjust."

———

The first clinic on Hawthorne Boulevard in North Torrance didn't bring any results. The office apparently had a big turnover, and no one remembered Dr. Khazin. However, the practice on Lomita Boulevard was bigger and more sophisticated. The young Hispanic receptionist said the office manager was expecting me. The office manager, a brisk middle-aged woman with a shock of salt-and-pepper hair, immediately took me to an older physician who appeared to be of Indian descent. She introduced him as Dr. Brar, and I introduced myself.

"Please be seated. How may I help you?" Dr. Brar indicated a chair in the corner of his small medical office for me, while he remained seated at his desk.

"We are investigating Dr. Khazin for murder," I said formally. "And we understand he used to work here."

"Yes, that's correct," he said. "But I have not seen him since he left." He crossed his long legs, and his poor posture made him slump forward in a chair that seemed too small for him.

"He's also on the FBI's radar for defrauding Medicare and taking kickbacks or consulting fees from pharmaceutical companies."

"I *have* heard about that. But not a murder investigation," Dr. Brar said and shifted his weight in his chair, re-crossing his legs. "But I really know nothing about it."

"I understand, but I think you do remember him as a skirt chaser." I looked at him and smiled.

"Well, he did have a way with the ladies." He smiled too. "And I disapproved of his behavior here."

"Are any of these women still working here?"

"Yes. Let me call Nurse Lola. She'll know more about it." He picked up the phone on his desk and asked that the nurse come into the office.

"Do you know if any of his relationships produced a child?"

"No, I never heard that. I'm sure he took precautions. I mean, he is a doctor."

"True," I said, and flashed another smile.

After a few minutes, Nurse Lola entered. She was a large and colorful woman with black wavy hair and lots of makeup. Dr. Brar introduced me as an FBI agent. I didn't contradict him as I should have and searched my purse frantically for a Kleenex, pretending not to hear him. I told the no-nonsense, stout and sturdy nurse why I was there.

"Yes, he played a little too much with the nurses and was let go, as I understand it. Right, Dr. Brar?"

"He became somewhat of an embarrassment after a while," Dr. Brar said cautiously. He was not one to commit one hundred percent, it seemed.

"Did you know that he was married during the time he worked here?"

"I had heard something like that, yes," Dr. Brar answered. "And I think some of us found that to be awkward." The doctor seemed uncomfortable talking about a former colleague's behavior.

I turned to Lola. "Do you know if any of his affairs resulted in a child?"

"No. I mean, no, I don't think that any of them got pregnant. That I would have heard. After all, he is a doctor, and if one of the girls had become pregnant, he would surely have taken care of it, performed an abortion, probably. He was not what I would call a man of high principles or moral standards."

"I see," I consciously worked at keeping a professional demeanor. "You may have already read in the local paper the grand jury's decision to indict Dr. Khazin for the murder of his wife."

Dr. Brar remained stoic and may not have heard or read about it yet. Lola visibly blanched despite her make-up, although she soon regained her composure. As an experienced nurse, she had probably seen her share of betrayal and death.

"Dr. Khazin has fled to Lebanon where he's originally from," I continued. "He still has a large family there. We are trying to bring him back to this country to stand trial. We wonder if he left any children behind here."

"I see," Lola said thoughtfully. "It would be highly unlikely, in my opinion."

I rose and thanked them both for their time. Then I excused myself and left. I had a lot to think about during my drive up the mountain. The sick-child trick didn't seem to be such a good idea after all, but I had one more person to talk to before I called Hoda once more.

———

Although the sick child ruse seemed to be at a dead end, I wasn't ready to let go of it yet. Unfortunately, another blow to my plan came in a message from Hoda the next morning, confirming what she had said earlier: Ray did not bring any children with him when he returned to Beirut. Nor did he have any children in Lebanon.

Before abandoning my idea altogether, I decided to check with one more person—Ray's brother, Richard Khazin, in Rancho Cucamonga. I verified his address and called him at the number I'd paid to obtain earlier. An answering machine picked up. I introduced myself, explaining my relationship to Ray. I left a long message that I'd like to talk to him, telling Richard I had a meeting in Rancho Cucamonga near his home the next day.

"I assume you still live at the same address," I rattled off the address I'd paid for. "Ray told me that he stayed with you for a few days after his wife died. If it's okay, I'd like to stop by for a few minutes after you come home from work or earlier, if that's more convenient. I seem to remember you telling me that you worked from home some days." I gave him my cell number and ended the call.

Richard Khazin did not call back that day, so after breakfast the next morning, I went out on the deck and called again. This time he answered after a few rings, and I repeated my request for a meeting. I had only a few questions, I said, and it would take but a few minutes.

"Sorry," he said. "I'm leaving town for a couple of days. Maybe I can answer your questions over the phone." His voice was tense, as if he were in a hurry to leave.

"That's okay," I said. "I'll wait. It's not urgent. I can come over when you return the day after tomorrow. Will you be home, or do you prefer to meet at your place of work?"

"No, I'll be home early afternoon."

"Perfect. What about two o'clock?" I suggested.

"A little later would be better. Maybe three or three-thirty."

"Okay."

"What's the problem?" he asked impatiently.

"No problem. Ray's back in Lebanon, right?"

"Yes. My father is ill."

"I'm so sorry. I hope he'll have a speedy recovery." I paused for a moment, letting the silence stretch. "We'll talk the day after tomorrow, then. Take care."

I ended the call and sat back in my chair to think about that terse conversation. Richard sounded tense, a little anxious even. His voice had an edge to it. Maybe he thought I would be satisfied with the information that Ray was back in Lebanon.

There was nothing else to do but wait. I worked on my novel, played with JP, and discussed plans for the fall term with James. As I had predicted, he and Ed were over here more than they were at their house. Maria liked to have Ed and James here too. She was okay with me, but she clearly preferred Ed and James and seemed to adore JP.

A little after noon two days later, I set out for the meeting with Richard Khazin in Rancho Cucamonga. The two-story house had curb appeal with tiled front steps that led to a tall oak door. Richard Khazin looked like his brother, but smaller and thinner with short black hair, olive skin and a small goatee. He was dressed like a typical Californian in a Hawaiian shirt over dressy shorts and flip-flops. He greeted me formally and led me into a sparsely furnished living room.

"Can I bring you something to drink?" he offered as I walked over to the couch and sat down.

"Thank you. A glass of water would be nice."

I looked around the room while Mr. Khazin fetched the water. A large landscape photograph, possibly of the Lebanese countryside, hung above the small fireplace. A Persian carpet decorated the floor. With only the couch, a coffee table and a couple of wooden chairs, the sitting room looked bare.

"So, what can I help you with?" Khazin asked in perfect English as he handed me the glass of water and sat down on one of the wooden chairs, crossing his legs.

Before I could answer, he continued. "You know, I wasn't really that close to Ray's wife. We met a few times, but I never got to know her well, so I don't know what information I can help you with."

"I understand that," I replied. "I'd like to learn more about Ray."

His eyebrows rose slightly, and he shifted uneasily in his chair, both feet now planted on the floor.

"You know that he had a mistress."

He laughed. "So what? Is that what you wanted to confirm? We're Arabs. We like women."

To him, being Arab and liking women explained everything.

"As a matter of fact, he had several mistresses."

He seemed to think that funny if the lurid smile on his face meant anything.

"You said Ray returned to Lebanon because your father is ill," I said. "Did he give you any other reason?"

"No. No other reason. Did you have anything in mind?"

"I'm sorry about your father," I said. "What's the matter with him?" I didn't think this man was going to give away much on his brother. Family meant everything to Arabs, the same as it did to folks like Maria.

"That's what we don't know. That's what Ray wants to find out."

"I see. Did he take anyone with him when he left?"

"No. Who would he take?"

"Any of his mistresses, for example."

"No. That's absurd."

"Or a child? I heard he had several children with these mistresses."

Richard Khazin's jaw dropped. His goatee almost touched his chest. "Where on earth did you hear that?" He looked at me hard. "Did his wife tell you that?"

"No, but one of the nurses whom he had an affair with said that her little boy was seriously ill and that Dr. Khazin was her son's father."

"That is an absolute lie!" Khazin practically shouted. "He would never leave a sick child. He has no children. To tell you the truth, that was a sore point with him. I assume his wife couldn't conceive, and that may be why he took mistresses. No Arab would hold that against him. For us, having no children is a shame, something that is not talked about. Swept under the carpet." He made a sweeping motion. "Sometimes, among Middle Eastern men, Ray would tell everyone that he had three sons."

"Really?" I said. "I had forgotten. I used to live in the Middle East with my first husband." I paused and delicately lifted one brow, giving him a womanly glance. "So, do you have any children, Richard?"

"Yes, two. A son and a daughter. They're with their mother. We divorced two years ago. Unlike Ray, I'm not a US citizen—I didn't see any benefits to it at the time—so I lost custody of my children. In the Middle East, the children go with the father in cases of divorce. Not so in the United States. Fortunately, my ex doesn't want to deny our children their father, so I'm still involved with them, especially my little girl."

I was glad I had been able to get him to talk.

"So now you know our whole story. Tell your friend, whoever she says she is, that her sick-child story does not fly in this family."

"Hmm. I see." I sat up a bit straighter, perhaps the better to run if this next question hit an anger button with Richard. "May I ask you another question? I understand several of your countrymen meet at Ray's club in San Bernardino, right?"

"So what?"

"Oh, nothing. I heard that you're part of a group working to change things in Lebanon."

He leaned forward a little, his hands on his knees. "Where did you hear that?"

"My fiancé and I went down to Ray's club one evening. As I said, I lived in Lebanon not too long ago. I had an apartment below Hamra Street. It's a lovely city, but I learned firsthand about the corruption and the inability of the government to manage the country in general and the economy in particular. I understand that the educated people who now live in different parts of the world want to take back their country."

"If I may be frank, I think you're sticking your nose into things you don't understand and that are none of your business."

"True, but you may be surprised to learn that I'm on your side, and so was Ray's wife. She had lived in Lebanon too and had seen firsthand the corruption everywhere and the mismanagement of that lovely country."

"Really?" He gave me a searching look.

I was dying to tell him about the grand jury's decision to indict Ray but held my tongue. Richard would alert his brother, and Ray would smell a rat in whatever ruse we'd come up with.

"I'm so sorry," I said simply and meant it. "I was curious why Ray had disappeared. Now I know. Please tell Ray I said hello if you talk to him. Forget about the mistress and her child. She probably smelled money. Women can be devious and mean, as I'm sure you know." I finished my water and stood, ready to leave. "I'm so happy you agreed to see me, and thank you for talking with me. *Shukran.*" I used the Arab phrase I'd learned overseas to tell him, *Thank you.*

He rose and nodded his head, in a semi-formal type of bow. "A*ssalamaleykum*—peace be upon you," he said.

"That brings back memories."

"*Ahlanwasahlan,*" he said simply, and looked away. As he walked me to the door, he seemed to rethink what he had said earlier. "You're right," he said slowly. "It is unfortunate how the present regime has ruined the entire country with its corruption, lawlessness, and ignorance. Its inability to manage the economy. We have to take back the country."

I nodded in agreement, thanked him again, and said goodbye.

Driving up the mountain, I mulled over the information that I would never have obtained over the phone. I thought about the group of expatriates who wanted their country to be like it was when they lived there. Lebanon had been a beacon of light in the dark valley that was the Middle East. New ideas were starting to hatch in my mind, and I had much to discuss with Ed tonight.

———

What Richard Khazin had revealed to me about his brother Ray opened up new avenues in my investigation, and I mulled over the possibilities all the way home. James and JP were playing catch when I got there. I joined them and was glad for the exercise. The long drive had left me stiff, and after spending the day in the LA smog, the fresh mountain air felt good. Ed texted me to say he would be late and not to wait for him. Maria had already gone, so James, JP and I sat down to a dinner of cod fillets in a cream sauce with rice and mixed vegetables. JP was not overly fond of fish, but since James loved it, JP said he loved it too. I was anxious to tell Ed about Richard Khazin's revelations, but it was after nine before he finally walked through the door.

"What happened?"

"Another shooting in a Mexican restaurant in Arrowbear," he replied, as he gave me a quick peck on the cheek. He unbuttoned his uniform jacket and loosened his tie before he unloaded his guns, hung his gun belt on a peg high up by the door, then walked into the kitchen.

"Thanks," he said as I handed him a glass of water. "What are these people thinking, running around with loaded guns and getting into drunken brawls?" He shook his head for emphasis.

"It's still the Wild West around here, isn't it?" I said as I warmed a plate of cod with lots of cream sauce and rice for him. When I set the plate in front of him, he attacked it ravenously. "This is delicious," he commented between bites.

I sat down at the table next to him. "Feel better now?"

"Yes, much better."

"Are you ready to hear what I learned from Ray's brother Richard Khazin today?" I asked as he scraped up the rest of the sauce.

"Okay." He pushed his plate away and leaned back in his chair.

I told him what Richard Khazin had shared about Ray, his alleged desire to father a child, and what an impact this unfulfilled wish had on him in the macho Arabic culture. "So, now I have another way to get him out of Lebanon."

"Oh? And what's that?"

"We'll tell him that one of his mistresses is pregnant with his child. That there may be complications, and she is begging him to return and help her."

"And I take it you mean to involve Heidi again?"

"Why not? She realizes now that Ray betrayed her. She's both hurt and furious. She wants him back here to stand trial."

"Dr. Khazin may just call a specialist for her to see. He is a surgeon and not a gynecologist, remember?"

"True, but at least we'll have established an initial contact with him."

"Did your Lebanese friend find out what his address is then?"

"No, not yet, but I have no doubt that Hoda will come through."

"And if she doesn't?"

"We'll cross that bridge when we come to it."

"You're surely not thinking of going over there yourself, are you?" He rose, placed his dishes in the dishwasher and started making a cup of coffee.

"No, not really. At least not yet."

"Megan, I will absolutely put my foot down and nix any such trip." He slid his full coffee cup away from the coffee maker and gave me as serious an expression as I'd ever seen.

"Ed, I'm not planning to go anywhere. But just so that we're clear: You have no right to stop me from going anywhere I want to go." I walked over to the coffee maker and made myself a cup of coffee too.

"And just to make *my* point absolutely clear too, Megan, as a sheriff, I can forbid a private citizen from meddling in an ongoing investigation. I should not have let it go this far."

The bold statements left both of us silent, if not stunned. Ed put down his foot, and I clearly tried to put mine right on top of it, rather than stand beside him. We could work as partners. He'd put on his sheriff hat and laid aside the fiancé hat.

No comment came to my mind. Certainly nothing that would calm this situation. Ed didn't look as if he'd change his mind either. He headed to the living room, his coffee probably forgotten though he still cradled the cup. I followed him into the room, taking tiny sips of the hot liquid, without an idea of what to do next.

James came racing downstairs. He had been watching television upstairs and had not heard Ed come home.

"Hi, Dad," he said quickly, already at the door, keys in hand. "I'm going out with the guys for a while, okay?"

Ed glanced at his watch. "This late?"

"It's not that late. I'll be home in a couple of hours."

"Be home by midnight, son," Ed said firmly. "Between midnight and five am, no one should be on the road unless they have to. That's when all the trouble happens."

Once again, and maybe unwisely, I stepped in to defend James' actions and help Ed see that his son wasn't a child anymore. "James is a grown man now, Ed. He can take care of himself." I nodded to James. "But I agree with your dad, James. Between midnight and five in the morning, most good people stay inside. See you tomorrow." The young man shot me a smile, and he was gone while Ed grumbled unhappily.

I turned back to Ed and tried to ease the tension. "I thought you said that you had dealt with a shooting today during daylight hours, Ed. Crime can happen anyplace at any time."

He picked up the local paper that I had put on the coffee table earlier and started flipping through the pages. I finished my coffee and checked my phone for messages. A new message from Hoda came up. She had obtained Ray's email address without any subterfuge. I quickly wrote back to thank her and to tell her that it was all we needed for now.

"My friend in Lebanon just texted Ray's email, Ed. Isn't it remarkable how easy it is to find people all over the world now?"

"Yes," he said, seemingly absorbed in an article in the paper. "But I have enough trouble catching criminals close to home."

"I'm sorry, Ed. I know I'm supposed to follow your lead, but you were so slow to acknowledge that my friend could have been murdered. I was frustrated and afraid we'd miss important evidence."

He put the paper down, and looked at me. "Well, from now on, you have to let me handle things. I'll let you know, and you can assist when appropriate."

"I know we live in a country of law and order and I will confer with you and Garcia about any hunch I have so we can work together."

"Okay. Let's see if you follow through on your promise." He rose and walked toward the hallway. "I'm tired, Megan. I'll take a long hot bath and go to bed. We'll start over tomorrow, okay?"

I nodded. Tomorrow I'd talk to Heidi about our new plan.

———

The next morning, I called Sally Ferguson at the FBI. She wasn't in, so I called my other contact and old friend Carrie Jensen. She picked up her phone on the first ring. I talked about the Arabic culture and the importance of a man fathering children.

"Dr. Khazin's brother Richard told me that his brother felt ashamed and was suffering from a deep-seated pain because he had not been able to have any children. A nurse that Dr. Khazin had an affair with told me he wanted to have sex with her right after she ovulated. She was convinced he was trying to impregnate her," I took a deep breath and cleared my throat. "She was furious when she heard that Dr. Khazin had other affairs. Now, she feels betrayed and angry that he left her without a word."

I paused for Carrie to respond, but she remained silent.

"Are you with me?" I asked her.

"Yes, and your point is?" Carrie said slowly.

"I think Dr. Khazin will return if he learns that one of his mistresses is pregnant. What do you think?"

"I don't know. Most men I know would run away if their mistresses got pregnant. And I'm sure you know of murder cases where husbands have killed their pregnant wives."

"I know. But this is different. Your scenario would truly be rare in the Arabic culture. All the Arabs I know love children."

"Really? Well, it's an idea," Carrie admitted and paused before she continued. "We are in contact with Interpol in Cyprus, and they're working on a ruse to lure him over there. It's only a short hop from Beirut."

"And I assume we have an extradition agreement with Cyprus then."

"We do."

"My idea would be cheaper." I didn't want to push, but time was running out to get Ray back and get justice for Lizzie.

"Yes, that's true. And who knows? It may be worth a try."

"I'll keep you posted," I said. "If it doesn't work, I'm glad we have a backup."

Later, when Ed came by for a quick lunch, I told him not to worry about me going anywhere or doing anything without his approval. "The FBI has a good plan. They'll set up a trap in Cyprus. Interpol will apprehend Ray there, and a couple of agents will escort him back to the States."

"Sounds like a good plan."

"Yes, I suppose as long as no one screws up." I'd never dealt with Interpol nor researched them for my novels so I wasn't sure if their plan would go off without a hitch.

Ed paused in the middle of his meal and looked around. "Where's everyone?"

"Out. JP is still at school, and Maria left. She'll pick up JP later. I have no idea where James is."

He looked at me with a glint in his eyes and came closer. He was not one to hold a grudge. I smiled and hugged him. He felt warm. "How about an afternoon nap?" he said and embraced me more seriously. "We have to take advantage of our alone time." He was back to his calm self, and I had the feeling he wanted more than just a nap.

———

After he left to go back to the station, I texted Heidi

*Can you come to my house tomorrow before lunch? I got Ray's email through a friend of mine.*

Heidi called me back a little later. "Tomorrow is my day off as a matter of fact. I can come over any time."

"Good. I think I have discovered his Achilles' heel, so to speak."

"His what?"

"Never mind. I think I know what his problem is. I believe he really wanted to have a child with you, Heidi, and I think you alone will be able to convince him to return to our little resort town. If you want to. I'll work with you."

"How?"

"I haven't completely figured it out yet, but we'll put our heads together tomorrow."

"Okay. What time?"

"Around ten or so. Is that good?"

"Yes, that's fine," she said, no longer snippy, sad or sullen. Now there was an eagerness in her voice.

I explained how to get to my house, and she said she'd find it.

"Do you have a laptop?" I asked.

"Yes. Do you want me to bring it?"

"Yes. We'll write an email together."

She chuckled in a truly wicked tone. "I wonder what he'll have to say for himself when he realizes that I've found him."

"Well, we'll see, won't we? See you tomorrow at ten."

As soon as I put down my phone, I started to draft a loving email to Ray, although I realized that we couldn't use my wording. I would read whatever I had written, then ask Heidi to write the message in her own words. I felt certain he still had her phone number, but she would include it to remind him. I predicted that he would call her right back. I'd help Heidi prepare a response.

Eager she might sound, but would she stay cool under the influence of his charm, even long distance? At least she wouldn't be able to see him, and he wouldn't be close enough to embrace her and whisper in her ear. It would be better not to mention pregnancy complications. As Ed noted, Ray was not a gynecologist, and he might just refer Heidi to a specialist. He would then confer with the same specialist and learn the truth.

No, that wouldn't work.

Although the email was just a preliminary part of the ruse, I would let Ed know exactly what I had in mind. I already had Carrie's go-ahead, so all was above board.

# 12

## AN ALLURING EMAIL

Maria had just returned from shopping and was putting the groceries away when Heidi arrived the next morning. I opened the door for her and led the way out to the deck. I brushed off a cushioned chair for her to sit down, and she put her big bag with her laptop beside her. "Nice house."

"Thank you." I remained standing. "How about a glass of juice or ice water?"

"Water will be fine if it's not too much trouble."

"No trouble at all." I went into the kitchen to pour two glasses.

"I make a light chicken salad for lunch," Maria said. "Ed, come over and probably James. What about your friend? She stay for lunch?"

"Yes, I think so. Yes, make enough for her too. Thank you, Maria."

"*De nada.*"

I carried the water outside and set one glass on the side table next to Heidi's chair. She already had her laptop out and was ready to go.

"So, what should I write?" She looked at me with wide blue eyes, fingers poised over the keys. "Hello Ray?"

"How about Dear Ray?"

"I don't feel like writing, *dear,*" she protested.

"Okay, I understand." I said, fidgeting uneasily with my hands. This whole business was awkward. "I have thought of a few things to write. But I don't want to dictate. It has to be in your words. Have you ever written Ray an email before?"

"No. We either talked on the phone or texted. I would text him the times we should meet, the right time to have sex and so on, as I told you. He would text me if he was going to be late."

"Okay, this email can be a little more formal, but not much. You want to ask him how he's doing first and how you felt when you heard he had left the country. Maybe ask him why he didn't say goodbye or contact you."

I watched Heidi's fingers as she typed. "You're fast!"

"I use computers a lot in my work now," she explained.

"Then maybe explain that you haven't been feeling well lately," I continued. "Tell him that you just found out that you're pregnant with his child. That you've not been with anyone since he left. Ask him what he wants you to do and when he's coming back. Tell him how much you love him and want to see him. Remind him of the plans both of you made together and what he told you. Did you have a special pet name for him?" I asked. "Use that if you can."

Heidi kept typing and whenever she finished a section, she would give me an expectant look.

"Be sure to include your phone number just in case he doesn't have it handy. Remind him that you're longing to hear his voice. Whatever he decides, you want to have this baby. Maybe put in a few hearts."

As she finished, she leaned back and grinned at me. "Oh, this is good."

"Okay, read it out loud," I suggested.

She did, and it sounded very much like her voice.

"Great, Heidi. Do a blind carbon copy to yourself so you'll have a copy of this then click on Send."

When she was done, I held up my hand for a high-five, and she joined in.

Heidi remained silent for a few moments. "What now?"

"Heidi, the reason I wanted you to come over early was that there's a ten-hour time change between California and Lebanon. It's almost 10 o'clock at night over there, and if he's still up, I predict that he'll call you right away."

"Oh, my God! What am I gonna say?" Her unsteady voice mirrored the tremor in her hands that now clasped the laptop.

"Let's think about it. Have something ready for when he calls. Do you think you can stay cool?"

"I told you I'm stronger than I look."

"You look strong, Heidi," I said untruthfully. I knew that she had not yet lost her naiveté. "But remember that Ray is older and more experienced than you. He'll lay on the charm and lay it on thick, but you don't need to commit to anything. If he calls now, I'll listen in if that's okay. If he calls later today or this evening, you're on your own."

"I can handle it. I'm a big girl," she assured me.

"Good." I rose and stretched my legs. "I hope you can stay for lunch in case Ray calls. Maria has made chicken salad." I heard Ed's chirp and his car door slam. "That's Ed. He's coming over for lunch."

"The sheriff?" she said in a bewildered tone as Ed appeared in the doorway in full uniform.

I introduced Heidi to him.

"Sorry, honey, I didn't know you had company."

"I told you yesterday, Ed, but never mind. Maria has made a big salad for all of us. James is helping Thomas' family with inventory at their store."

In the kitchen, I introduced Heidi to Maria. Maria has never met a stranger and promptly urged Heidi to sit down while I helped set the table. Maria treated us to another one of her delicious meals, and for a while, the conversation revolved around the email we had sent to Dr. Khazin.

"And how are things at the hospital?" Ed asked Heidi in an effort to change the subject. "Are your patients behaving themselves?"

"Most of them are, but we have a few oddballs. One older man, a real mountain man, attacked me a couple of days ago. He was so combative that a male attendant had to take him on."

"How long have you worked up here now?"

"A little over a year. It's a beautiful place."

We continued with some more small talk.

Maria excused herself as soon as she finished eating. Ed rose to leave too. He said goodbye to Heidi and gave me a quick embrace and a peck on the cheek.

"See you later, honey."

Heidi looked at me with raised eyebrows. "I didn't know that you and the sheriff were an item," she commented as I started to make coffee for both of us to take out on the deck again.

"Well. Yes. We're planning to marry one day, but in the meantime, we each have roles to play in this investigation. I was actually married to Ed's brother Chris, who died last year. I thought it was the end of the world. He was the father of my small son. But as you can see, Heidi, life goes on. One relationship ends, and another comes along." I squeezed her hand in an effort to comfort her.

We returned to the deck to sip our coffee.

"So, the sheriff will be working with us to bring Ray back to stand trial."

"Yes, as will the FBI."

"My goodness! This is a big deal, then."

"Yes. It's a big deal, Heidi. And your role is very important. You're the most important pawn in this game right now." We drank our coffee in silence. "It's doesn't look like Ray is going to call until this evening when it's morning over there," I said finally.

She set her coffee mug down and rose, ready to leave. "I should go home and finish my laundry and do some cleaning. I have a full shift again tomorrow. Thank you for lunch and for letting me help bring in Ray."

I walked her to the door. "We depend on you not to succumb to this man's charm, Heidi. He'll be full of lies again. Be prepared."

"I am," she said and raised her chin defiantly.

———

It was almost eleven o'clock in the evening when she texted me and said that Ray had indeed called. I called her right back.

"What happened?" I was so anxious I was almost breathless.

"Ray called! He actually called. I can't get over it. He wants to come back to me." She sounded like a teenager whose ex just called to say he wanted to make up. Which is exactly what Ray did—using Heidi's feelings for him to seduce her into this mindlessness.

My heart sank. "And what did you tell him?"

"That I was pregnant. He was so excited."

"That's what I expected, Heidi. But you know when he finds out that you're not, he'll betray you again."

I could hear a heavy disappointment in her voice. "Yes, but he sounded so wonderful. He said this was his first child. He hadn't really wanted to have a baby with anyone but me."

"He is a fraud, Heidi. Pull yourself together."

"I know."

"When is he coming back?"

"He said he had some business to take care of over there, but as soon as it was completed, he would be back."

"When?"

"I don't know exactly. He wanted me to meet him in Paris, but I knew that wouldn't work, so I told him I couldn't travel that far right now."

"Good job, Heidi. Paris is no good. We need him on American soil."

"Yes, he said he was going to try to arrange it."

"Soon?"

"He was a little vague about the time, but he said he was anxious to come as soon as he could. He said that when his business is completed, he will hop on a plane immediately."

"You done good, Heidi. We'll get him. If he calls again, stay cool, okay?"

"I'll let you know."

"We have to be careful. I'll let the sheriff and the FBI know."

Ed was already in bed, reading. I joined him and told him Ray had called Heidi back.

"And what did he say?"

"That he'd be returning soon."

"When?"

"He didn't say exactly." I repeated what Heidi told me. "So now the waiting game starts again."

———

As soon as the house was quiet after the morning rush, I texted Carrie at the FBI and asked her to call me, which she did right away. I told her the news, and Carrie listened without interrupting me.

"It sounds like we've got him," she said.

"He first wanted to meet Heidi in Paris, France."

"No, France won't work. That's another country that doesn't cooperate with us."

"Fortunately, Heidi said that she couldn't travel that far. Ray told her that he had business to take care of first but would return to California after that. He admitted to her that he didn't have any children and that she was the first one he wanted to have a baby with. According to his brother, he's wanted a child for some time. I don't know what the problem is, but sometimes it's the male and not the female who is unable to produce a child."

"Yes, I know." I could hear Carrie tapping, probably a pencil. Something that helped her think. "He'll probably travel back here through France as the connections will be better through Paris. As soon as he steps on U. S. soil, we'll nab him. Any idea when?"

"No, not yet, but I'll stay in touch with Heidi. I just hope she can stay cool and not fall for his charm. Although I never fell for him myself, many otherwise smart women, like my friend Lizzie, couldn't resist his good looks and charming manner."

"Beware of good-looking men."

"It's funny you should say that. It was one of the last things my friend Lizzie said to me."

"Smart woman."

"She got smart too late."

———

148

I called or texted Heidi every day. She reported that Ray had called her several times to ask how she was feeling. As far as I could tell, Heidi was able to stick to our plan. On Saturday morning, before everyone was up, I was out on the deck surfing the Internet on my laptop when I saw *Breaking News* flash across my screen. Then I caught the headline: *Massive Explosion Rocks Beirut.* I kept scrolling through photos of billowing brown smoke and crumbling buildings. I sat there, my mouth gaping, frozen in my chair. Further destruction of this beautiful city. Unbelievable! I read the first article slowly, trying to absorb what could have happened.

BEIRUT — *A massive explosion shook Beirut, the capital of Lebanon, early Friday morning, causing widespread damage. The blast occurred near one of the busiest ports in the eastern part of the Mediterranean Sea, destroying much of the country's grain supplies stored in a warehouse near the site, adding more fuel to the minefield of Lebanese politics and inciting public rage against the current corrupt regime. In a scathing criticism of government officials, opposition leaders called for a nationwide revolution against the system, maintaining that the government was at fault and could have prevented the disaster.*

*With the destruction of much of the port, the country will be unable to import basic goods, throwing Lebanon into deeper political and economic turmoil.*

*According to the Associated Press, highly explosive ammonium nitrate used in fertilizer caused the blast. Local officials say that such dangerous material should never have been stored so close to the port.*

*Last month, tens of thousands of mostly peaceful protesters demonstrated against the current regime for its inability to provide basic services and prevent financial ruin. After the explosion, the number of demonstrators has grown into hundreds of thousands who have gathered in town squares all over Lebanon. One opposition group, supported by wealthy Lebanese-Americans, stands ready to step in...*

I closed my laptop and looked out over the dark blue lake, unwilling to read the rest of the article. My hands were numb. My thoughts were numb. My heart… People died. People were injured. My thoughts immediately went to Hoda. Was she safe? I didn't want to call and tie up the telephone lines, so I messaged her instead.

"I'm good. In shock. More later." Her text was short with no details, of course, but it confirmed she was alive.

That was a relief. But what about Ray? Was he involved? Was this the business he had to take care of before returning to Heidi? Had he been hurt? Or worse? And what about his family? Were any of them hurt? Would Ray be able to leave the devastation and return to the States?

How would this affect Heidi? She was working long shifts both Saturday and Sunday this weekend. I would call her at lunchtime.

I watched the time closely so as not to miss Heidi in her lunch hour. From time to time, I looked for updates on the Internet and learned that dozens had been killed and hundreds had been injured. At noon, I texted Heidi some of the information and told her I would call her. She called me instead, and I filled in what details I'd learned in the long morning hours.

Heidi was at first speechless. "Ray?" she finally asked with an unsteady voice. "Is he hurt?"

"I don't know. It happened Friday morning. Did you hear from him yesterday?"

"No. I haven't talked to him since Wednesday. Should I try to call him?"

"No, wait. We don't want to tie up the phone lines. Read the story on the Internet and email him instead. I think that's okay, but if he doesn't answer, don't worry. There could be a problem with communication."

"What about your friend?"

"She messaged me that she's fine, and I'm sure Ray is fine too. The whole affair may be part of an effort by a group to overthrow the government. I believe Ray is part of this group of his countrymen who want change in Lebanon. Because he may have known about it, I believe he probably was far away when the explosion occurred."

"Is that why he couldn't come back right away?"

"It's possible. Right now, I think Lebanon needs him as a doctor. He may need to stay to help care for the injured. I'm not sure. I'll try to find out and update you."

"But maybe that's why he couldn't take me with him when he left," she said with hope in her voice.

"No, Heidi," I said firmly. "Don't let him fool you into thinking something like that. Don't waver. Stay strong."

She didn't answer.

I made her promise to stay cool before we said goodbye, but worried that any promise to me would fall by the wayside in the light of Ray's charm.

I called Carrie Jensen and caught her in the car on her way to downtown LA. "Don't you take Saturdays off?"

"I do, but I need to check on something."

"Did you see the news about the accident in Beirut?"

"Yes, but I didn't read the whole story."

"I don't think Dr. Khazin will travel any time soon now. He may feel obligated to stay and care for the injured."

"We can wait."

"But this may also be a time when he'll have to hop over to Cyprus for supplies or help those who may have escaped there, or maybe just to breathe some fresh air."

"We'll be ready."

"I hope so. I guess you've had experience in handling such affairs." I realized too late that I sounded a bit sarcastic.

"Yes, ma'am. Give us some credit. We've done this before."

"I know. But I feel that the wheels sometimes turn slowly in your big machine."

"We have to follow the law." She paused before she continued. "But be sure to update us if you hear anything."

"I will." Either her phone or mine seemed to be breaking up. I lost the call. Since I didn't really have anything else to say, I didn't call her back. I realized that willingly or not, I had become an FBI informant.

———

The summer holiday season was in full swing in our resort town, and Ed worked most weekends but came home early when possible. We'd take drinks out on the deck, and I would listen to his laments: the rise in traffic violations, petty thefts, burglaries, disorderly conduct, and domestic violence. "And it's just a matter of time before we have our first boating accident and drowning."

A couple of days after the explosion in Beirut, I showed him pictures on my laptop of raging fires, smoke, windowless buildings, rubble and debris from the accident.

"People are so hell bent on creating misery for each other," he said, rattling the ice in his glass. "It's not enough that we have earthquakes, fires, hurricanes, floods, and other natural disasters. No, we have to make our own disasters too."

"Lebanon is such a beautiful country. In the west lies the glittering Mediterranean Sea. A perennial breeze and swaying palm trees cool the shoreline. In the east are snow-capped mountains with ski slopes and evergreen cedars. The country has everything including many historical sites, monuments and artifacts from Greek and Roman times. People used to come from the other Arab states with plenty of money looking for some freedom from religious restrictions." I could hear the sadness in my own voice.

"Sounds like a paradise."

"It was." I let my mind wander back in time to our beautiful strolls along the Corniche and Hamra Street, our visits to the ancient ruins of Baalbek, and our drives up to the mountains to frolic in the snow. The numbskulls running the place now should be put in prison for mismanaging the resources and destroying the place.

Ray and his group had a good point in trying to take back their country. However, they weren't doing it the correct way. The explosion could have been an accident. But most likely not. If the government was involved, it may have been because it suspected that an opposition group had stored weapons and dangerous materials in the warehouse.

———

Speculations about what caused the explosion and the ensuing fire in Beirut abounded on the Internet. Without a doubt, the situation had become more ominous than first reported. I waited several days before I called Hoda.

"I'm good. None of my close friends and no one in the Khazin family was hurt as far as I know. They all have second homes in the mountains, and many have already left Beirut for the countryside."

"I hope Dr. Khazin will be able to travel soon because his girlfriend is pregnant." I hated to deceive Hoda, but she could provide support for our ruse, and I would explain everything to her later.

She didn't question it, nor did she seem surprised by my mendacious statement. "Well, flights in and out of the airport have resumed, so he should be on his way in a few days."

"How's the situation over there now?"

"Terrible. Unrest and demonstrations everywhere. People are demanding that the crooks in the government resign. It couldn't be worse. But I feel confident that when all the chaos is over, we'll be alright again. If people would just calm down and mind their own business, life would quickly return to normal. We're a resilient people. We have gone through a lot, and we'll emerge from this crisis too and become stronger in the process."

This was my friend Hoda, the epitome of wisdom and eternal optimism.

I already knew that Ray was fine. He had finally called Heidi, and she and I kept in touch.

"Ray and his family are good," Heidi said breathlessly when she called a few days after the explosion. "The communication lines were down for a short time, but all is well now." She seemed eager to continue, so I didn't interrupt her. "Ray is really busy now, caring for the injured, but he wants to leave before more unrest erupts. He's with family members and friends. Several of them will fly together to France. From there he will take a direct flight to Los Angeles."

I could hear eagerness in her voice as she continued without much of a pause.

"He told me he doesn't want me to meet him at the airport. He'll call when he arrives in Los Angeles." She cleared her throat. "I'll meet him at his hotel or at his brother's house, or he'll come up here. Then he wants me to go back to France with him." She sounded so excited and hopeful. That hopefulness worried me.

"Heidi, listen. Try to calm down. The FBI will place him under arrest as soon as he steps off the plane. They will put him in shackles, Heidi. How do you feel about that?" I was merciless because her fickleness irritated me.

"I don't like it," she said softly. "Why are you always so negative? You might be wrong about him, you know. He says he still loves me. He sounded so caring and concerned for my wellbeing."

I shook my head at her naiveté and took a deep breath. "What do you think he'll say when he discovers that you're not pregnant?"

"I'll tell him I lost it. Maybe he'll want to try again."

"I'm sorry, Heidi," I used a more conciliatory tone. "It won't come to that. Be sure to call when you know what flight he's coming in on. The FBI will check the manifest to confirm. They'll be checking passenger lists of all incoming flights from Paris in the next few days." I swallowed and cleared my throat. I needed to be strong, but deep down I also felt sorry for Heidi. She knew so little about the world outside her own sphere. "Trust me, Heidi. Ray is no good. You deserve better, you hear?" I once feared his charm would woo her back to his point of view. Now I feared that's exactly what had happened. What if she told him the FBI would be waiting?

After Heidi and I talked, I checked the Internet for flights from Paris to LAX. Air France flew nonstop flights between Charles de Gaulle and LAX every day. Other flights went through London or had stopovers at US airports.

———

The next day, I talked to Carrie Jensen. "Dr. Khazin is still in Beirut. I talked to Heidi yesterday. His plan is to fly to Paris and from there go on to Los Angeles."

"Any idea when?"

"No. It will be a few days. Will you have agents ready?"

"We will when we know the flight."

"Is agent Andrew Wells still there?"

"I believe so, yes."

"In charge?"

"He may take charge, yes. Why?"

"He did a good job with our ruse that led to the arrest of the big New York mafia boss last year, remember? Do you think I could call him directly?"

"I'm sure he'll remember you, but let me talk to him."

"Okay. Sounds good."

"We'll check the manifest of all incoming flights from Paris. There should be plenty of time for a couple of agents to drive to the airport and set up base at the gate. They'll book him the minute he comes through customs."

"As I said, it may take a few days. He's in touch with Heidi Hillstrom, and so far, he seems to trust her."

"Hmm." I assumed Carrie didn't know anything about Heidi and may have had her doubts. I too was still unsure that Heidi would stay strong and not double cross the FBI or me.

———

Two days later, Heidi called. "Ray will be on his way in a couple of days. I don't know why he doesn't want me to meet him at the airport, but he said he'll take the shuttle to his brother's house, and he'll call from there."

"Great job, Heidi! Stay strong."

As soon as we ended the call, I punched in Carrie's number and told her Dr. Khazin's plan.

"Okay, we'll take it from here," she said confidently.

I had butterflies in my stomach because I was not so confident. I knew that if anything went wrong, Heidi could be in danger. They would have to send an agent with her if she was going to meet Ray. She could not go by herself. I tried to figure out how to check the flight manifest myself, but I didn't have all the codes.

After we were in bed that night and Ed had turned off the lights, I asked him if he knew how to access the list of passengers on a flight.

"Let the FBI handle it, Megan. It's their job."

"I know, but what if Heidi crumbles and won't tell anyone that she's meeting him?"

"The FBI will make sure she doesn't, okay?"

I didn't answer. I sat up and swung my feet to the floor. I turned a light back on, rose and walked over to the closet. I reached up to the top shelf and took down my Chic Lady.

Ed looked at me curiously. "What are you doing, honey?"

I took my little handgun out of its box and showed it to him. Although I had a permit to carry a concealed weapon, I didn't keep the gun itself with me anymore.

"It's pretty, ain't it?" I said, mimicking country folk in my home state of Wisconsin. It was very light and the rose-colored mother-of-pearl handle with pink rivets glowed in the dim lighting. "Now that I'm a police informant and your deputy, I ought to be better prepared for trouble, don't you think, Ed?"

Ed smiled. He had gone with me to the range before and given me pointers and praised me for being a good shot. But he might have thought I was pushing too hard. "Me…gan," he drawled in frustration.

"Help me with a refresher course?" I waved the empty gun in the air, one hand on my hip.

# 13

## PRACTICE AT THE RANGE

It was midmorning when I drove up to the range and parked my Subaru next to the gate. A few men and women were lined up downrange. Ed had texted that he was on his way. I had just loaded my little Chic Lady and put on my earmuffs and safety glasses when he came walking up behind me. After greeting the people already lined up, he reminded me of the correct stance. I aimed and pulled the trigger, trying hard not to jerk back. No bull's eye but close. I had always had good eye-hand coordination, sharpened by the years as a softball pitcher in high school, although that was a long time ago.

"You're doing good," Ed said in a rare moment of praise.

"Thank you. Now, let's see you."

Ed hit the target smack in the middle. "I have more practice," he said. Like a showman, he swung around and shot one more bull's eye. I tried some quick draws too, and although they were close, they were never perfect.

"Enough. You're good," Ed concluded. "Now let's go home and see what Maria has for lunch."

I called Heidi every day to make sure she didn't falter. I also asked Ed if a deputy could keep an eye on her in case she decided to meet Ray by herself. He said he would.

Finally, one day Heidi called to say that Ray was on his way.

"What time did he leave Paris?"

"I'm not sure, but he said that if I couldn't reach him, he would be on the plane. I think he'll arrive this evening according to the schedules I have seen on the Internet."

"Good, Heidi. You're a smart woman. The FBI should get him at the gate even before he goes through Immigration, but just in case, be on the alert in case he calls you."

"When I spoke to him yesterday, he said I'd have to fly back to France with him. Maybe even to Lebanon. I'm so excited, Megan."

Her excitement showed in her voice and sowed doubts in my mind. "Don't be a fool, Heidi. He'll be picked up by the FBI at the airport."

She didn't answer, but at least she had called and alerted me. A good sign.

I was on the phone with Carrie Jensen, giving her a heads up that Ray was on his way, when I heard Ed's little chirp. I quickly ended the call, put down my phone, and went outside to meet him.

"Glad to see you," I said as he slid out of his car and came toward me.

"Well, that's good to hear."

"Heidi called to say that Ray is about to leave Paris or may possibly have already left. I just called the FBI. But Heidi is ready to go down to meet Ray in Rancho Cucamonga. He wants her to return to Paris with him. Do you have a deputy at her house, keeping an eye on her in case she decides to take off by herself to meet him? If he somehow manages to call her, I'm afraid he'll sweet talk her into doing what he tells her. Both of them could be back on a plane once more, never to be seen again."

"You don't give up, do you?"

"That's right. And you are a law enforcement officer and want to see justice done too."

"I know you're right. But I rely on others too. I don't try to do everything on my own."

"I guess I grew up with the expectations that I become self-reliant. That's the Midwestern code, in case you didn't know." I hung my head a little, feigning exasperation. We were still standing outside, and he slowly opened the front door. No one was home. As soon as we were inside, he pulled me close to him and kissed me. "And that's why I love you."

"Because of my self-reliance?"

"Well, that too." He paused. "I have someone keeping an eye on Heidi, but I don't think she'll be going anywhere anytime soon. The FBI has a lot of manpower and can handle it."

"I know. It's just in case." Ed was very reassuring, and I felt better about Heidi.

I called Heidi in the evening, and she calmly told me that she was getting ready to meet Ray in Rancho Cucamonga in the morning.

"What?" I said incredulously. I was flabbergasted. "How did he get through Immigration and Customs?"

"He said he came in on a flight from Atlanta."

"Atlanta?"

"Yes, the flights to LA were full."

I was speechless. "Where is he now?"

"At a hotel near his brother's house. He wanted a good night's sleep before we met."

"Heidi, I'll go with you."

"No. He said he loved me more than ever, and I told him I'd go with him wherever he wanted."

"He'll find out that you're not pregnant."

"As I told you, I have a plan. Please, Megan. I know you mean well, but just stay away. Let me go alone."

"No, Heidi. I'm coming with you whether you want me to or not. I got you into this mess, and I'll get you out too. Ray is wanted for murder."

"Please let me handle it my way, Megan."

The connection went bad and broke up our conversation. I immediately texted Carrie and then went to cry on Ed's shoulder.

"Maybe you're overreacting, Megan," Ed said. "But I'll go with you both and call in the FBI myself. This is unacceptable. The man is wanted for murder, for Christ's sake. There's a warrant for his arrest." He was clearly exasperated.

"Ed, the FBI acted on the information I gave them, information Heidi gave me. Ray is not stupid. He told Heidi a lie, sure that someone would be using that information, and he was right. He played us all."

"That's right. The guy is a slippery snake. I've never seen anything like it."

"Heidi is adamant that she wants to go by herself."

"We'll follow her in an unmarked car. She won't notice. The good doctor will be in for a surprise."

———

Ed called from the station the next morning. "Your nurse friend just left in her green SUV. The deputy is on her tail. He'll keep in touch, and I'll go down behind him. If you want to come along, I'll pick you up in twenty minutes."

"Of course, I want to go along, but maybe Heidi is just out running errands."

"That may be, but if she's going down the hill, we'd better be around."

"What if she spots you in her rear-view mirror?"

"She won't. The deputy put a tracker on her car, so he doesn't have to stay right on her tail."

"Good. I'll be outside waiting for you."

No sooner had I put the phone and my Chic Lady in my pocket and pulled a brush through my hair than I heard Ed in the driveway. I grabbed my purse and ran outside. He was in his unmarked white sedan. I quickly slid in next to him. He put the red emergency lights on the roof, and off we raced over to the highway and down the hill, red lights pulsing all the way. But no siren.

"Did you call the FBI?"

"Yes, but we don't know exactly where she's going. We'll call when we know something definite."

The deputy updated Ed constantly. He was heading west on the 210 freeway toward Rancho Cucamonga. Ed turned off the emergency light and slowed down when we saw Heidi's car ahead of us. After a while, she slowed down to exit the freeway and continued on surface streets. The traffic was light, and we soon picked up two local police cars. I recognized the streets. We were going toward Richard Khazin's house.

"It's time to call Heidi." I said. I pulled out my phone and hit her number, all the while keeping an eye on her SUV.

"Damn stupid woman," Ed mumbled and swore under his breath. "How the hell does she think she can get away with this game unobserved? Doesn't she know we have technology to find almost anyone anywhere these days?"

"I know, but she's not thinking straight."

Heidi did not pick up. She may have seen my name or number on the screen and decided that she didn't want to talk. I tried again with the same result.

"Do you remember the address?" Ed asked. "It's the same place you went the other day, isn't it?"

"Yes." I said and checked my contact list.

"Copy the deputy, and tell him to park away from the house," Ed said. "I'll call the FBI agent on the case."

As soon as we stopped, Ed jumped out to direct the local officers on the scene. I remained in the car and could see Heidi walk up to the door and Ray coming out to greet her. They embraced and hugged passionately before Ray led her into the house. I felt sorry for my new friend and wondered why the officers hadn't grabbed Ray while they had a chance. Finally, I saw what I thought to be two FBI agents banging on the door. They shouted something but I couldn't hear. I opened the window, but by that time, someone had already let them in. I don't know where the other officers were but assumed that they had surrounded the house. Although I didn't know what to expect, I took it for granted that they would bring Ray out in handcuffs. However, nothing happened.

After what seemed like hours but was probably only a few minutes, Ed came running toward the car. "Get out and take an Uber home," he shouted breathlessly. "The bastard escaped. Heidi told the officers that Ray was in the bathroom, and the idiots waited politely two minutes before going in. By that time, the bathroom was empty, and the doctor somehow escaped out the back." Ed watched me as he restarted the car. "Move," he said sharply.

"Forget it," I said. "I'm staying right here."

"Damn it." He shifted gears and drove off, sirens blaring and lights flashing. "Now the bastard is putting everyone in danger. Who does he think he is? Batman? No one escapes these car chases alive. Hasn't he ever watched television?"

"Is anyone else with him in the car?" I asked. "I hope Heidi remained in the house,"

"I don't think anyone is with him, but we'll see when we come closer."

The hot pursuit continued west on the 210 Freeway again, heading toward LA.

"Now he can add one more charge to his rap sheet—evading arrest," Ed said sarcastically.

I sat completely still. Luckily, Ed had enough sense to hang back and let the local officers lead the chase. It was their jurisdiction. Ray segued onto the 605 and then west again on the 91.

"Ray is headed for Torrance," I said. "Maybe one of his girlfriends from one of his old practices will take him in." I glanced over at Ed who had his eyes glued to the road. "What a fool. Poor Heidi. You should have tapped her phone, Ed."

"Now you're starting to talk nonsense too," he said in an irritated tone. "You may be able to do that remotely, but the FBI had very little time."

"Sorry. I guess I should have stayed on her more, been more persuasive."

"Damn well you should have. Now she'll be charged as an accessory, aiding and abetting a fugitive."

I chose to remain silent and looked straight ahead. The caravan of cop cars moved on to surface streets in Torrance until Ray crashed into a delivery van on Crenshaw Boulevard. Officers from Rancho Cucamonga quickly surrounded his car and arrested him without further incident. Ed stopped and left the car without saying a word and walked up to the arresting officers. When he returned, he backed the car up, turned it around, and we drove back the same way we had come.

I called Heidi again, and this time she picked up. "Where are you?" I asked and clicked on the speaker phone so Ed could hear.

"On my way home," she said slowly with a big sigh.

"What happened? Are you alright? Did any of the officers talk to you?" I waited for a few moments to give her time to say something. She didn't. "I thought you were meeting Ray."

"I was, but police officers swarmed the house, and Ray drove away."

"From his brother's house?" I wanted to make sure Heidi knew what went down.

"Yes. How did you know?"

"You told me yesterday."

"So you told the police?" She paused, probably waiting for me to say something, but I remained silent.

"I asked you to stay out of it," she continued. Her voice was unsteady. "It was so wonderful to see him and hold him again." She started sobbing.

I waited before I answered. "Heidi, pull over at the next pullout-spot and wait for me. You can't drive safely if you're crying."

"No, I'm okay. I'm almost home."

"Heidi, the man is wanted for murder." I tried to sound friendly, but my tone probably revealed frustration.

"He is innocent," she sobbed.

"The court will have to decide that now."

There was nothing but silence at the other end.

"Heidi, we'll talk when you get home."

More silence.

"She must have it hard," Ed commented. He reached over and put his right hand on my arm as if he wanted to apologize, but he didn't say anything. I looked straight ahead, and he kept quiet, focusing on the road the rest of the way home. I realized he needed time to assess the situation. He dropped me off at home and immediately took off for the station. At least that's what I assumed. He didn't return home until almost midnight. I was in bed but awake. However, Ed was in no mood for cuddling or sex.

———

The next day, Ed's disposition had improved some but not much. I made some progress on my novel about Nabila Brown's murder and was so absorbed in my imaginary world that I hardly noticed when Ed returned home later in the afternoon. I was out on the deck with my laptop.

"You won't believe what I'm going to tell you," he said. He tossed his hat on the table beside my computer and loosened his black tie as he flung himself down in a chair.

"What happened?"

"Someone posted bail for Raymond Khazin. A million dollars."

"Oh, my god," I exclaimed. "I can't believe it. Don't they realize that he's a flight risk?"

"That's why the court set the bail that high"

"Did they put an ankle bracelet on him?" I asked, but knew they probably hadn't.

"No, I don't think so. And even if they had, he would have had it cut off somehow, even though it's not that easy." Ed said thoughtfully, looking down at his boots.

"He may be on his way to the airport as we speak."

"I know."

"How did you find out that someone had posted bail?"

"An FBI agent called me."

"Maybe they can catch him before he gets on the plane."

"Maybe," he said, but shook his head.

"I better call Heidi. Maybe she knows something. This is insane." I said, taking out my phone.

"It's possible she knows, I guess, but he's no dummy. If he's with her, he'll have both their phones turned off and left behind somewhere so neither of them can be tracked." Ed paused as if to ponder something.

"I feel guilty in a way," I said. "I dragged Heidi into all of this, and I've got to get her out of it." I hesitated, thinking Ed would contradict me, but he remained silent. "But what can I do? She's so intent on incriminating herself."

"Right. She had her chance, and you can't be blamed for her bad decisions."

"If she'd just called me or notified the FBI directly as soon as she heard from Ray, she could have avoided trouble."

"Yes, but she didn't, and the case doesn't look good for her. The doctor's family posted bail. We're talking about a family with some serious money and connections here."

I stared out over the calm waters and tried to think. I hardly noticed the sailboats floating along on the glittering lake. Ed left quietly. He may have said a perfunctory goodbye, but I didn't hear it. As soon as he left, I picked up my phone and punched in Heidi's number.

"Heidi, is Ray with you?" I asked, coming straight to the point.

"No, I haven't seen or heard from him since he left his brother's house, chased by the police. I can probably thank you for that," she said in an accusing tone.

"Heidi, he was arrested, but someone posted bail. One million dollars. He's now on the run. He's a fugitive. Do you know what that means?"

"Maybe he'll go back to Lebanon again. And I'll remain here." Her voice was shaky. "Or maybe I will join him there," Her breathing revved up, perhaps with excitement over the possibility.

I gave her time to compose herself. "Heidi, you've already failed to notify the FBI about Ray's reentry into the country and you helped him escape by delaying the agents. You're already in trouble for aiding and abetting a suspected felon. You're adding more to those charges the longer you help Ray," I said. "Do you know what the penalty for that is?" I paused to let her think it over.

I heard nothing on the other end. Not even sobbing.

"Years in jail, Heidi, not a place you want to be. Are you sure he hasn't tried to contact you?"

"Yes. I didn't even know they had caught him. And now you say he's already out on bail."

"Yes," I said firmly. "And you've got to help capture him. Do you understand what I'm saying?"

"Yes. I understand."

"If he contacts you, call the police immediately, so they can locate him by tracking his phone. Promise me, Heidi."

She said nothing.

"Heidi, this is serious."

A click of her phone ending the call was all I got for my seriousness.

I had tried to be as persuasive as I could, but Ed was right. From now on, Heidi was in charge of making her own decisions, of plotting her own destiny. I wasn't convinced she understood the severity of the situation, but I was at a loss as to what more to say or do. I put down my phone and went inside. I was really rattled and sat down at the piano. After a few wild chords, I ran through a few Scott Joplin ragtime pieces again to release some of the excess energy that was building up inside me. Then I put on my hiking boots and took Duchess for a long hike along the lake. Maybe Ed would have good news when he came home later.

———

Ed didn't have good news when he came home. Ray was still on the run. The FBI had located his phone. The last ping had come from a cell tower near his brother's house, but the phone had since been turned off or destroyed. Ray had most likely bought a prepaid phone that was almost impossible to trace. Agents had scoured a number of local phone companies and shown Ray's mug shot around to see if anyone could remember if the man in the picture had come in to buy a phone using cash. He was smart enough not to use his credit card that could be traced. He would need a lot of cash to get around Los Angeles. Without plastic, it would be difficult to book a flight to Paris or Beirut.

"I guess he could go to the airport, buy a seat to Paris, and, like an airline employee, try to fly space available," I said. "But it would be expensive." We were sitting on the couch in the living room. The house was quiet. Maria had left, and James was out. JP was asleep.

"According to the FBI, the doctor is still in the country. I feel confident that the Bureau will not let him slip through their fingers again. The only reason they lost him the first time was because he lied to Heidi about his flight then used her as a cover in order to escape custody."

I had to agree—that's pretty much how this case had gone down so far. Ed leaned back as he crossed his legs. He looked very comfortable, but I felt unsettled. "Let's go up to the media room and turn on the TV to see if any of this has been picked up by the news media," I suggested.

Murder and mayhem are common in Los Angeles, and we heard nothing about our case. The big news was the fire danger. The Fourth of July was coming up, and the governor announced a fireworks ban in many parts of California this year.

"I suppose that means our little village, too," I said, and looked at Ed for confirmation.

"People will grumble, but it makes my life a whole lot easier." He made himself comfortable on the leather couch that still looked new. We didn't use this room much.

"Duchess will be happy too," I said. "Loud noises scare her, particularly fireworks. Remember last year? I had to hold her in the kitchen to calm her. I missed the entire show."

"I remember. I'll sit with her next time," he said. "I've seen enough fireworks to last me a lifetime."

I had lost interest in the television and inched closer to him. I remained silent for a few minutes, thinking about my four-legged friend. "How old is Duchess now?"

"I'm not sure," Ed said uncertainly. "Chris bought her from a breeder for his daughter when she was five or six. Emily died when she was about eight. That was five years ago, so that would make Duchess about eight or nine? Her records and pedigree certificate should be among Chris's papers in the office."

"She's a great dog."

Ed nodded. "Chris took her to a training course right after he bought her, and she is very good with children. Emily loved her, and James used to play with her whenever he came over. JP seems to think of her as a member of the family."

"I'm glad she took to me right away," I said. "I think she realizes that I'm her main caretaker now."

Ed looked at me with a faint grin. Since nothing was mentioned about any FBI fugitive or investigation, Ed didn't seem interested in watching television either, so we turned the TV off. I decided to go out to check on Duchess. It was dark, and Duchess was in her bed. She knew that was where she was supposed to be even though her eyes were wide open. I put more fresh water in her dish. She had eaten all her food. I fed her only once a day, so she'd have to wait till the morning for another meal. How I loved that dog…a cherished part of my family.

# 14

## DUCHESS'S FATE

The next day saw me on the deck pecking away on my laptop. The mystery in my new novel deepened, and the plot thickened. I was on a roll and took only a short lunch break and continued into the afternoon. My murder victim Nabila Brown was a good lawyer, but she had poor taste in men. Her current love interest was a fitness instructor at a local gym. He had been cheating on her with another instructor, an attractive woman from Eastern Europe. Both the fitness instructor and his East-European paramour might have had a motive for murdering Nabila.

JP and Maria brought me back to reality. Ed came home early as well, and that put an end to my writing. James stopped by for a change of clothes and said he'd sleep over at a friend's house. Ed and I went to bed late, and I slept uneasily.

At around two o'clock am, I woke up and thought I heard noises outside. I heard Duchess barking and listened for a while but didn't get up. Bears seldom came near the house, but they were around. Coyotes would pass by now and then, and I figured it would have to be one of the two, so I went back to sleep. Ed didn't stir.

I woke up before dawn and went out on the deck. It was a moonless night, and all was quiet—too quiet. When I made myself a cup of coffee in the kitchen, I had a strange feeling that I was missing something but didn't know what it was. As the sun rose and bathed the lake and everything around it with daylight, I went out to let Duchess out of her pen for her short morning run. She usually whimpered when she heard me to let me know she was there, but Duchess made no noise this morning. I realized that what I missed earlier was her whimpering.

The first thing I saw was the gate to her pen swinging back and forth. Duchess was nowhere in sight. Both her water and food dishes were empty. I remembered specifically that I had filled the water dish to the rim the night before. I hadn't double-checked that the gate was locked but couldn't imagine that I had left it open. I went down the path to the deck and called her. I tried to imitate the way Chris used to whistle, but there was no sign of Duchess. I felt confident that she would return when it was time to feed her, but I continued along the trail a little longer before I turned and headed back, calling and whistling to no avail.

When I came back inside, everyone was up getting ready for school and work.

"What were you doing outside so early in the morning?" Ed wanted to know. "I thought I heard someone whistling and calling."

"That was me," I said. "I was calling Duchess."

"Duchess?" he said quizzically as he poured a bowl of cereal.

"Duchess got out last night. I went out to look for her, but she appears to have taken off."

"Maybe she heard a coyote or something and broke out to chase it," Ed suggested as he added milk to his cereal.

"Maybe," I said. "I hope she didn't get in a fight." I took a bowl from the cupboard and filled it with cereal and milk too. Maria was getting JP ready for school. After several rounds of hugs and kisses, JP and Maria left.

"I heard noises in the night, but I didn't think anything of it and went back to sleep."

"She'll show up when it's time to eat," Ed assured me. He rose and embraced me before he too left.

After I finished my cereal, I sat down at the piano and worked on some new finger exercises that had given me trouble. After a few runs up and down the black and white keyboard, I dove into the first movement of

Edvard Grieg's Piano Concerto in A Minor. The piano truly had a brilliant sound. All the keys worked evenly and responded to the lightest touch. I had always wanted a Steinway, and now I had one.

Afterward, I put on my hiking boots and went outside again. I wondered if Duchess might be hurt, so I set out to search for her all the way up to Deerskin Lane and down again through the brush, but all I saw were a few squirrels scampering about and a couple of gophers sniffing at me with their funny noses. Back home again, I checked the pen to see if against all odds, Duchess might have made it home by herself, but no such luck. I filled her dishes with water and dog food and left the gate open before I went inside to work.

James came over, and we both went on another wild goose chase. As we walked back, we met JP and Maria in the driveway followed by Ed. We now were able to form a real search party and set out once more. JP loved the water, so he and Maria hung out near the lake edge.

Suddenly JP called out to Maria *"Aqui esta."* (Here she is.)

We all rushed down to the water, and there Duchess lay, half covered by water. She was dead. We stood next to her, stunned, frozen like statues. I had trouble breathing, and Ed put his arm around me. He didn't say a word. Maria lifted JP up and held him, while James stood beside them and held JP's hand. Tears ran down my cheeks, and JP held out his arms toward me as if he wanted to comfort me. I took him from Maria and held him close. He didn't fully understand, of course, but seemed to grasp that something important was going on.

Ed went down and pulled the limp body to drier ground. "I'll call Animal Control to come get her," he said to no one in particular and pulled out his phone.

I went up close but didn't see any marks on Duchess's head, legs or body in general. However, her eyes were glassy, and her tongue hung out of her mouth. Ed held out his phone toward me. All I could hear was elevator music.

"I'm on hold," he whispered.

"Hang up…please," I said. "I want the vet to look at her. She has no scratches anywhere that I can see. She drank all the water in her dish that I filled to the rim last night. I think she went down to the lake because her mouth was dry or burning. She was thirsty." I had to stop to catch my breath. I was now seeing a whole scenario in my mind. "I think someone gave her something poisonous, and she was literally burning up inside. I think that's what I heard in the middle of the night. I clearly remember hearing Duchess barking at something." Ed clicked the cell to end the call to Animal Control.

Sadness filled James's eyes. "What do you think Duchess was barking at, Megan?"

"I don't know. I thought she was barking at a coyote or a bear or another four-legged animal rummaging around outside, but now I wonder if it was a two-legged animal."

Ed looked from me to the lifeless Duchess. I dried my tears. JP had started to squirm and wanted down. He started for home followed by Maria.

"Duchess was in her prime," I said. "Even if she was hurt in a fight with a coyote or something, we would see signs of that on her body. She's been poisoned. I feel it. That's why she wanted to drink."

Ed looked like he didn't think much of my suspicions. He probably thought I had poison on the brain. Before he had time to say anything, I added, "I know, Ed. You think I'm overreacting again. But I grew up with animals, and I know how resilient they are, especially cats and dogs. How strong their survival instinct is. If Duchess had been older, she might have had a heart attack after too much strain, but she was still young and in good shape. You have to believe me." I had regained my composure and watched him defiantly.

Ed coughed and cleared his throat. "No, I don't think you're overreacting," he said calmly. "I think you may be right on. It looks very much like someone wanted Duchess hurt and gave her something to harm her." He pulled out his phone again and dialed the veterinarian. "We'll have my friend Andy examine her."

My mind had cleared after the initial shock, and my suspicions grew. "Ed, I'm afraid Duchess's death is connected to Lizzie's death and Ray's arrest. In the Middle East, revenge is an obligation—an eye for an eye, a tooth for a tooth, and so on."

Ed nodded quietly.

"Or, it's a message to me to stay away," I said slowly. "I'm sure Ray and his brother figured out that I had something to do with his capture. Heidi may even have told them. Even if she didn't say anything, Ray knows that I'm somehow involved. Too many phone calls and then my visit to his brother."

James looked at me with a bewildered expression. I had not told him of my suspicions that my friend's killer was her husband Dr. Khazin. "What did you say or do, Megan?"

"I may have helped get my friend's murderer arrested," I said and turned to Ed. "What do you think, Ed?"

"This case is now edging a little too close to home. We'll have a necropsy done on the dog. It's too much of a coincidence, and I don't believe in coincidences."

It didn't take long for the local veterinarian to arrive. Being an old friend of Ed's and Ed being a sheriff might have helped speed up the vet's arrival. Ed stayed to greet his friend and talk to him, but James and I went up to the house. I didn't particularly want to see what the vet would do in order to learn how Duchess died.

No note or message of any kind had been left anywhere as far as I could see, but none was needed. If Duchess had been poisoned, the message was clear: *Stay out of the way from now on and mind your own business. Next time it could be you or even worse. Next time it could be your son.*

But this *was* my business. My friend had been murdered, and I promised to help find the one who killed her. I had made it my business to investigate the circumstances surrounding Lizzie's death, and I wanted to know not only *who* but *why*. The death of my dog only added impetus to that promise rather than halting it.

---

Later, two deputies from San Bernardino arrived to dust her cage and bowls for fingerprints, but I was skeptical that it would do any good. Whoever was behind Duchess's death would have worn gloves, and no way would Ray have come up here himself to do the job. He or his cohorts would have hired someone to do the dirty work.

Ed had a serious talk with Maria in Spanish, and I understood that he asked her to watch JP carefully. He thought she would be fine, he told her, but JP was at risk. Ed also decided to post a deputy at the house every night for a few days. If these people had any more antics in mind, life was going to be a whole lot more difficult.

———

Everything was quiet for a couple of days, but Ed was not satisfied that it was over. I also knew that people in the Middle East had long memories. Forgiveness has traditionally not been part of their culture.

"Instead of having the deputy here, I suppose I could rent a house in Newport Beach for a few days as we did last year," I suggested to Ed one day. I stood against the kitchen counter, and Ed sat at the table, his legs crossed. He remained silent, apparently having no opinion or another suggestion.

"Of course, I hate to take JP away from his friends in his play group unless we have no other option," I continued. "Another possibility is for me and JP to move into your house for a while. I don't think James would mind, and I don't think Maria would mind taking a break from the routine either. It would at least mean a change of scenery, and I have a suspicion that your house could use some deep cleaning as well."

Ed leaned back in his chair and looked up at me. "Yes," he said with a deep sigh and a broad hand over his face, as if wiping away memories. "No one needs to stay around to take care of Duchess anymore."

Duchess lay wrapped in a blue tarp some distance from the house but protected from marauding animals or insects. Andy had taken samples from the contents of her stomach to a lab somewhere, and we had to wait for the result.

"Since Duchess is still on the grounds, we should bury her remains," I said. "Have a little private funeral to provide some closure for James and JP especially, but for us too. It's legal, isn't it?"

Ed smiled indulgently. "Oh, I don't think anyone cares about an animal. Where do you want to dig the grave?"

"I don't know." I looked over to the north side of the property. "How far out does the property line go?"

"Quite far. The county has a little wooden property marker with the lot number out there somewhere. I'm surprised you haven't noticed it—although it's pretty well covered with leaves and debris."

"It must be, because I think I've walked all over the place." I paused. "But out there would be a good place, don't you think?" I pointed over to where I thought the property line would have to be. "I'll text James and ask him if he can come over. He may know where the marker is and if not, he can help me find it. If we agree, we could even start digging."

"Sounds good." Ed smiled. "So, you have the afternoon mapped out for yourself. And I'd better get back to the station. Don't forget to include JP in your grave digging project."

"I won't. It will be good for all of us to have a little ceremony to say goodbye to Duchess."

I texted James and told him that I needed him to come over to the north side of my house, where I would be rooting around among pine needles and gopher holes. That should intrigue him.

I still had on my boots, so I tramped up and down about a hundred feet north of the house where I thought the property line might be but saw nothing but sticks and low brush. The entire property was what landscapers called *au naturel*. No one had attempted any sort of gardening or landscaping. Very few people around the lake had anything that resembled a garden. Despite the lake, we often experienced droughts in the mountains. The water level in the lake could go way down, and then watering was rationed or even prohibited. And no one wanted vegetation close to the house in case of a forest fire.

I had not rooted around long before I heard—and then saw—James's Range Rover in the driveway. I waved to him. He spotted me and loped through the brush to where I stood. He too wore boots, shorts with a T-shirt, and a baseball cap. I told him what I had in mind, and it didn't take him long to find the marker. It was much farther out than I had thought.

"Where do you think the grave should be?" I asked him.

"I don't know. Maybe as far from the lake as possible, close to the sunny southern property line."

We went a little farther uphill and staked out a place. "I'll get a couple of shovels," James said and went back to the storage room under the house. He returned with a big shovel and a small one. "The small shovel was mine to use when I came over here to help Uncle Chris," James commented. "Or maybe it was Emily's, and I borrowed it." He pulled a measuring tape from his pocket and started to mark an outline. Then we started digging, James with the big shovel at one end and I at the other end with the small one. In between, I texted Ed to prepare him for a funeral this evening.

Maria arrived with JP in tow, and James explained to him what we were doing. JP hung onto every word James uttered and wanted to help. He ran back to the house and got his little plastic sand shovel and dug next to James.

The dirt was loose and easy to remove. By the time Ed arrived, we had a four-foot deep trench. Ed and James dragged over the tarp with Duchess's remains. There was a faint foul smell but not as bad as I had expected. "I expected her to be worse," I said.

"Andy covered Duchess's body with lime before wrapping her up."

I nodded. Ed and James placed the tarp with Duchess's body in the makeshift grave. Maria had found a rake in the storage room, and we all helped cover up the poor dog. We gathered heavy stones and piled them on top of the loose dirt to discourage wild animals from digging up the remains.

The funeral could now start with James in charge.

"And now Duchess is on her way to animal heaven," James announced formally.

"Why do we have to put Duchess in the ground and cover her up to go to animal heaven?" JP wanted to know.

James thought for a few moments and made up a story on the spot: "Deep down in the earth are underground tunnels where the seven dwarves live."

"Why do they have to live down there?" JP asked.

"Because if they come out of the ground, they will die." James looked at JP who watched him with wide eyes. "Since we started digging her grave," James continued, "The seven dwarves have been waiting for Duchess to be buried so they can carry her all the way to the ocean."

"I've been to the ocean." JP interjected.

"At the end of the tunnel, where the ocean begins, a special sailing ship with five angels is waiting. As soon as the angels lift Duchess into the boat, they raise their special sails and fly up into the sky,"

"Oh," JP said. "Will the doors go with them?" His little brain cells seemed to be churning as he ate it all up.

"Dwarves," James said slowly. "Like Snow White and the Seven Dwarves. And no, the dwarves cannot go with them because they have to go back in the tunnel to pick up another animal."

We were all silent as James concluded the ceremony.

"That was a nice eulogy, son." Ed said and slapped James on the back. "Because of all this, Megan, JP and Maria will be moving in with us for a few days." Ed turned to JP. "What do you think about that, JP?"

"About what?"

"About moving in with James and me."

"Mommy too?"

"Yes, and our *mamacita"*

JP was all for it and started jumping up and down. "Can we take my new tricycle?" He had already forgotten Duchess.

Ed headed back to the station while I packed up a few pieces of clothing and toiletries. I put JP's tricycle and a few toys in the trunk of the van and JP in his car seat. Leaving my Subaru in the driveway, I drove the short distance to Ed's house. Maria had driven her own car over ahead of us and stopped at the store to pick up a few items. We made ourselves at home, and when Ed came in later, James and JP were already outside tossing a football back and forth.

Duchess had loved chasing wayward balls. The boys didn't seem to miss Duchess as much as I did. At least they didn't show it. Young people and children are resilient and learn to adapt quickly. I would adapt to life without her, but I had lots of memories of her and our walks.

"So, I see you've already settled in," Ed said jovially.

I gave him a hug. "It's not as comfortable as my own house, but it will do."

"It's only for a little while," he said and put his arm around me. Ed was a great comforter, and we stood watching the two boys play. James may not have been overly enthusiastic, but he was a dutiful young man and older soon-to-be brother. JP loved every minute of it.

Ed and I went back into the kitchen, and I grabbed an apple and some grapes from the fruit bowl on the table. "Did you buy fruit for us?"

"No, I didn't have time. Maria must have put it there." He took a few grapes too. We nibbled on the fruit while I walked around the small but efficient kitchen, looking into the cupboards to learn where everything was.

"The FBI is searching for Ray," I said. "I've already paid for Ray's arrest—or rather Duchess paid—and if they stick to their *tooth for a tooth* axiom, we're now even." I took several big bites of the apple before I went on. "I called Carrie about Duchess, and she was sorry for our loss. She remembered Duchess from the time we all hiked together. She said she'd relay the information. The Bureau definitely seems to take the case seriously."

"This whole thing would be ridiculous if it weren't so serious," Ed said irritably. He took two mugs from the cupboard. "Want some coffee? I'll show you how my coffee maker works. It's a little different from yours."

"Ed, I know how to operate a coffee maker," I said mockingly.

Ed shot me a quick glance. "Okay. I'm just trying to help."

I leaned against the sink, still eating my apple, and Ed offered me the first cup.

"I drove by your friend's house on my way over here, and it's up for sale," Ed said. "A realty sign has already been placed next to the driveway."

"That was fast," I said. I blew into the cup before I took a sip while Ed doctored his coffee with milk and sugar. I walked ahead of him into the small living room that had a worn couch with lots of pillows and a glass coffee table with magazines and papers. A recliner stood in front of the fireplace. Instead of sitting down, I continued out on the deck to watch the boys. Ed followed.

Although there was no lake view, we had a beautiful vista of tall pines and oaks. We sat down on two deck chairs and put our cups on his round table, that was inlaid with a mosaic of brown and beige tiles. Not knowing what to do with the apple core, I tossed it over the rail into some bushes. It would serve as a snack for the squirrels and gophers.

"Do you know who the listing agent is for Lizzie's house?" I asked.

"No, but you could ask Vee. She knows everything that goes on around here."

"Yes, I remember Vee," I said with a snide snort. Vee had had her claws in Ed long after Ed and I started to date formally. Probably not her fault, though. Ed may not have told her. He wasn't in the habit of volunteering information, especially private information. I took several sips of coffee. "Maybe I'll call her and pretend to be a buyer," I said in as civilized a tone as I could manage. I noted that my opinion of Vee didn't register with Ed.

———

As soon as everyone left the next morning, I braided my hair and put on my hiking boots and sunscreen. I grabbed a hat, my phone and a bottle of water and started out for Lizzie's house. Lizzie had lived in our lake community less than a year, but I'd known her for a long time. I wondered how much she actually knew about Lebanese politics and the uprisings. She probably knew more than anyone realized.

She had worked in the Foreign Service in Beirut and might have discovered both Ray's political ambitions and his other shenanigans. She might have threatened to bring it all out in the open. Had she blackmailed Ray and told him she would remain mum about his group's plot against the Lebanese government, but only if he stopped seeing other women?

Could such a demand have cost Lizzie her life? The thought gave me more to ponder.

It was a beautiful day. A few small sailboats bobbed along the shoreline while farther out bigger boats crisscrossed the lake. Gophers sniffed at me with their whiskered noses; squirrels scampered about, and I missed Duchess's joy of chasing them. As long as I lived on the mountain, I would want to have a dog, a big dog, maybe a Labrador or an Alaskan Husky. Maybe a German Shepherd. A breeze played with my hair. I pulled my hat down so it wouldn't blow off. No sense my hat being part of the boat traffic on the lake.

Lizzie's house stood shuttered, looking lonely and forlorn. I read the telephone number on the realty sign, pulled out my phone and called. The sign did not list an agent, but after I gave the receptionist my name and told her where I was, I asked for Vee anyway.

"Vee doesn't work here," the receptionist said. "But I can connect you with Lorraine. I think it's Lorraine's listing."

When Lorraine came on the line, I told her that I was at Lizzie Khazin's house and gave her the address. "Actually, I'm already working with an agent," I said. "But could I ask you the list price?"

Instead of just giving me the price, I had to give her my full name and contact information, an irritating practice that realtors have. I should have looked up the listing on Zillow.

"$995,000," she finally said. "Is that in your price range?"

"No," I said. "But thank you anyway."

"No problem."

I Googled Vee and found her number. She picked up right away. I told her my name and asked if she remembered me. She did, of course. I told her the house I was looking at and told her that I had talked to the listing agent.

"Are you in the market for a new home?" She sounded surprised.

"Maybe," I said untruthfully. "Do you have time to meet me at the property today?"

"Sure. I can come by right now," she said like a true salesman. "Just give me a few minutes."

"That's wonderful, Vee. I'll just walk around a little until you arrive."

Vee drove up in a new white Cadillac SUV a few minutes later. She punched in the code on the lockbox hanging from the doorknob. The box popped open, and she took out the key to the front door. Her hair was as fiery red as ever. She must just have had a new color job. She wore a lot of make-up to cover up her freckles and was dressed professionally in white slacks and a loose multi-colored top while I was in my walking shorts and a T-shirt. I followed her in a bit hesitantly. I saw nothing, not even the few pieces there when Lizzie died. No trace of Lizzie remained.

"So, are you and Ed having problems?" she asked as she pranced around in her high heels. "Are you finally tired of his condescending behavior and ready to move on?"

I now remembered why I detested this woman. So patronizing and annoying!

"No. What gives you that idea?"

She looked at me and cocked her head. "Ed came over the other night and stayed past midnight. He seemed very down and depressed, and I immediately knew that something was wrong at home."

"Really? And he told you it was because of me?"

"He gave me that impression, yes. He was not happy."

I was dumbstruck. Blood rose to my cheeks. I remained unable to speak for several minutes, so I pretended to be interested in the kitchen appliances. "When was that?" I finally asked.

"Oh, a few nights ago. He said he was working on a difficult case that might put some people close to him in danger, and I took that to mean James."

I looked away, for I remembered exactly what night it was. So, that's why he had come home so late. I had foolishly thought he was at the station or at his house with James.

"I ran into him in the Village," Vee continued. "I thought he looked miserable. I told him I had just made his favorite carrot cake with lots of cream cheese and invited him over. After we had cake, I thought he was going to fall asleep on the couch."

I tried to pull myself together. "Yes, he's been a little stressed these days." I continued walking through the house. "Actually, I'm house-hunting for a friend. But I don't think this is what she wants."

"The price is negotiable," Vee said. "Where does your friend live now?"

"In Rancho Cucamonga."

"Really? What a coincidence! That's where the owner lives. His brother used to work as a doctor at the hospital up here. He's selling the house for his brother who lives overseas somewhere."

"Does the doctor's brother have power of attorney, then?"

"Yes, I believe so. And he's anxious to sell. I have a sense that he'll be willing to sell low enough to cover the loan. The loan is almost $800,000, so I think he'll accept anything close to that. This is a good deal. Have your friend call me. I have several other properties too."

"I will, Vee. Thank you for coming over so quickly."

"I didn't see your car. Do you need a ride?"

"No, but thanks. I'll hike back. Need the exercise."

It was a long hike. It was warm, and I was exhausted by the time I got home. I went straight into Ed's bathroom and took a shower. I was just coming out with a towel around me when I heard Ed walk in the door. I greeted him casually before I went into the bedroom to put on clean clothes.

"So," I said as I was about to enter the kitchen where he was fixing a snack of cheese and crackers. "I'm sorry I don't have any carrot cake with lots of cream cheese."

Ed didn't say anything but looked at me with raised eyebrows and a bewildered expression.

"That is your favorite cake, isn't it?" I continued sarcastically.

"What the hell are you talking about?"

"Just wondered why you never told me that carrot cake with cream cheese was your favorite. I would have made it for you too, you know." I leaned against the doorframe between the kitchen and the living room.

Ed continued preparing his snack. He put the plate of crackers covered with cheese in the microwave while he poured a glass of ice water that he carried over to the table. He went back for his plate and finally sat down. He didn't appear to be in any hurry to talk to me.

"I'll get you a paper towel, Ed," I said and walked over to the counter to grab a towel. "That can be messy." I gave him the towel and stood by the table, facing him. "I saw Vee today when I went to see Lizzie's house. Vee met me there and showed it to me. She wanted to know if I was moving out. If I was going to buy a place for myself. She had heard that you and I were having problems."

Ed put a cracker with melted cheese in his mouth and slowly wiped his fingers on the paper towel.

"Are we having problems, Ed?"

He glared at me before he spoke: "I didn't think so, but you seem to want to start some kind of a fight."

"So you went to see Vee the other night and ate some of her carrot cake. I wondered why you came home so late that night. I thought you were working on something."

"I stopped by an old friend's house. Am I not allowed to do that?" he said in an irritated tone.

"You stayed until past midnight. You told her that you and I were having problems and she thought you would fall asleep on her couch."

"Is that what she told you?"

"You deny it?"

"Yes, I do." He frowned, and his face turned red as if he were on the verge of getting seriously angry. "I did not say we were having problems," he continued emphatically and paused to take a deep breath. "And I did not fall asleep on her couch. I came home *before* midnight and went to sleep next to you."

"But you ate her cake?"

"And that's supposed to mean something?"

"Maybe not. But Vee seems to think it meant something."

"Vee is crazy. I have no particular interest in her whatsoever. I've known her for a long time, ever since we were in school together years ago."

"So why did you go to her house?"

"I was exhausted, and she invited me over for a piece of cake."

"Ed, this is a small place. She's probably telling the story all over town." I leaned over and took one of his crackers. Then I sat down on his lap. "I don't think anything happened, Ed, and I don't care if people gossip. But you should care. You're a respected law enforcement officer, and you don't want your reputation smeared."

He sighed, and the muscles in his face relaxed. "I'm sorry, honey. I should have told you," he said sheepishly.

"That would have been nice. I was pretty shocked when she told me you had fallen asleep on her couch."

"But you didn't believe her, I hope."

"I didn't think that anything happened, I suppose, but it was awkward." I got up from his lap and pulled him up. I put my arms around his neck, and he embraced me for several minutes before he spoke.

"You're a reasonable woman, Megan. I should know better than to try any shenanigans with a sleuth like you for a fiancée. You would expose me immediately."

"That's right," I confirmed playfully, "and don't you forget it." We both laughed, and the tension disappeared.

———

What had puzzled me all along was Ray's medical training. What happened to *First do no Harm*? Isn't that what physicians are taught? Ray seemed to have done a lot of harm. I was convinced that he had killed his wife Lizzie, even if not directly. I knew that he went to medical schools in Lebanon. Although no medical schools there and the surrounding Arab countries ranked higher than one-thousandth on the global scale, at least some were approved by the American medical society. However, to practice in the United States, he would also have had to complete his residency here.

Ray may or may not have been involved with the explosion in Beirut. That may have been an accident. But why were ammunition and weapons of mass destruction stored together with ammonium nitrate used in fertilizers and highly inflammable so close to the harbor? Nothing made sense, but so much of what happens in the Middle East doesn't make sense to our Western way of thinking.

Though it was early, I texted Hoda to see if it was convenient to call her. She called me instead. Curiously, it was cheaper for Hoda to call me than for me to call her. I filled her in on the latest regarding Ray.

"Ray was arrested, but his family posted bail. A big bail, by the way. Now he seems to be on the run and is on the FBI's fugitive list."

"I heard. And I also heard that he's on his way back here."

My mouth fell open. "No," I almost shouted into the phone. "That is impossible." I was shocked. How could he have boarded a plane here without the FBI knowing and stopping him? Yes, he had several passports, but the FBI knew that, would be on guard. I took a deep breath and made myself relax. It simply could not be true. I changed the subject. "Aside from that—which staggers me—can you find out if he attended more than one medical school in Lebanon, I mean, without too much trouble? His last medical school is in the public records here, but did he attend others before that?"

"Okay, sure," she said without a beat. "He would have gone to a Catholic university, most likely Saint Joseph's, but I'll check. If Saint Joseph's didn't have his specialty, he might have transferred to Beirut University. That's the best one we have. I'll find out."

"Great, Hoda. You're a treasure," I paused for a moment or two. "How's everything over there now?"

"Much has been cleaned up," she said. "We still have demonstrations, but the shops are back in business. The city is once again buzzing with life. How's LA?"

"I don't live in LA, Hoda. I live in a small town up in the mountains above LA now, and just like your social circles in Beirut, everyone here knows everybody's business except that the people in your circle are more sophisticated."

"And what about your man?"

"Which one? The big one or the little one?"

Hoda laughed. "Both, I guess."

"They keep me busy. I'm also working on another mystery novel. And what about you?"

"I'm settling down too. I'm seeing a Jordanian businessman who does much of his business in Saudi Arabia."

"A man with lots of money, I assume."

"Yes, but I have my own."

"Good for you." We chatted for a few more minutes. After we ended our call, I Googled Ray's medical bio. I read that he had indeed graduated from Beirut University Medical School and done his residency at a small hospital in Oklahoma. I knew that he couldn't have faked his residency. I wondered how he had ranked at his Lebanese school. Not too high, I expected. He had charm and was good at selling himself, but I doubted his academic intelligence. Hoda would soon find out from his records. I wouldn't be surprised if she knew someone at the school.

When Ed came by for lunch, I told him what Hoda had said about Ray being on his way back to Lebanon.

"No. I don't believe it," he said firmly and shook his head for emphasis.

"He has multiple passports."

"It doesn't matter. The FBI knows that, and the doctor is not going to outfox our FBI a second time."

"He could hire a private jet. The family has money to burn. It's pretty easy and not as expensive as it once was."

"He still has to show his passport if he's on the way out of the country—"

"He could slip into Mexico or Canada and leave from either of these countries."

Ed looked at me with a lifted brow, as if he'd rather leave Ray to the Feds. By now, we were in the kitchen making sandwiches for ourselves. "I guess it could be done," he said finally and shrugged his shoulders

"It would be difficult," I said. "A small jet would have to make many stops along the way to refuel, and it would be hard to find a company with pilots willing to go into Lebanon at this time. But, then again, for a price…" My voice trailed off. We sat down at the table and started to nibble at our sandwiches. "Interpol is involved too," I said between bites. "They would keep an eye on flights arriving from Canada and Mexico too. Besides, there are no direct commercial flights from either of these two countries to anywhere in the Middle East."

"In any case, I have to leave this whole case to the FBI. In no way can our small department handle all this in addition to our local crime sprees."

We had coffee on the deck before Ed had to return to his office. After he left, I sat down at the piano and played half a dozen scales and Hanon exercises before I once more launched into the first movement of Grieg's Piano Concerto. It still needed a lot of work. At the same time, I was trying to think of ways to catch the wily doctor.

The next morning, I had a text from Hoda. As predicted, Ray had attended Saint Joseph's then transferred to Beirut University where he graduated in the bottom half of his class. BU had a high ranking in the Middle East, but it is way down on the global list. All instruction at Saint Joseph's had been in French, while at BU all the classes were taught in English. Ray had done advanced studies, although he did not appear to be a brilliant scholar. Since I knew that he couldn't have faked his way through his residency, I figured that he must be an adequate physician.

That evening, as I was sitting on the couch reading the newspaper, Hoda called again. "I heard another tidbit about Raymond Khazin last night that you might find interesting."

"Really? What?"

"I know a couple of people at St. Joseph's," she continued. No surprise there! "And someone I've known for a long time told me that either right before or after Ray graduated, they had discovered irregularities with his initial application."

"What kind of irregularities?"

"Well, with his application, he had submitted another student's tests, all top scores by the way. The Khazin family had contributed big money to the school, and since Dr. Khazin did graduate and was admitted to advanced studies at BU, no one wanted to deal with it."

"I can't believe it," I exclaimed. "No, wait. I can believe that. Money can buy anything. And his family has that kind of money."

She cleared her throat before she went on. "Buying your way into school...it's not that unusual. It goes on where you are too. I read that even one of your presidents had cheated his way into a university."

"I know, but Ray was my friend's husband. How could she fall for someone so slick? He gets in trouble time and again, but every time, whatever it is, he glides to the surface."

We chatted a few more minutes, then ended our call. I sat there looking at the newspaper without reading it.

———

The next day Hoda sent me another text telling me that Dr. Khazin had not yet returned to Beirut. Ed was right. Ray must not have left US soil. Maybe his family had sent out rumors that he was on his way to sow confusion. My guess was that he was still in the area. He wouldn't stay at his brother's house. Agents had that house covered. He wouldn't come up here where people would immediately spot him. His cronies were well-to-do and would live in upscale suburbs. Train and bus stations would also be covered. No, most likely he would stay in a hotel in a crowded area like downtown Los Angeles. Probably one of the big hotels with a lot of traffic passing through. Maybe he would move from place to place until things died down.

I called Carrie Jensen and asked her what she thought of my theory. She said agents were on it, canvasing LA hotels with pictures of Ray to see if any of the hotel staff recognized him.

"How can I help?"

"Relax, Megan. The FBI has dozens of agents to put on the case."

"That's good to hear."

"But we might call on you again. I'll think about it. It's a dangerous business. He'll pay with cash, of course, and he'll not use his real name," she said.

"He may also be in disguise," I said. "Then how will the agents be able to recognize him?"

"Well, maybe that's where you could come in again."

# 15

## THE VET'S ANALYSIS

I missed Duchess every day but especially when I put on my boots, sunscreen and hat to hike along the lake. Everyone on the trails seemed to have at least one dog, and some had two or three. Most had their dogs on a leash, but a few dogs ran around freely just as Duchess had done, chasing scampering squirrels and barking at gophers, scaring the animals into their holes. I briefly thought about offering my services as a dog walker. I felt rather useless hiking to nowhere by myself.

I thought of Lizzie, too, and wished we could have spent more time together, taken walks and reminisced about our happy college days. I decided I would call Susie and invite her up soon.

―――

Although we remained at Ed's house, I often went back to my own house. I left my car in the driveway and checked the dock, the boat and the rest of the property. Then I hiked my familiar loops.

One day when I returned from another lonely hike, I saw Ed's car in my driveway. "Hi," I shouted as I came closer. Ed was standing by the rail on the deck.

"Oh, there you are," he called back. "I saw your car and knew you'd come over here to take a walk."

"It's lonely without Duchess. We should walk together more, Ed. The exercise will do you good too."

"Sounds like a good plan," he said agreeably, then added with a tinge of sarcasm, "Except for the fact that I have to go to work."

"I know. But whenever you can get away early, we should spend time on the trails instead of puttering around the house." I took the shortcut up to the deck and gave him a quick hug before I slumped down in a chair. Ed sat down in the chair next to me.

"Andy, my veterinarian friend, stopped by with the result of the analysis of Duchess's stomach contents," Ed said as he took out a piece of paper from his pocket.

"That was pretty fast. And what did it say?"

"Duchess was poisoned with…" He paused and looked down at the sheet in front of him. "She was poisoned with a high dose of sodium fluoroacetate." He pronounced the word carefully, one syllable at a time. "It's used as rodenticide, but in Australia it's used to kill wild dogs."

"Oh, no. Poor Duchess. I should have fed her the night before. I know she was hungry."

"Doc said that the poison may have been administered in what he called *savory dog biscuits*." Ed was reading the last part. "Doc said the poison has no taste, odor, or color."

I was at a loss for words and sat staring at the water below. Two sailboats bobbed along far out and looked like little paper boats. There was not much wind.

"Doc also said that this particular poison doesn't cause much pain," Ed said. "But I'm still surprised that I didn't hear her bark. You said you heard her, though."

"Yes, I heard noises, barking too but thought an animal had scared her." I hesitated for a moment. "I did wonder why she ran down to the water, but you said sodium something or other."

"Yes, sodium fluor…something." Ed gave up on trying to pronounce the word a second time.

"Sodium indicates salt. I wonder if the sodium made Duchess so thirsty that she drank a full dish of water and then wanted more, so she ran down to the lake. She must have either jumped in or fallen in."

———

Nothing new developed in the search for Ray over the next few days. I didn't know how many agents had been posted at the hotels in the overcrowded downtown Los Angeles where Ray would blend in well with all the Latinos. He could easily be taken for a Central, or South American businessman. I was reluctant to go down to the inner city as I stood out. I could perhaps change my Nordic looks, but I could not hide my five-foot-seven stature. However, the next day, I called Carrie to see if there was anything I could do.

"Be patient, Megan. We do have a plan, and we will need you to make a positive identification."

"What do you think of me going down there? That way, I'll be on the spot when they locate him. I'll make myself invisible."

Carrie remained neutral but did not nix the idea. I left Ed a message that I'd be helping Carrie locate Ray in LA. He was at the other end of the county checking out another fire. I called a rental company that picked me up in a non-descript beige Honda that I rented for a week. I found an old woolen hat and put on a pair of dusty hiking boots that I wore only in inclement weather. Driving west on the 210, I stopped at a shopping center that had a big Goodwill store. I found two outfits that resembled ethnic Mexican dresses and a big cloth bag made in Peru. At a department store nearby, I bought a black wig, and at a shop next door, I bought a bag full of Mexican snacks. In the public bathroom nearby, I stuffed my hair under the wig and changed into my new outfit before I headed for the big parking lot on Figueroa and 3$^{rd}$ Street where I made sure the attendant saw me. In my woolen hat, worn Mexican dress, and dirty boots, I blended in well with the homeless and the drug addicts and didn't want to risk the attendant telling me to leave my car alone.

I staked out a busy corner on 1$^{st}$ Street and sat down on a wooden crate, munching on my snacks and observing life in Los Angeles. A few passersby in suits, carrying briefcases—they looked like attorneys—were either going to or coming from the courthouse. Some tossed me a few coins, even a few dollar bills.

I knew my phone would look out of place and took it only halfway out of the bag periodically to check for messages. I called Carrie and told her where I was.

"But you won't recognize me. I'd take a selfie, but it would blow my cover." I kept the speakerphone on as if I were talking to myself like many of the others around me. "Have any of the agents had any luck?" I asked Carrie quietly. I knew a lot would depend on luck in this case.

"No, not yet. But they are around with photos, checking with hotel staff and business owners."

"He could be moving from place to place too."

"Oh, we expect it," Carrie assured me.

"Okay. I'll sit here during check-out time and see if he's on the move. This is a fabulous place to disappear in," I admitted. "People stroll, run, and push their way in every direction, business people with rollaboards as if they were going on a flight, a few women in heels and derelicts drinking out of brown paper bags. I've already seen two drug deals go down right in front of me."

Carrie remained silent.

"To me, most of the people appear to be Latinos or possibly Middle Easterners. As many times as I've seen Dr. Khazin, I would have a hard time distinguishing him from the others here."

"Do you want one of the agents in the area to contact you?"

"I don't know. What do you think?"

"It might be a good safety precaution."

"I'll try to take a selfie and text it to you."

"Oh, they'll find you without one. I'm sure at least one of them has already spotted you."

"Maybe, but I doubt it. I'll hang around the Omni and the California and later the Biltmore. I have my handgun. And yes, I do know how to use it, and you know I have a permit."

"Yes, I know you do. Do you think Dr. Khazin is armed?"

"I have no idea. But I doubt it. He did not grow up here as you know, but he may have a gun if he's involved in a gun running operation."

"How long do you plan on hanging around?"

"I'll be out of here before dark or when the shops and businesses close. Ray won't be out on the streets in the evening." I noticed a couple of my fellow beggars staring at me. I wondered if they had seen my phone and were planning to steal it. I rose and carrying my crate and cloth bag, I moved to another spot near the Plaza.

It did not take long for an agent to notice me. He suddenly stood right in front of me, very anonymous and nondescript—a crumpled black T-shirt and shorts, a scruffy beard and hair, medium height and weight. "You okay?" he asked softly.

"Yes," I said. "Any luck?"

"Not yet, but if this guy is around here, we'll catch him."

"He's pretty slick."

An LAPD officer approached, and the agent turned around. "Move along, buddy," he told the agent.

"Yes, sir," the agent answered obediently, giving the officer a small bowing nod. "You too, lady," the officer continued

"Okay, okay, officer," I said, trying to mimic my grandmother's accent. I rose slowly as if my arthritis was bothering me and started toward the Biltmore.

A brawl broke out behind us. The officer swore, and I hurried along before he could follow me. I found a bench from which I had a good view of the entrance to the Biltmore and the various groups that entered and left the hotel. But I realized that surveillance was like searching for the proverbial needle in a haystack.

When the shops closed and the traffic diminished, I placed my wooden crate beside a trash can and walked back to the parking lot. I stuffed my woolen hat into my bag and straightened myself up as best I could. I was afraid the parking attendant wouldn't let me pick up my car, but I walked briskly past him and managed to drive out without being harassed.

The freeway out of town was packed, but the car had the necessary transponder on the windshield, and I maneuvered into the express lane and was at Ed's house in less than an hour and a half. Maria and JP were out on the deck. I quickly showered in Ed's bathroom and changed into my jean skirt and a T-shirt before going outside to join them.

Ed appeared shortly afterward. "Whose car is that outside in the driveway?" he asked, a bewildered expression on his face.

"It's a rental car."

"What happened to your car?"

"Nothing. But I took a trip downtown Los Angeles today, and I didn't want to take my own car in case someone is trying to follow me."

"Where did you go?" Ed asked with raised eyebrows, a suspicious tone to his voice.

"I just walked around for a while. I left you a message. Didn't you get it? I'm almost positive Ray would try to hide in plain sight down there. I was really struck by how easy it would be for him to blend in among the Latinos. FBI agents are searching the hotels, showing Ray's pictures around, but I'm sure it will be hard to distinguish him from the others."

"Did you talk to any of the agents?"

"Yes, one. And he was really well camouflaged."

"Yes, they're good."

I didn't want to go into detail about my downtown expedition and shifted the conversation over to Ed, who seemed eager to tell me about the fires and recount the day's local crime log.

---

The next day, I repeated my adventure in Los Angeles. I drove the rental car and stopped at the same public restroom to disguise myself. I found good observation spots near the Sheraton and later Hotel Figueroa. I suspected the FBI agents were around and that they knew where I was, but they were well-hidden. My respect for the famous agency rose. These people were highly trained. However, stakeouts require much patience, in my case a trait in short supply, and at the end of the day I once more I returned home empty-handed.

I called Carrie and asked her if the agents were on surveillance at any of the hotels in Hollywood. "With his good looks, Ray could easily be taken for an actor, even a star."

She answered in the affirmative, and I told her I'd be around there the following day.

The next day, well before noon, I was once more in my disguise, parking the rental car in a lot near Hollywood Boulevard. Even though it was a regular weekday, throngs of tourists pushed their way along the sidewalks. Would-be actors and entertainers performed their routines and asked for money, as did bag ladies and drunks. I easily blended in as one of them and found a ledge to sit on. If Ray were hiding in plain sight around here, it would be even more difficult to spot him.

I moved to another ledge to observe people entering and leaving the Walk of Fame Hotel with no luck. By now, people looked all the same. Maybe the FBI agents were more discerning, but I was starting to grow more and more hopeless.

Toward the end of the day, I suddenly felt my phone vibrate. The connection was spotty, and I didn't hear the agent's name, but the message was clear: "Move over to the Roosevelt Hotel as soon as possible."

Because of the mass of people on the sidewalks, it took me almost half an hour to push my way over there. An agent met me before I reached the entrance, and we walked a few steps down a side street where he showed me several pictures on his phone of a man who looked like Ray. Although they were grainy, they were close-ups.

"How were you able to snap pictures so close?" I asked.

"I posed as a celebrity photographer but transferred the photos to my phone. They're not entirely in focus."

The photos showed a man from both the front and the side. He looked very much like Ray, although I wasn't a hundred percent sure. "Yes, that's him as far as I can tell," I said.

The agent had checked with the hotel manager, and the man in the picture was indeed a guest at the hotel. The manager let me sit near the entrance and served me a cup of hot coffee as if I were a charity case. I sipped my coffee slowly and hoped an agent had followed Ray because he was evidently in no hurry to return to the hotel. I surreptitiously texted Maria and Ed, saying I would be late and urging them to go ahead with dinner.

It was almost dark when the same agent came over to tell me that the man they thought was Ray had checked out of the hotel by phone and had left a message that he would send for the rest of his luggage later.

"Is someone watching him?"

"Yes, don't worry. He's not going anywhere."

I told him I needed to leave, that I had family to take care of at home. "But I can be back tomorrow morning."

---

Ed, James and JP were still up when I returned home. Maria had gone home. I took over JP's bedtime routine from James. JP had had a busy day and was soon fast asleep. In the kitchen, Ed had reheated two chicken fajitas. I sat down at the table and let Ed serve me.

"Well, did you get him?"

"No, not exactly."

"What do you mean, *not exactly?*"

"The FBI believes they have him under surveillance at the West Hollywood Hotel on Hollywood Boulevard. He ordered room service and appeared to be ensconced in his room for the night. Tomorrow morning I'll meet with a couple of agents to help verify that the man they have in sight is indeed Ray Khazin."

"Are you sure you're dealing with real FBI agents and not some of the doctor's henchmen?"

"Why would you say that?"

"Okay, finish your food first."

"And then what?"

"We'll go over to your house. I want to show you something."

"Bad?"

"Nothing that can't be fixed."

I finished the last fajita. James was watching television in the living room.

"I'm taking Megan over to her house for a few minutes," Ed said to his son. "Can you keep an eye on your cousin until we get back?"

"Sure. What's up?"

"Nothing," Ed answered enigmatically. "I want to show Megan something. We'll be right back."

"No problem."

"There may be a problem, James," I said. "But your dad is not going to tell me."

"Dad, what's going on? Has anything bad happened again?"

"Don't worry. It's a small thing this time."

James looked at us with his mouth open for a few seconds. "Okay, but if there's trouble, let me know so I can take care of JP." Ed gave him a nod and James turned his attention back to his TV show as we walked out the door. Ed took the wheel in his white sedan, and I slid into the seat beside him.

"What is all this about, Ed?" I said, annoyed at his secrecy.

Ed kept his eyes on the dark and narrow mountain road. My Subaru stood in the driveway where I had left it. That was a relief.

"Take a good look at it," Ed said as we both came closer. Then I saw a big gash in the paint all the way around.

"Damn!" I exploded. "Someone keyed my car. Who on earth would do such a dumb thing?"

"I don't know. It could be some of the hoodlums around here. What do you think?"

"Do you think it could be another warning to stay away?"

"Could be. Maybe it's time to find out if your contacts down there really work for the FBI or someone else."

"Ray wouldn't have this kind of manpower," I said a bit doubtfully. "He wouldn't have enough people who would know how to keep me under surveillance. This has got to be a random act." I paused and thought about other solutions for a few moments. "Then again, Ray has lots of compatriots from the restaurant who might be willing to help. When do you think it was done?"

"It could have been last night. Or it could have been several days ago. I didn't drive by here yesterday, and if I did the day before, I would have noticed if the car had been gone or if the tires had been flat, but I didn't check the paint job."

"I can't believe it. You'd think they would have done this first before getting more desperate and killing poor Duchess." Frustration and resentment hit at the same time.

Ed remained silent as he scrutinized the big gash that circled the car like a necklace. "I'll find out if the FBI had agents stationed downtown the days you said you were there and walked around. If you interacted with someone, can you give me the approximate times?"

"Yes, I believe I can pinpoint that time pretty accurately," I said. "I can check my phone. I made a call at the time."

"Good," he said, and I gave him the exact times.

"Thank you, Ed. I'll text Carrie right now too and ask her if she can verify that agents had interacted with me at the times I had called her."

Instead of texting back, she called from her cell, and I told her about my keyed car. "It may be a random act," I said. "But under the circumstances, I'm worried. First my dog and now my car."

"I agree," Carrie said. "I'll check for you and call you back tomorrow morning."

"Tomorrow I'll be back on Hollywood Boulevard. I hope to God we have the right guy." I paused to take a deep breath. "I'll have my phone on vibrate, but if I don't pick up, I'm in the middle of a situation."

"Okay. I'll text you as soon as I have any news."

James was still sitting in front of the TV when we returned, and Ed and I joined him. "I'll go into Hollywood early in the morning before the rush-hour traffic," I said. "No need for anyone to get up, but can one of you make sure Maria is here before you leave?"

James looked at his father. "Yeah," he said. "I'll be here. I can take JP to school too if you want."

"Thank you, James, but Maria should be here unless she has an emergency."

Ed pretended to be interested in the TV show, but I knew him better by now. He was thinking about something else.

"I shouldn't have let the FBI take advantage of you like this," he said and eyed me with demonstrative anger.

"Ed, the FBI hasn't taken advantage of me. I asked to help, and they're letting me." I looked him straight in the face. "Besides, I don't like to be told what I can and cannot do. We're not married yet."

"Doesn't that engagement ring give me some rights? I know we agreed to keep our engagement under the hat for a while because some people might think it happened too soon after Chris died, but it's still official."

"Okay, Ed, I'll listen, but I made a promise to Lizzie's mother to find out what happened, and I intend to keep it. I'm lucky to have a good friend like Carrie who understands that I have a personal stake in this case. I don't want Ray to be filed away as another cold case or end up on the list of fugitives where he'll stay for the next ten years. I'm going to make damn sure that Ray pays for what he has done."

16

## THE FINAL CHASE

I awoke early the next morning, starting out on what I hoped would be my last adventure in this particular case. I had my wig, hat and old boots but added a pair of loose cotton pants that I wore only when I raked leaves around my house in the fall. To complement the outfit, I put on a long-sleeved T-shirt that I had worn once when I had attempted to paint the fence around the old cabin that my first husband Robert and I bought. The T-shirt sported plenty of brown paint stains. In my ragtag outfit, I thought I looked like just another homeless person.

My rental car was brand new, but it was dirty and the color subdued. It looked the epitome of anonymity. To my knowledge, no one followed me, but to make sure, I exited the freeway in Pasadena and parked for a few minutes while I crammed the wig and my hat over my hair. Then I continued on to Hollywood.

I parked in an expensive lot on a side street and texted the agent who had shown me the pictures of Ray the day before. He texted right back and told me to go to West Hollywood Hotel on Hollywood Boulevard and hang out by the door. "I'll have someone serve you coffee in a paper cup. You'll blend in with no problem," the agent texted. He would keep an eye out from across the street. My sign when I saw Ray was to raise my arms behind my head as if to stretch.

Carrying my worn cloth bag around my shoulder, I sauntered over to the hotel and hung out with other drifters. When a druggie left his makeshift seat on a ledge, I claimed it. Sure enough, someone offered me a cup of coffee.

An hour passed, but no sign of Ray. My phone pinged, and I muttered something into the bag while I checked who had messaged me. It was Carrie Jensen. She verified that my contact yesterday was Agent Chuck Collin, and the description matched. Another agent had been in contact with me in downtown Los Angeles at the time I had given her. I breathed a sigh of relief. Agent Collin had evidently told Carrie that it was imperative that I stick around to confirm that the male in the photos he had shown me really was Dr. Khazin.

I looked from my bag to the hotel entrance. If Ray escaped once more, I would be in trouble. I did not fear for my life—although I probably should have—I was more afraid of what I would find at home. The Lebanese restaurant group and the Khazin family would not want another accidental death or even bodily injury attributed to them. They might cause more inconveniences for me, like blow out my tires or burglarize my house. Or God forbid, hurt someone in the family.

I moved to the other side of the street and assumed Agent Chuck Collin or another agent kept an eye on both the hotel entrance and me, waiting for the agreed-upon sign.

An olive-skinned male finally exited the hotel. He wore a white cap with HOLLYWOOD stitched in big letters on the front. He was pulling a Rollaboard suitcase as if he was on the move again. Wearing a white souvenir T-shirt and sunglasses and sporting a five-o'clock shadow even though it was before noon, he looked so much like a tourist that I had to watch closely. Again, I lost my confidence for a moment.

Tourist Ray crossed the street and turned up the sidewalk no more than ten feet away from me. As he passed, I caught a glimpse of the man's hands. I often notice people's hands. Ray's hands were short and fleshy, with black hair. Above the wrist was a brown mole that I remembered. It was Ray. I was sure of it.

I looked at my own hands and realized that I should have worn gloves. Fortunately, I had left my engagement ring and other jewelry at home, but these were not the hands of a homeless person or a drug addict. My fingernails were clean and trimmed short, and my fingers were nimble from keyboarding and playing the piano. I raised my arms high as if to stretch but didn't see any agents.

I followed Ray as closely as I dared. The crowds had grown and would continue to grow as the afternoon progressed. It was hard to keep up the pace. A big red double-decker sightseeing bus pushed its way through the traffic. When it stopped for just a minute at a red light, I lost sight of Ray. It stopped again to let tourists hop off and hop on. No sign of Ray. He must have boarded the bus that was now heading toward the end of the Boulevard.

I got on the next bus right behind and texted Agent Collin. He texted me back that he had made a momentary pit stop and had missed my sign, but another agent was in the area. I was aghast. A sudden pain shot through my stomach, and I felt blood rise to my cheeks.

Since I was on the bus, I decided to call my new FBI contact and moved to the back as the bus came to a stop. I looked up and down the street to see if Ray had gotten off the bus, but no tourist in a white hat pulling a Rollaboard was walking on either side of the street. I saw the Hotel Roosevelt sign again on my left and wondered if Ray could have darted into the hotel and disappeared.

I called Ed and told him what had happened. He swore. "Damn it, Megan. You're a god-damned mystery writer, not a trained FBI agent or detective, no matter what you think!"

"Calm down, Ed. I'm in no danger. I'm just following a guy that I think is Ray. I'm texting back and forth with the agent."

"Megan, this is insane. You shouldn't be doing this!" His temper, fear for me or both hadn't settled.

"Ed, can you make Maria take JP to her house after school? Just so they won't be alone?"

I didn't tell Ed about my stomach ache and my difficulty breathing.

Ed, bless his heart, was mad at me, scared for me, most likely, but he agreed to contact Maria. At least JP was taken care of, and Ed would make sure no one was hurt.

My thoughts went back to Chris's crazy wife who had set the house on fire. I debated whether or not to call Ed back to remind him of a possible fire, but he would already have thought of that.

The Roosevelt was the last hotel before the bus entered the residential areas. When the bus left the crowds behind, I decided to hop off and walk back. I texted Chuck Collin and told him where I was and shared my theory about Ray disappearing into the Roosevelt. He texted me back that he was almost there and said another agent was in the area as well, although I didn't see anyone.

"I'm worried," I texted back.

"Well, let's check out the Roosevelt," was his reply. It didn't sound very reassuring. This plan meant another wait, and Ray might have changed into another outfit by now.

Suddenly, Ray appeared from around the corner and jumped into a taxi. Damn. The guy was a real escape artist, a Harry Houdini without chains. Another taxi came up alongside me, and when it stopped, I opened the door and slid into the backseat.

"Hey, lady. This is a taxi. Not a welfare van. I'm picking up someone."

"Yes, me," I said. "Follow that taxi that just turned around and headed west." I dug out two twenties and flung them into the front seat. "I'm in disguise—undercover," I corrected myself. "I'm working with the FBI." Lying was easier than I realized.

"Okay," he said and dutifully turned his car around to start a slow chase. "The FBI, eh?"

"Yeah. And don't get too close." Since I was now well ensconced in a taxi, I called Agent Collin and told him what street we were on. "We're headed west, and my guess is that he's trying to get to Santa Monica."

"Why Santa Monica?"

"Because he'll be looking for another crowded area. Bel Air or Beverly Hills doesn't provide any area to hide. I'm trying to use psychology to follow Dr. Khazin's reasoning. If I were on the run, I'd try to hide in crowded places like Hollywood Boulevard and Santa Monica Beach."

"Good point." He paused. "I'm sorry I missed him earlier."

"Yes, so am I. We really need to catch him today," I said firmly. "I'm positive he realizes that I'm behind this pursuit. He has a group of co-conspirators that want to take back their country of Lebanon. The funny part is that I agree with them in principle. It's a beautiful country that has been mismanaged for decades now. But I don't agree with their method or their use of violence."

"Yes, I heard, and I do understand your predicament."

"Predicament?" I said sharply. "I firmly believe they killed my dog and keyed my car. I don't believe in coincidences. Although I don't believe they want to have another murder on their hands, one never knows. And I have a small son." My voice was starting to shake.

"Yes, I know. And please don't worry. We'll get him."

"I know you will eventually, but I'm scared."

"I understand, and we appreciate it." He was clearly trying to sound calm and reassuring, but I'm a realist—at least sometimes.

"If we don't catch him today, I may have an accident on my way home or find my house on fire."

He remained silent, as I tried to take a more optimistic tone. "I drove a rental car here, and I don't think I was followed. I should be alright."

"Good. I'll call in for more back-ups to meet us in Santa Monica. The doctor will not escape this time."

---

Ray's taxi stopped in Santa Monica on the 3rd Street Promenade, and he slipped into a small restaurant. "Stop," I told the taxi driver. "How much?"

"The forty you gave me will cover it."

I had already pulled out another ten and shoved it to him as I scooted out in time to see Agent Collin bolt into the restaurant after our suspect. From a vendor, I grabbed a colorful button-down shirt and put it over my paint-stained T. The sign said $14.99. I gave the woman a twenty and told her to keep the change as I hurried into the restaurant. "Did you see two men come in?" I asked the young greeter. "A tourist in a white cap and a

T-shirt with a Hollywood logo, and a middle-aged white male, casually elegant with short brown hair?"

"Yes," the young man replied politely. "They both just came through and went out the back."

I tried to avoid running and walked briskly through a narrow door into the kitchen then into an alley. In my mind, I had an image of Ray gliding toward the ocean like a slithering snake. Surely he didn't have a boat anchored there. The pier seemed longer than I remembered, and someone could be waiting in a dinghy. I called Agent Collin again and asked him if he saw any boats around, but he answered in the negative, so I continued on to 1$^{st}$ Street. No sign of either Ray or Agent Collin.

I finally gave up and sat down on a bench in the sun. People were everywhere, jogging, bicycling, strolling along this way and that way with no discernible goal. Without an apparent worry in the world. The whole affair was starting to weigh on me.

It was hot, and I removed my woolen hat. It looked out of place here. Couples ambled toward the water or along the waterfront as if they had nothing else to do, as if this was what they always did. I rose and moved closer to the water. Frothy waves crashed against the shore and farther out, a sailboat with full sails cruised along, propelled by the wind. Beyond the distant Channel Islands, the sea met the cloudless sky. Surfers, swimmers, and sunbathers were everywhere. The sand stretched north and south for miles, and in all of this vastness, I was trying to find a man who blended in perfectly with thousands of people milling about everywhere.

My phone vibrated. It was Chuck Collin. "He's still wearing his white hat, and I spotted the hat walking, looking up at a ten-story complex facing the ocean, just south of where I saw you last."

I left the sand and slowly resumed my trek south on the bike path. "Okay. I think I see the building."

"Walk on."

I crossed the street and walked along on the sidewalk, furtively looking around me. "And where will you be?"

"I'm right behind you."

At first, I saw neither a white hat nor anyone who resembled Ray, but then I spotted him entering the complex. Santa Monica Beach Hotel, the sign said. I assumed Agent Collin had seen him too, but I called him just in case he hadn't. "Dr. Khazin is inside the Santa Monica Beach Hotel."

"Yes, I saw him enter."

At the entrance, I stopped for a moment, not entirely sure whether I should enter. But the sun was starting its descent, and I felt an unsettling sense of urgency. When my mind cleared, I rationalized that I might be safe. If Ray was indeed part of a political group plotting to overthrow the current Lebanese government, it was unlikely that they would risk another death here in the States. Lizzie's *accidental* death, now classified as a homicide, may have taken them by surprise. Their business was political. Violence might be part of their plan to change the government of *their* country, but I bet they had not planned on a murder charge brought up against them in *this* country.

Entering the reception area, I stood for a while letting my eyes adjust from the bright sunlight to the dark lobby.

"Excuse me," I said to the young receptionist on duty. He was impeccably groomed, wearing a dark red sports coat that looked like part of the hotel's uniform. "I just saw an old friend enter. He's Lebanese, around forty, and speaks with a slight Middle-Eastern accent."

The young man looked at me curiously, and I tried to flash him my most innocent and friendly smile. "He made a reservation only this morning. He requested a room with a fire escape. He said he was deadly afraid of the fires all over California." He picked up the hotel telephone, still keeping his eye on me. "I'll call his room and tell him a young lady is here to see him."

There was no answer. I could hear the phone ring at the other end. "He doesn't answer, ma'am," the man said apologetically.

"No worries. Thank you so much. I have his cell phone number somewhere. I'll text him that I'm coming up." I pretended to look in my contact list, but instead I texted Chuck Collin. I thought the clerk pushed 600 on his phone but was not entirely sure. "Did you say his room number was 600?"

The clerk looked at his computer. "Yes, room 600. The elevator is over there." He pointed to a hallway on the side of the lobby.

Before I clicked to send my text to Collin, I added *room number 600 with fire escape.* By the time I reached the elevators, Agent Collin was already there, looking intently at his own phone. As I entered the first elevator with three other people, I quickly looked back at the receptionist who was on the phone again. Agent Collin did not follow. I assumed he would come up on the next elevator. I pushed the sixth-floor number and took a deep breath.

The ride up seemed to take hours. We stopped at every floor whether someone wanted to get off on that floor or not. On the sixth floor, I had to orient myself as to how the numbers ran, but soon found room 600 and knocked on the door. I waited and then called out. "Ray, I saw you downstairs and wanted to say hello."

Silence.

I called Agent Collin. "I'm outside room 600. I've knocked and called, but he's either dead or escaped down the fire escape."

"Hang on," he said. "I'll be right there with the manager."

"I hope to God you have someone at the bottom of the fire escape." I whispered furiously though I wanted to shout impatiently.

At that moment, I saw Collin exit the elevator followed by another employee. I called out, "Over here," then knocked at the door again, but not a sound. Could Ray have seen no other way out than to take his own life? No, I decided. He was not the type.

It didn't take long for the agent and the manager to open the door with a master key. Collin entered first with his gun drawn and identified himself as the FBI. The manager waited in the hall, but I followed Collin into the room. The Rollaboard was there but no sign of Ray. "I hope you have another agent at the bottom of the fire escape," I repeated a bit sarcastically.

Agent Collin frowned and looked at me. "We do," he said calmly, and opened the sliding door to the fire escape. Collin descended first, and I followed.

At the bottom of the stairs, a police officer in uniform and a young man that I assumed to be the other FBI agent had detained Ray without incident. As I came closer and saw Ray's face clearly, I nodded to the agents, signaling that their detainee was indeed Dr. Raymond Khazin.

"Ray, what on earth are you up to?" I called to him from the bottom of the stairs.

Ray scowled but shot me a quick glance. He remained silent.

"I saw you enter the hotel and wanted to come up and say hello," I continued and shook my head.

As Ray bowed his head, the uniformed officer read him his rights and handcuffed him.

"Where are they taking him?" I asked Agent Collin. I was still standing at the bottom of the stairs.

"To the downtown detention center," Collin replied.

"Downtown Los Angeles? The detention center on Alameda Street?"

"Yes, that's the one." Collin smiled faintly. "You're familiar with it?"

"Yes, I've been there."

"Not as an inmate, I hope."

I shook my head. "Correct. I was there last year with Carrie Jensen clearing up another case."

"Quite the detective, I hear," he said, with a slight trace of condescension in his tone.

The officer and the other agent led Ray away to a waiting black and white, while Collin and I followed. "I hope he's held without bail this time," I said to Agent Collin. "You know he slipped away before, right?"

"Yes, I know."

"I wonder if we can persuade Dr. Khazin to confess," I said quietly to Collin. "It would sure simplify things."

"Not likely, but who knows?"

I could tell he was anxious to follow the police car that just pulled away. "Well, thank you for your good work," I said.

"I guess you'll sleep easier tonight, eh?" he said with a grin.

"I will. You heard about my dead dog and my keyed car, didn't you?"

"I did. You need a ride somewhere?"

"Where are you going?"

"To Long Beach."

"Oh no, thank you. That's too far out of your way. I have my car parked in Hollywood. I'll just take a cab."

"Okay, but I'd be happy to drop you off. You've been of great help in this case."

I glanced at him. "I have a personal stake in this case. My good friend was murdered, and everyone wanted to call it an accidental death. I even heard suicide mentioned. It was all too ridiculous. I hope our man, a doctor no less, won't see the light of day anytime soon."

"He won't," Collin said, then walked away.

I hailed a taxi. On the way, I texted Carrie and asked her to call when it was convenient. She called a few minutes later, as the taxi entered the onramp to the 10 freeway east. Skipping the formalities, she almost shouted, "Where are you?"

I told her. "And we nabbed him!" I said exuberantly.

"Yes. I just heard. You did it again, my friend."

"The LAPD were on hand, and they cuffed him without a hitch at the bottom of the fire escape behind the Santa Monica Beach Hotel. He had specifically reserved a room with a fire escape because he was mortally afraid of all the fires we have in California, the receptionist told me. They took him to the detention center downtown Los Angeles, the very same place you and I went to interview Johnny Frazzano's wife last year"

"Good for them, and good for you."

I took a deep breath and leaned back in the comfortable sedan. "I hope to God they book him without bail. He has influential friends."

"I know."

"I wonder if we should go down to Alameda Street tomorrow and see if we could coax a confession out of him before he gets all lawyered up. Remember, we did it last year."

"Yes, I remember. Maybe he'll see the benefit of avoiding a very public trial."

"Good point," I said. "A public trial would damage his political ambitions."

"And he'll get a lawyer immediately, anyway. It's the first call he'll make."

"Another good point. I'll try to think of arguments for a plea deal. Second degree murder, perhaps. I'll try to paint pictures of the headlines for him if he goes to trial: *Lebanese Physician Murders His American*

*Wife for Money.* Or *Middle-Eastern Doctor Accused of Medicare and Insurance Fraud to Fund Plot to Overthrow Lebanese Government.* Maybe he'll want to avoid that kind of publicity and agree to manslaughter charges and avoid a real spectacle."

"It's an idea," Carrie said. "Let's talk later,"

I removed my black wig and stuffed it in my bag with the scarf and a sweater. Then I called Ed and told him the whole story. He didn't interrupt me even once.

# 17

# RAY BEHIND BARS

M y rental car stood in the parking lot as if nothing had happened. The car had Bluetooth capability, and I connected my phone before I took off. I found Mrs. Wurtz's number and called her as I merged onto Hollywood Blvd East. She answered, and we exchanged greetings.

"Ray has been arrested, accused of Lizzie's death. That may not provide much consolation, but I hope it will mean some kind of closure." I paused to let it sink in, but she remained silent. I cleared my throat. "Ray is involved in a political group that was plotting to oust the corrupt Lebanese government. Lizzie understood more than most about Lebanese politics. She and I often talked about the Middle East since I too had lived over there. I believe we both agreed with the opposition group in principle, but not their method of violence. Lizzie may have threatened to expose the group's illegal weapons smuggling, and it cost her her life."

"I didn't know any of that," Mrs. Wurtz said quietly.

I didn't mention anything about Ray's mistresses. It would be too hurtful. Lizzie had discovered a secret plot, and that discovery turned out to be lethal. That's all the mother needed to know.

Mrs. Wurtz started sobbing.

"I'm so sorry, Mrs. Wurtz. Lizzie was a smart woman, and she died an honorable death. I think she bravely stood up to her husband and his cohorts and tried to stop illegal and dangerous activities. I'm convinced she saved countless innocent lives." I paused for a few moments before I continued. "I too miss Lizzie dearly. She was a good friend. We had a lot in common."

"Thank you," she sobbed.

"At least Lizzie didn't die in vain. And her killer is now behind bars." I heard Mrs. Wurtz heave a shuddering sigh. "Nothing will bring her back. But time will ease the pain. I know from personal experience. Although the sorrow will never go away completely, it will diminish with time."

"I know," Mrs. Wurtz said. "And thank you." She had regained her composure, and we finished our conversation with a few stories in remembrance of Lizzie.

Ed was waiting for me at home. "How did it go?"

"Fine," I said without any enthusiasm. I wanted to tell Ed the whole story. About Ray's capture and how the officers had taken him to the Los Angeles Metropolitan Detention Center, seemingly without incident, but I didn't know where to begin. I was too agitated to go to sleep, but when we were finally in bed and I lay comfortably in the crook of Ed's arm, the entire story, detail by detail, spilled out of me like beans from a ripped sack.

———

Two days later saw FBI agent Carrie Jensen and me driving along the 105 and the 110 freeways toward the Los Angeles Detention Center on Alameda Street in downtown Los Angeles to visit Dr. Khazin. Ray had now spent two days and nights in a jail cell, long enough, we figured, for him to think his situation through. The experience was surely a new one for him. He was used to cheating his way through life and having his influential family and wealthy friends bail him out. This time, no bail had been set, but his lawyer or lawyers had most certainly been there to give him advice.

"You ready?" Carrie asked as we exited the freeway. She was at the wheel and kept her eyes on the road.

"Yep," I had been wired so that Carrie could listen to my conversation with Ray.

"Nervous?"

"A little," I said casually, trying to hide my uneasiness. Without the recorded interview, in which I hoped Ray would compromise himself or even confess, our trip would not be of much use.

"They're expecting you," she said as she maneuvered her way through the traffic. "It's all been arranged." She had her ID ready around her neck and looked the epitome of a professional woman.

"I'll do my best, as my students used to say."

"Yeah, your students. You miss them?"

"Of course. And I'll be back in the classroom one day soon, perhaps when my little boy starts kindergarten." I glanced over at her. She was a tough cookie, hardened by her job, no family of her own. "Aren't you going to slow down, take some time off and have a family too, Carrie?"

"Maybe one day," she said as we approached the huge angular detention center, a light gray stucco building in typical 1980s architecture.

"I may get a private investigator's license."

She shot me a quick glance. "Why would you want to waste two years of your life on something like that? You already know the tricks of the trade."

"Is that how long it takes?" I was surprised.

"I believe so."

"Getting a PI endorsement though would give me credibility with law enforcement. They'd see a professional rather than a nosey mystery writer."

She said nothing more as she swung into the parking and found an empty spot near the entrance.

"I'll check your wiring one more time and go in with you to make sure everything is okay. Then I'll sit in the car with my speaker on and hear the entire conversation. You gonna be okay with that?"

"I think so," I said. "Students often used to tape my lectures."

Last year she had come with me into the visitors' room, but this time she had suggested that I see Ray by myself. I was not bound by all the regulations and restrictions that an FBI agent had to observe and could more easily ask the intimate questions I had in mind. The visit would also seem less official and make it easier for Ray to confess.

"Okay. You know the ropes. You did great last time," she said.

"Thank you."

"Good luck."

I took my Chic Lady out of my purse and put it in the glove compartment before I slid out of my seat. As soon as Carrie showed her badge, we passed through security. "We're here to see Dr. Raymond Khazin," Carrie explained to the guard, a tall middle-aged African American. "She'll go in by herself."

The guard nodded.

"I'll wait in the car," Carrie said and left.

"Follow me," the guard said and led the way to the elevator.

"The visitors' room is on the second floor," he said when we were in the elevator.

The small room was plain in basic beige with light aluminum chairs. No pictures on the wall. No posters or distractions of any kind. I sat down and waited. A few minutes later, a guard escorted Ray in and directed him to the chair opposite me. He looked tired and haggard, slightly bent over. Dark circles framed his eyes. His usually tanned face was pale.

"Hello, Ray," I said. "I'm so sorry to see you under such circumstances." Truly, I felt sorry for him. Though he'd lived in the States several years, he was in a culture completely foreign to him, a culture where no one cared about his overseas high social status and family wealth. He must have felt so bewildered and alone.

"I thought this was where you wanted to see me," he said. He may have meant his tone to be sarcastic, but instead he sounded utterly defeated. "This is hell. I haven't slept for two days."

"I'm sorry, Ray. I know you probably have a team of excellent lawyers already lined up, but I'm here to help you avoid publicity and embarrassment, not only for yourself but also for your family." He shot me another quick glance. "Both Lizzie and I agreed with you that the current government in Lebanon is a disaster for the country, and that the time has come to throw out these bastards. But not with violence and illegally smuggled weapons from the United States. Lizzie and I could have helped, but you killed her. Why, Ray? Why?" I looked at him sternly, and he shifted uneasily in his chair.

"I didn't kill anyone," he said with scorn.

"Lizzie is gone, but I, like your group, want to keep the cause alive. It will all be lost if you go to trial. The publicity will ruin everything. It's no use, Ray. The FBI also has you under surveillance for Medicare and Medical fraud."

"They have no proof," he shot back. He had regained a little of his old defiance.

"Maybe not, but the accusation will be there as will the suspicion that you've been involved in gun-running."

He snorted and broke out in an evil-sounding laughter.

"The news media here can be vicious, and they'll go to town with all of it. The news will reach all the way to Lebanon. You're in a different culture inside these walls, Ray. No one here gives a crap about the Khazin name and your family's money. In fact, your family's money will make the news stories even more salacious. Like you, I love Lebanon, Ray. It's a lovely country. I lived over there too, and I saw firsthand the corruption and the destruction of the place." I looked at him in search of a reaction but saw none. "It's true that the evidence against you is circumstantial, but one thing that can be proven is the false exam papers you submitted with your application to Saint Joseph's Medical School. You submitted another student's grades, all top scores no less, I discovered. That's another little tidbit that the media will blow out of proportion. Another embarrassment to your family and powerful friends."

Ray shifted uncomfortably in his chair and looked up briefly with raised eyebrows. He may not have realized that this detail too would be part of the conversation. "What does that have to do with anything?"

"To a jury it will say something about your character, Ray. I know it's common to pay your way into top schools and high position, not only over there but here as well. But Americans frown upon such practices and probably much more here than in Lebanon."

Ray watched me more seriously now and seemed to pay closer attention.

"I know you graduated and completed your residency in Oklahoma," I continued. "So you must be a competent physician, but an American jury will resent that you cheated your way in here."

Ray bit his lip as if he were thinking this over. I gave him some time to let it all sink in, but I was on a roll. After a moment of silence, I went on, "Ray, I know how to avoid all this unpleasantness."

He looked down at his unfamiliar and ridiculous prison suit and shoes.

"Ray, will you listen to me?"

"Okay," he said quietly. "I'm dead tired, but I'm listening."

I took a deep breath before I finally decided to lay the cards on the table. "You can avoid a very public jury trial by taking a plea deal, Ray. You can confess to killing Lizzie. The other issues will not be brought up, and the whole case will go away quietly."

"I didn't kill anyone. I'm innocent. You have no proof."

"Ray, we have a ton of evidence. The autopsy revealed that there was residue of potassium cyanide in Lizzie's body. We also found a capsule in one of Lizzie's pockets, a pill like the ones Lizzie said you had prescribed for her. The capsule had been injected with potassium cyanide. Only a medical professional would know how to do that. The FBI can trace where you bought the potassium cyanide online. To whatever pharmacy or dealer you used."

Ray's mouth fell open. This piece of information took him by surprise.

"I didn't do what you said. I'm innocent," he repeated in a feeble effort to sound convincing.

"Lizzie found out about your mistresses and your illegal weapons smuggling. She threatened to expose you, so you decided that she must disappear."

"Where's your proof?" he repeated again, but his defiance had changed to resignation.

"Make a plea deal and avoid the death penalty, Ray. Confess to second-degree murder or even manslaughter. Serve a few years in prison, and you'll be free to go." I wasn't going to tell him that his second-degree plea deal could carry as few as fifteen years or as many as fifty.

"I won't confess to something I didn't do."

"Listen, Ray. A jury will convict you without a doubt. Let me be frank with you. The way the climate is today, Ray, an Arab killing his American wife will have as much chance of acquittal as an ice cube in hell. All your mistresses will testify against you. Heidi too. I don't know if you've learned that she's not pregnant after all." I was merciless and pressed on. "Everyone will hear about your obsession with trying to father a child and your infertility. Your entire miserable life will be laid bare. Is that what you want, Ray?"

Ray bent over and held his head in his hands, his elbows on his knees. "Okay, I wanted to get rid of Elizabeth. She said she had been to a gynecologist who told her that nothing was wrong with her. Her eggs were healthy, suggesting that I was the one with defective sperm." He kept holding his head in his hands and didn't look at me. "Do you know how it feels for a man to hear that?"

"I'm so sorry, Ray. And I do understand. I was married to Robert. You remember Robert, don't you?"

"Yes, I remember him. Why?"

"We were married for eight years, and we couldn't have any children." I didn't want to lose the momentum and break the spell by telling Ray that I now had a son. "So that's when you took mistresses to find out if it was true," I said. "I think Lizzie threatened to expose your personal secrets in addition to your political ambitions."

Ray sat there, his head still down. I let him have time to think things over.

"You wanted revenge, didn't you Ray? I can understand that. And so, you prescribed some pills, supposedly diet pills, and injected them with potassium cyanide."

"I didn't mean to kill her. There wasn't enough cyanide to kill anyone."

"I see. Just enough to impair her balance and give headaches. Then, if she had an accident, it would be her own fault."

He remained silent except for some heavy breathing.

"Am I right, Ray?"

More silence. Then some quiet sobs.

"And why did you have to kill my dog, Ray? Did one of your friends poison my dog to scare me away?"

Ray raised head slightly. "It was just a dumb dog."

I remembered well the contempt Arabs had for dogs. To be called a *dog* was the ultimate curse.

"And who keyed my car?"

He looked at me with his mouth open. "What?"

He didn't seem to know what I was talking about. He may not have known exactly what that expression meant, but he seemed to realize the game was over.

"Confess to second degree murder, and save your own life, Ray."

"My life is so messed up anyway. What does it matter?" he mumbled between sobs.

I had had enough. He had clearly confessed. I hoped to god that our conversation was audible to Carrie.

"Smart move, Ray. Your lawyer will work out the details of the plea deal. Tell him…" I knew it would be a man as Ray would never hire a female lawyer. "Tell him exactly what you told me. I understand your position, Ray. You're making the right decision."

———

The interview with Ray went as well as could be expected, and I should have felt happy that I had pulled a confession out of him. He didn't realize that we had recorded everything, of course, and I felt sorry for him. He had been brought up in a culture where social position and money played a much bigger role than in the United States. Nepotism and bribery were ingrained. It was not unusual to be offered a job because of your family connections rather than your ability to do the job. It was a culture of *who* you knew, not *what* you knew, which might be universal but more so some places than others. It was also not unusual to be accepted by a good school for the same reasons. No big deal. That practice occurs in the Western world too, but more subtly.

My FBI friend waved and had a big smile on her face as I approached her parked car. She leaned over to the passenger side to open the door for me. "Great job! You were right. I couldn't have asked the same questions."

I scooted into the seat beside her. "Did you hear everything?"

"Absolutely. And clear as a bell."

"Was it enough?"

"More than enough. I don't think his lawyer or any lawyer would try to screw this up. A plea deal is his best shot. No way would a jury let this bastard off the hook"

"I have to agree."

"I'll have the tape copied before I hand it over to the district attorney's office. And no way would a prosecutor be dumb enough to try for a first-degree murder conviction without any physical evidence."

"I hope you're right." I undid the wire from my bra, wrapped it around my hand and placed it in the glove compartment.

Carrie started the car and drove slowly onto the street. "Relax," she said. "The case is over, finished, *finito*! Got it? You hungry? You want to stop for a bite to eat before we try the freeway again?"

"Actually, I am." I had eaten only a little cold cereal for breakfast. Although the trip and the interview had not been physically challenging, I was mentally drained. I looked at my phone. "I can't believe it," I said. "It's almost noon."

"Well, you were inside the detention center for almost two hours."

"Really?"

"Yes, really."

"I guess time flies when you're having fun," I tried to chuckle in an effort to lighten my mood. But there was little humor in the situation. "You have an expense account, don't you?"

She shot me a quick glance. "You have some place fancy in mind?"

"Maybe. There's a place on Grand by the Music Center with underground parking right there. Or we could go all out and try the Water Grill. We could park in the library lot."

"Okay. I know the Water Grill. Let's do it."

The plush restaurant was half-full of men in suits and women in heels and professional office attire. Lawyers and business people most likely. The ambience provided a stark contrast to the inside of the county jail. Carrie kept the conversation light, and by the time we walked back to her car, the gloomy detention center with Ray and his sorry circumstances seemed like a dream.

No one was at my house when I returned home. I made myself a cup of coffee and brought it out on the deck. I needed to think this day through. It was hard to believe that it was all over. Ray had understood the advantages of a plea deal. Carrie would deliver the tape to the district attorney as soon as possible. After hearing the taped confession, any reputable defense lawyer would agree that a plea deal would be in the client's best interest. The lawyers' job would now be to negotiate the best deal they could for Ray.

I was deep in my thoughts when Ed's chirp brought me back to reality. He came out on the deck in his summer uniform, a light brown shirt and a black tie that he loosened as he sat down, crossing his legs leisurely. "So, how did it go this morning?"

"How did what go?"

"You and your FBI friend were going down to the LA Detention Center today. You had a plan."

"Yes, we did. And yes, I did. Carrie Jensen drove us. Everything went according to our plan. At least, I hope so." I paused, but he didn't have any comments. "With a wire hidden in my bra, I met Dr. Khazin in the visitors' room, while Carrie sat in the car listening to the whole interview. Ray confessed to everything. It was almost too easy." I recounted all the details and described how Ray had finally broken down and confessed. "He finally saw the logic of accepting a plea deal. There will be no trial as far as I can tell. It would be foolish for a defense attorney to go before a jury after he learns that the jury would have access to Ray's recorded confession, don't you agree?"

Ed shook his head slowly, his mouth open. "What a devious little devil you are! So what are you going to do now?"

"Maybe take a few days off."

"Or maybe I should bring you another case."

"Do you have one?"

"No, but there's a box full of cold cases down at the main office." He reached over and took my hand.

"Ed," I said after a while. "What about taking a vacation? Go someplace like Thailand? Have you ever ridden an elephant?"

"No. Is that what they do in Thailand?"

"Some do. Or maybe we could go to South Africa or Kenya."

"And what do they ride over there? Tigers?"

"No, Ed. Tigers don't live in Africa. They live in Asia."

"Oh, that's right," he said a bit sheepishly. "I forgot that."

"Well, what do you think?"

He let go of my hand and re-crossed his legs. "How about Ireland? Or maybe Italy?"

"Yes," I said, eager to keep the momentum going, my mood growing lighter. "We could go to Ireland first to see the country your great-grandparents left. Maybe we'll find some of your cousins. Then we could take a Mediterranean cruise."

"That sounds interesting. But what about James and JP?"

"It will take some time to prepare. You can't leave until the summer crowds wind down. By that time, James will be well ensconced at USC. His paperwork is all done. The tuition and fees are paid. I guess you haven't noticed that a chunk of money has been withdrawn from your bank account." I laughed and went on. "JP could either come along with us or stay with Maria. He will miss his little friends at the nursery school, but it would only be for a couple of weeks, and it would be an educational experience for him."

Ed didn't say anything and stared at the lake. Several sailboats glided back and forth in the distance.

"What are you thinking about, Ed?"

Ed didn't answer right away. "Well," he said after a minute or two. "I was thinking maybe we should get married first. It would seem more appropriate."

"Ed, you're so old-fashioned. But I wouldn't be against it. Then we could call the trip our honeymoon."

I cleared my throat and took one last sip of my cold coffee before I continued, "There's one problem, though."

Ed looked up with raised eyebrows.

"When the town sheriff takes a bride, it's a big deal."

"Not really. By now, most people think I'm married, anyway. And Maria wouldn't mind taking care of JP for a couple of weeks."

"I have no doubt about that. She will be so happy for you, Ed. She thinks of you as her own son."

"I know. And I love her as much as my mother."

"So, do you want me to go ahead and plan for both a wedding and our honeymoon, then?"

"Well, you have the time, don't you? You said you wanted to take a few days off from crime. I still have to go to work, you know."

"I'll be glad to take care of it all."

And while Ed was staring at the sailboats, I started thinking about the details and where to start.

A few minutes later, JP came running out on the deck followed by Maria. While JP updated me on the goings on in nursery school, Ed talked to Maria in Spanish. I understood only bits and pieces like *las bodas* and *luna de miel*, which I guessed meant he was telling Maria about our wedding followed by a trip.

"So excited," Maria said to me in English. "I take care of JP. No problem."

When we were getting ready for bed that night, Ed was unusually amorous. "We have to practice for our wedding night," he said and dimmed the light.

———

The Mediterranean Sea bears little resemblance to our mountain lake. The water in the Mediterranean is rougher, a brighter blue and salty. The air is balmier, and at this time of the year, the sun is warm as soon as it leaves the dawn horizon.

I was leaning back in a lounge chair on the forward deck of the Nordic Spirit, a smaller cruise ship than the ubiquitous floating theme parks that plow the world's oceans. In this early morning hour, no one was around, and, except for the din of the engines, all was quiet. We had left Barcelona the night before, a little delayed, after a sumptuous dinner of stuffed salmon with a divine oyster sauce. Now we were gliding past the spectacular French Riviera toward our first landfall—Monte Carlo.

Ed was asleep in our cabin below. He still suffered from jetlag. I texted him and asked him to come up to the top forward deck so that he could see the famous skyline of Monaco as we sailed into the harbor with its myriad of yachts against a backdrop of a precipitous cliff topped by Prince Albert's expansive palace.

A few moments later, I saw Ed accompanied by an attendant coming out of the glass elevator. I put out another lounge chair and asked the attendant, a young Filipino, if we could have coffee and croissants brought up here.

*No* was not in the vocabulary of any of the attendants on this ship, and croissants and coffee would come right up.

"Isn't the view from up here gorgeous, Ed?" I said as he adjusted his chair and sat down. He looked fresh and neat in his white golf shirt and khaki shorts.

He nodded. "Sure is, Mrs. Cronin," he said with an affectionate smile and shot me a mischievous glance.

We had only been married for a week and were officially on our honeymoon. We had spent five days in Ireland furiously sightseeing everywhere before we flew down to Barcelona. Now we had a week to relax.

"How long till we go ashore?"

"Soon." I told him about my short visit there by car a few years ago. "I suggest we take a bus tour to Grasse to see the perfume factory." I gave him a wickedly seductive glance. "The travel agent said they make a cologne for men that makes them irresistible. Then we'll go on to a little cobblestoned village for lunch."

"Sounds like a good plan," Ed said agreeably and smiled indulgently.

"But most of the day we'll stroll along the harbor, watch the magnificent yachts, and snack on crepes. Then we'll inspect the famous casino."

"And maybe we'll see James Bond. Isn't this where James Bond used to hang out?"

I shot him a quick surprised glance. "I didn't know you watched James Bond movies."

"Not lately," he said with a sigh. "But I read a couple of the books."

"Really?" I hadn't actually seen Ed read much of anything but newspapers and reports.

After we finished our breakfast and the waiter had picked up our dishes, we leaned back in our chairs and enjoyed the breeze as the ship plowed its way forward.

"I wonder what's happened to Heidi."

"She's probably moved on to another predator," Ed said dismissively.

"I talked to Cheryl, and she told me that Heidi was still at the hospital but was looking to move down to Rancho Cucamonga."

"Why on earth would she move there?"

"Cheryl said that Heidi had hooked up with Ray's brother Richard."

"She's crazy." He lay back in his chair and closed his eyes, dismissing the fickle woman. "Oh, in all the commotion, I forgot to tell you that one of the deputies caught a gang of hoodlums who went around the resort keying cars as a gag."

"So, it was nothing more serious. What a stupid thing to do. Ray admitted a friend had poisoned Duchess—to Arabs, dogs are lowly creatures. I may decide to pursue that when we return home."

Soon hundreds of yachts and the enormous cliff, dotted with white apartment buildings and houses came into view.

"The folks around here sure have a lot of boats," Ed commented.

"And not a single one under a million dollars," I said. "And see the impressive palace on top of the cliff," I pointed. "That's where Prince Albert lives and rules this tiny principality. Pretty spectacular, eh?"

The debarkation was quick and orderly. We saw only a few passengers our age. Most were older. The bus tour was informative, with the guide talking nonstop. Like many of the older men, Ed closed his eyes and probably took a catnap.

After the ride and lunch, we walked along the harbor admiring the majestic yachts and watching the slow traffic. "I don't think I've ever seen so many Porsches, Lamborghinis, Maseratis, Jaguars, and high-end

Mercedes in one place," Ed commented. "I doubt that Subaru and Honda are doing much business around here."

"This is a place for people with serious money," I said. "The apartments and houses you see on the slope above us are in the millions too."

"I could never live with all these people around me all the time. I think I prefer Ireland."

"Don't worry, Ed. You won't have to make that choice."

Ed was not impressed by the ornate casino. "If I were a gambler, I'd go to Las Vegas," he said as we inspected the inside. "Too small and cramped for me."

In the evening, after dinner, Ed had a beer on our private balcony while I had a glass of wine. From the balcony, we could see the French shoreline as the ship slowly made its way out of the harbor, toward the coast of Italy. Our thoughts went back home to JP, James, and Maria, and I emailed James.

"You know, I've been thinking of the poor woman who drove off the side of the highway and rolled down a cliff where she remained for weeks, or even months, with no one reporting her missing," I said. "What happened to that case?"

"Oh," Ed said as he looked out on the water that glowed like gold in the setting sun. "It has been filed away with a stack of other cold cases."

"That's what I thought." I paused for a moment or two. "I think I'd like to take a look at it when we get home. Can you show me what paperwork you have on her?"

"Sure," Ed said, shrugging his shoulders. "Just remember that cases like that remain unsolved for years, most of them forever."

"What I have in mind is to make the poor woman the victim of my next book. Then I'll document how I go about solving it. How's that?"

"You're crazy, Megan," he said with a chuckle. "Here we are on our honeymoon in the middle of the Mediterranean Sea, and all you can think of is solving another crime."

The Mediterranean sun had given him a glowing tan, and his eyes glittered. "But I still love you." I said, cocking my head as I met his gaze.

His eyebrows rose and now it was his grin that was wicked. "Then show me."

## THE END

———

**Don't miss out on your next favorite book!**

Join the Satin Romance mailing list
www.satinromance.com/mail.html